# THE SKELETON

# FAERIE

SEA OF INK PRESS

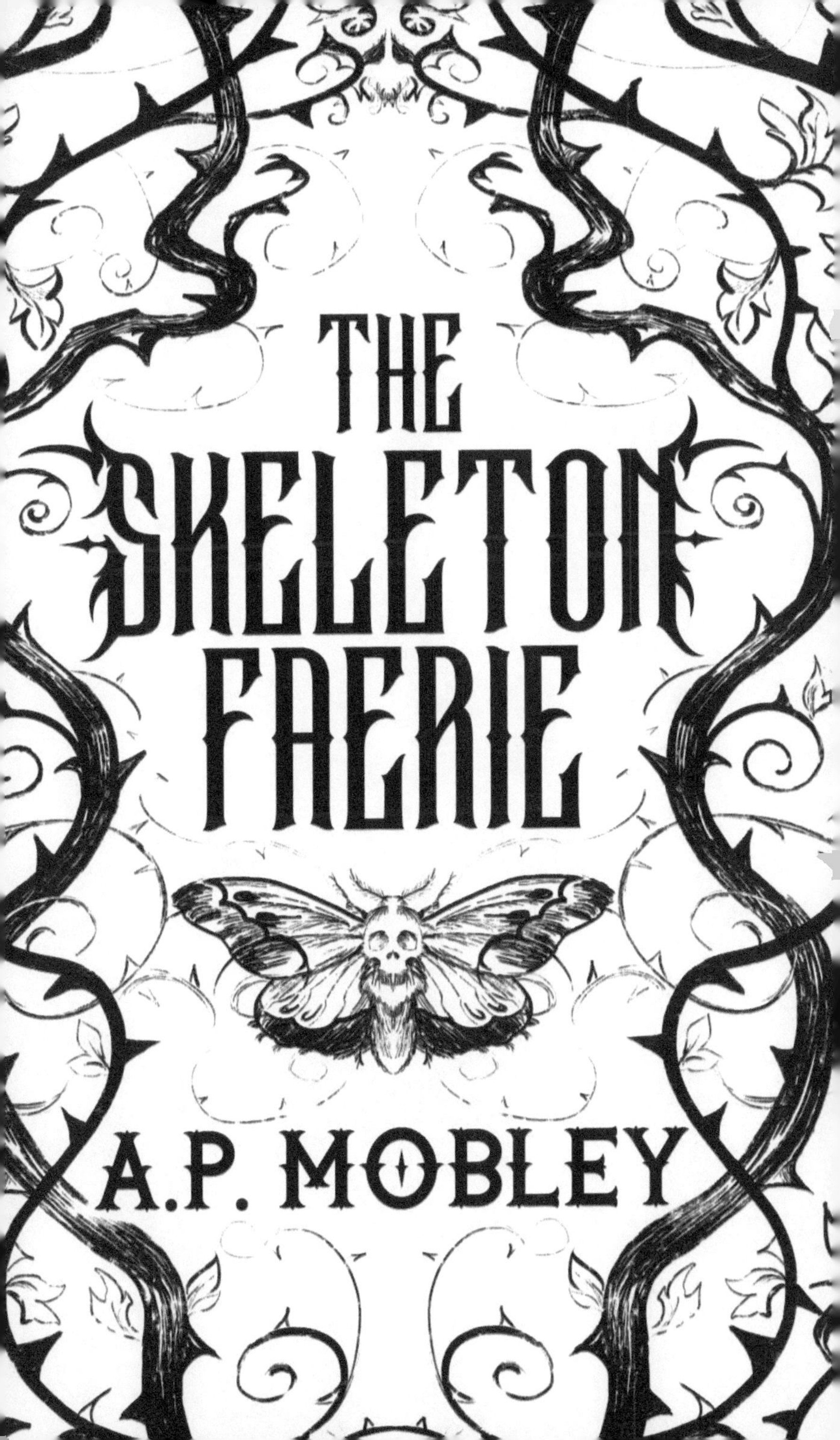

THE
SKELETON
FAERIE
A.P. MOBLEY

*For Grandpa Ron and Papa Don.*

*Can't wait to hug you both in the next life.*

# CONTENT WARNINGS

*The Skeleton Faerie* contains themes and elements that may be upsetting for some readers. A list of content warnings for this book and all other works by A. P. Mobley can be found at www.apmobley.com/books

# PRONUNCIATION GUIDE

## WELSH:

Pair Dadeni – payr-dah-den-ee
Mabinogi – mah-bin-oh-ghee
Tylwyth Teg – tull-with-teg
Annwn – ah-noon
Cŵn Annwn – koon-ah-noon
Arawn – ah-rown
Pwyll – pwh-ikh
Dyfed – dih-ved
Matholwch – ma-thoh-lookh
Efnysien – eff-nih-see-en
Branwen – brahn-win
Bran – brahn
Olwen – oll-win
Culhwch – keel-hookh
Ysbaddaden – us-bah-dath-en
Rhiannon – rhee-ah-non
Arianrhod – ah-ree-ahn-rhod

## IRISH:

Tír na nÓg – teer-nah-nog
Aes Sídhe – ay-shee
Merrow – mair-oh

Pooka – poo-kuh
Fomorian – foh-mor-ee-un
Lugh – loogh or loo
Brigid – bridge-id
Balor – bay-lor
Saoirse – sear-shah
Fiadh – fee-uh
Niall – nee-al

## SCOTTISH:

Elphame – elf-hame
Kelpie – kell-pee
Seelie – see-lee
Unseelie – un-see-lee

## IRISH AND SCOTTISH:

Samhain – sow-in or sah-win
Bealtaine – bee-al-ten-uh
Sluagh – sloo-ah

## CORNISH:

Piskies – pis-kees

# GUS'S PLAYLIST

1. All I Want (A Day To Remember)
2. Drown (Bring Me The Horizon)
3. When We're Dead (MOD SUN)
4. Alkaline (Sleep Token)
5. Never Too Late (Three Days Grace)
6. Running Up That Hill – A Deal With God (Lø Spirit)
7. IF IT DOESN'T HURT (NOTHING MORE)
8. Iris (MOD SUN)

# SAOIRSE'S PLAYLIST

1. The Cure for Breathing (VOILÀ)
2. DARKSIDE (Neoni)
3. World War Me (Hollywood Undead)
4. Teardrops (Bring Me The Horizon)
5. Fighting Myself (Linkin Park)
6. My Light (Dead by April)
7. Part Of Me (Evanescence)
8. Specter (Bad Omens)

THE COMPOUND
THE OLD LIBRARY
WALL 1
BLACK HILLS
THE PLAZA
CONSTRUCTION & MEP
WALL 2
APARTMENTS
MEDICAL
SUPPLY
SCHOOLS
WALL 4
FARMING
MILITARY POLICE & ARTILLERY
WALL 3
TO THE OTHERWORLD

ISLE OF BONE AND BLOOD
MOUND OF SKULLS
THE MARSHES
MOTH LAKE
FOREST OF GHOSTS
HILLS
WALL 2
LD
N

# PART ONE

# THE COMPOUND

# ONE

Long ago, there was a cauldron that revived the dead.

The cauldron was called the Pair Dadeni—the Cauldron of Rebirth—and it had various owners over the years. Eventually, it found itself in the hands of an Irish king.

The king was cowardly, spiteful. In his weakness, he brought a war upon himself, and during that war, he used the Pair Dadeni to reanimate the corpses of his fallen soldiers.

When the king's enemies discovered what he was doing, they destroyed the cauldron, rendering its powers useless. By all accounts, that was the end of its story.

Until now.

EARLY AUTUMN, NINETY-NINE YEARS
AFTER THE NUCLEAR WAR OF 1989

Trips to the library (or anywhere else within the ruinous cities, for that matter) were risky and reckless. Gus Brandon's compound elders forbid them, unless under certain circumstances.

But Gus was desperate enough to break the rules.

At twenty-one years old, he shouldn't have been obsessed with anything other than surviving, continuing humanity, and restoring the world to the glory of the Golden Era. He especially shouldn't have been obsessed with something as trivial as old folklore.

Yet here he was, ditching his scavenge-duty so he could scour a relic for the scraps of stories lost to time.

Again.

These woods offered little shade, the sun baking the air around him. As he darted through aspen and birch trees, sweat poured from his skin, and his throat felt drier than a crater left in the wake of a bomb. To make matters worse, the water in his canteen was already more than half gone. He paused, pulled it out, and took a swig anyway. The cool liquid spilled down his esophagus, offering temporary relief.

Soon the trees grew even more sparse. He crested a hill, and mountains of debris became visible in the distance. Although these ruins were less than six miles from the compound, he couldn't visit them often—because of his elders' rules, of course. *"It's too dangerous to visit a relic for recreational purposes,"* they said at assemblies. *"A waste of time and resources as well."*

If his teammates discovered where he'd been sneaking off to and told the military police about it, he'd most certainly receive a lashing in punishment. But even as he thought of whips shredding his flesh, he couldn't stay away.

He picked up the pace, sprinting toward the destroyed city ahead. Once he reached the wreckage, he was safe to slow down and catch his breath, hidden from sight by mounds of fragmented wood, brick, and concrete. He dove deeper into the ruins, his combat boots scraping against dry soil and splintered glass, and dozens of automobiles rusting with age began to crop up, dispersed all around him.

Human bones—skulls, rib cages, spines, femurs—started to appear as well. Sprawled-out skeletons coated with grime, their jaws hanging open in soulless smiles, were scattered across the destruction, and the farther he went, the more of them he saw.

He wondered who they'd been in life, and what it'd been like to live and die in the Golden Era. They must have been terrified when tensions between the United States and the Soviet Union reached a boiling point—when soldiers left home for the battlefields, when fights broke out in the streets, when explosives rained down on civilians.

*Try thinking of something less bleak*, he thought. And, in a way, it was easy. After all, how could he consider the horrors of reality when stories of fair folk danced in his mind?

Finally, he approached the library. It was a plain two-level rectangular structure that had (somehow) withstood the Nuclear War. Damage to the building consisted of shattered windows and doors, cracked flooring, knocked-over shelves, and a collapsed section in the back. Other than that, it was intact.

Gus had always found the library's stability to be strange, especially considering that everything around it had been so utterly demolished. Not that he was complaining; the building's survival meant he got to read something other than compound manuals and historical textbooks. It was just weird, and if he were more interested in his job as a construction worker, he might have investigated how it could have happened.

Too bad he hated the job he'd been assigned . . . Not that any job in the compound sounded particularly swell.

He glanced down to check the time on the black watch around his wrist—which Ronnie had given to him years back, when he'd gotten old enough for scavenge-duty—and cussed under his breath. It was half past three. He only had until six thirty before his scavenge-team would return to the meeting point and start the hike back to the compound. *I'd better make this quick. I still have to catch something.* He hastened up the concrete stairs, leapt through the broken doors, and jogged toward his section of choice.

A smile turned up his lips when he saw the sign that read "Fantasy: Myths, Folktales, and Faerie Tales." It was discolored and hung crookedly from the sagging ceiling, the tome-lined shelves beneath it overrun with the twisting, gnarled vines that grew up out of the fractures in the wooden-plank floor. At the back of the dilapidated section, an oak tree had even broken through the floorboards, its tallest branches brushing the ceiling.

Adjusting his aviator eyeglasses, he inspected the books' spines for compelling titles. He only had room for one or two in the secret sleeve he'd sewn on the inside of his backpack, depending on their trim size and length, so he had to decide what sounded the most interesting and narrow down his choices from there.

Several "modern" fiction titles (that is to say, published within the last two centuries—to his knowledge, no new novels had been produced since the Nuclear War) caught his eye, but what he most wanted to read were books that documented the beliefs and superstitions of the cultures that came before his own, not stories inspired by said beliefs and superstitions. Maybe someday, after he'd exhausted his nonfiction options, he'd move on to fiction.

Soon he found more of what he was searching for and narrowed it down between a collection of "real-life" encounters with changelings and an illustrated encyclopedia of Celtic deities. *Oh boy, what would the elders think if they saw me reading this?*

The elders had always asserted that there was no such thing as God or gods, that it was pointless to even contemplate ideas such as reincarnation or life after death. *"Focus on the here and now, what you can see and touch and know to be real,"* they urged, again and again. *"Focusing on anything else is a waste counterproductive to the compound's survival."*

Ultimately, Gus chose the book on changelings, and as he slipped the treasure into his backpack, there was a chittering noise nearby, then the familiar scurrying of tiny paws. He smiled. "Is that you, Rem?" More chatter, this time to his left. He turned that way.

The black-furred squirrel that seemed to live in the library—Remington, Gus called him—stood atop the shelf before Gus. The creature cocked his head, twitched his tail, and scampered forward.

With his free hand, Gus brushed some unkempt chestnut hair out of his eyes and stroked Remington behind the ears. Many animals in the area suffered from genetic deformities, their ancestors' DNA damaged by fallout, but Remington appeared to be a normal, healthy squirrel, identical to the old photographs Gus had seen in school.

"Hey, little guy," Gus said. "What's up? Haven't visited you in a while." In fact, he hadn't been here for months. He had scavenge-duty once every five weeks, and during his last two duties, he hadn't managed to get away from his teammates at all.

He'd missed picking out books, but he'd almost missed talking to and petting Remington more.

Almost.

The *creak* of floorboards sounded behind him. "You got a friend I don't know about?" he asked Remington, chuckling. He pivoted, sure he was about to see another squirrel, but was met with something much more surprising.

Shrouded in shadow, a woman stood less than twenty feet away. He couldn't make out her facial features, but he could tell she was on the shorter side. Her long-sleeved dress hugged her pronounced curves, the hem stopping just past her mid-thigh. For some reason, she was barefoot.

Gus dropped his backpack, his pulse quickening. Years of survival training kicked in, and he reached for his gun, ready to shoot, ready to—

Wait a second.

She was just standing there, wasn't attacking him.

Not yet anyway.

*What if she doesn't? What if I scared her as much as she scared me?*

His palm hovered above the worn leather holster at his belt. He cleared his throat. "Uhh, hello?"

Hesitantly, she stepped into a ray of light shining in through a break in the ceiling, and Gus got a better look at her. She was young, probably his age. Her straight platinum-blonde hair framed her full cheeks and reached a little past her collarbones. She watched him with large round eyes, her irises the same shade of green as her dress, her top lash line drooping as if she'd always been sad, as if she'd been cursed to a lifetime of sorrow.

"Hello," she said. She spoke differently from anyone he'd ever met—was that what they called an accent?—her voice high and melodious. "Who are you?"

"I'm, um—I'm Gus Brandon. And you?"

"Oh, what a nice name." She paced forward, slowly and carefully, and Gus's lips parted as he noticed her pale skin was covered with scars. Raised and pink, they must have come from surgical stitches, and they wrapped around her flesh like chains. No exposed part of her body was free of the marks—not her face, not her neck, not her hands or legs or feet.

How in the world had she gotten those scars? Had she been operated on by the deranged scientists the elders warned people on scavenge-duty about? If so, how had she survived such intense surgeries?

Not only that, but where had she come from? She couldn't belong to the compound. Hardly anyone there owned a dress, let alone garments in colors other than black, white, and gray. Also, nobody went outside without a good pair of boots. How was she supposed to protect her feet?

None of this was adding up. Something horrible had happened to this young woman. *Does she need help? The elders accepted Ronnie even though he was an outsider. Would they take her in too?*

"Thanks, I think." He dropped his hand to his side. It didn't seem there was anything to be afraid of. "What did you say your name was?"

She paused, her face brightening by the slightest of margins. Wait a second—was she *smirking* at him? "I didn't give it to you."

Okay, yeah, she was definitely smirking at him, but two could play that game. He did his best to mirror her expression. "Would you? It's not every day I get to meet someone in my"—he gestured at the bookshelves around him—"favorite place of all time. This is groundbreaking for me, really."

She giggled, her lips turning up in a full-on smile, and Gus's breath hitched. *She's . . . really pretty.*

Several moments passed before her laughter subsided, and she replied, "You can call me Saoirse, Gus Brandon."

"Sear . . . shah? Is that what you said?"

"Mm-hmm."

"How do you spell that, exactly?"

"S-A-O-I-R-S-E," she said. "Saoirse."

"*Saoirse*," he repeated. "That's beautiful."

A reddish-brown insect flittered in his peripheral, and he looked that way. It was a moth, one bigger than his palm, the kind he saw in the forest sometimes.

The moth flew straight over to Saoirse, and she lifted a hand toward it. It landed on her index finger, and she smiled sadly at it, then at Gus. "How kind of you to say." Glimmering, flickering movement winked all around her.

And then she disappeared.

It was as if she'd melted into the air, and Gus stood there, dumbstruck. What had *happened* to her?

He reached for his gun again. "What the hell?" He glanced around, but nobody else was in the library. *I'm alone.*

The moth fluttered past him, back from where it came, and he took deep breaths, removing his glasses and rubbing his eyes with trembling hands. Was he going crazy, seeing things? Had his "overactive imagination" finally "gotten the best" of him, just as Beverly always said it would? Or had his parents' passing, combined with Beverly breaking things off with him and moving on, become too much for him, and he'd snapped?

Sure, his relationship with Mom and Dad had been nonexistent at best, abusive at worst, and he and Beverly had wanted different things, so it'd had to end between them.

But still . . .

He sighed and put his glasses back on. So what if he *were* going crazy? Tons of people had lost their minds after the turmoil of the Nuclear War, and he wasn't convinced that even after all these years, every person in the compound was entirely sane. A bunch of folks probably saw people that weren't there, right? *Constantly. I bet they see people that aren't there constantly.*

He shook his head. There wasn't time to stand here and worry about it anyway. Now that he had his books, he needed to catch a hog or a deer or a goat or *something* so that he wouldn't get in trouble. So that there would be more animals in the compound to breed, to eat.

Chittering sounded on the ground next to his feet.

He looked down to find Remington nuzzling the side of his boot. "I'll see you next time, okay, Rem?" He knelt and quickly petted the black squirrel, then retrieved and zipped up his backpack, threw it over his shoulder, and left the library.

# TWO

It took over half an hour to track and capture the six-legged white billy goat. But once Gus had it tied up, he couldn't have been more pleased. It meant the compound would have a male to impregnate the females they'd been catching lately—their livestock supply was sorely lacking ever since that nasty virus killed so many people and animals last year. He'd be the hero of today's scavenge, and his teammates wouldn't worry about why he'd run off during their mission.

It was perfect, really.

He tugged the goat as he trekked through the forest, keeping the creature beside himself, careful not to let it run wild and gore him. He lifted his wrist; the time on his watch showed six o'clock. *Fantastic. I'm early.*

The woods began to thicken, and he reached his destination located at the edge of a ravine three miles north of the compound. Compared to its surroundings, the ravine was a lush oasis, with weeping willows hanging over a river. Moss blanketed the bark and rocks, and mushrooms dotted the grass.

As Gus stopped at the riverbank, the smells of damp soil and green vegetation filled his nostrils, the sounds of gushing water and splashing fish permeating the air. He breathed in deeply, savoring the scents and sounds. *Wish I could read out here.*

The goat bleated at something behind them, and he spun around. The rest of his team—yes, he counted all three of them in the distance—was fast approaching. Adam had a massive duffel bag slung over his shoulder, Oliver carried a bundle of dead two- and three-headed birds, and Nancy pulled along a live pig, the animal's skin covered in scarlet splotches.

At the sight of Adam's new bag, Gus's stomach dropped. *Great, he found guns. No one's going to give a shit about my goat now.*

Adam pointed at Gus. "You got a billy?" His freckled white skin was fried from being outside all day, his shaggy ginger curls shining in the sun like freshly polished copper. He patted the duffel bag. "Try again. I got some .22 long rifles with lots of ammo."

"Oh boy." Gus resisted the urge to pinch the bridge of his nose. That was a favorite make and model of artillery.

The three of them—all of average height, average

build—paused in front of him. Nancy put a tanned hand on her hip and watched him with a suspicious look in her brown eyes, her silky straight onyx hair tied up in a ponytail, her blunt bangs clinging to the sweat on her forehead. "Where'd you run off to?" she asked.

"Where do you think?" Gus jutted a finger at the goat. "I was tracking this guy."

"Come on, Gus," Oliver said. He looked like a short-haired clone of Nancy, as she was his older sister by two years. "You've got to stop doing this."

"Stop doing what?" Gus asked, feigning innocence.

"Sneaking into that relic," Nancy replied. "The old city."

"What? What are you talking about? Why would I—"

"You're putting yourself in danger," Oliver interrupted. "And the rest of us too. We have no idea what kind of crazies could be lurking around the ruins, just waiting for someone to prey on. Traffickers, cultists, cannibals, organ thieves—you name it, they're probably hanging out in there."

"To be fair," Gus started, "if there *are* any 'crazies' in the ruins, who's to say they aren't hanging out in the woods too? I seriously doubt the forest is any safer than a relic. Case in point: Where do you think those rifles came from? Our people have been scavenging since the war. If the guns had been out here all along, they would've been discovered before we were born. Someone must have lost them recently. Someone passing through."

He thought of the blonde woman he'd imagined seeing in the library, of her scars and sad green eyes. *Saoirse.* How much of her was tethered to reality? How many people like her were truly out there, wandering this hellscape of a world without a safe compound to sleep in at night?

Adam shook his head. "I don't know why you're so fascinated with that place, but today was the last time you'll visit it without permission. Because if you do so again, I'm informing MP."

"I already told you I didn't!"

Oliver balled his free fist at his side. "We saw tracks. Actually, we've *seen* tracks on multiple occasions. The difference is this time we wizened up and took a photograph of the pattern on your soles, and we were able to confirm that the tracks belong to *you.* You can't lie to us anymore."

"You got a *photograph* of my *soles?*" Gus cried, anger bubbling in the pit of his stomach. "When did you do that? How'd you manage to save the credits for something so frivolous?"

"We all worked doubles for a month to chip in for it," Nancy said. "Anyway, like Adam told you, you can't visit the relic anymore. Not without an approved mission. And if you break the rules again, we'll have to notify MP."

Gus laughed, but it was devoid of joviality. "Man, I can't believe this."

"Can't believe what?" Adam raised a brow. "That we're holding you accountable for your actions? That we aren't going to let you take so many risks and break the compound rules?"

"Oh, that's rich," Gus said with a snort. "Especially coming from you. If you're so worried about me taking risks and breaking rules, stop doing it yourself. In fact, maybe *I'll* go to MP. Maybe I'll tell them what *you've* been up to on our missions. You know, to 'hold you accountable' for your actions and all." He tugged on the goat and stomped around his teammates, ready to end this conversation and get back to the compound.

One of them seized his free arm and yanked him backward. He turned to see it was Adam. "What's that supposed to mean?" Adam demanded, a threatening look in his ice-blue eyes.

"You already know. You and Oliver both." Gus ripped his arm from Adam's grasp and kept on walking. He didn't want to call out Adam and Oliver for their secret relationship, but they were being hypocrites for threatening to inform MP about Gus's trips to the city, considering same-sex coupling was strictly forbidden.

Another asinine rule, but Gus understood why the elders had put it in place. How else would they restore the planet to the glory of the Golden Era if their people got to choose who to sleep with? Got to choose whether to pop out babies?

The compound needed as many little workers as it could get.

"Are you really going to rat us out?" There was a tremor in Oliver's voice.

Gus stopped. Let out a long sigh. It would make his

life easier, so much easier, if he held this over their heads. They wouldn't be able to tell *anyone* about what he was doing.

But he'd been on the receiving end of cruelty too many times before, knew just how much it hurt.

Finally, he said, "No, I'm not."

It seemed that, at least for now, the discussion was over, and without another word, they began the hike back.

# THREE

When Gus and his teammates were a mere mile from the compound, the sun had almost finished setting, and the temperature had dropped significantly. A breeze grazed the back of his bare neck and arms, sending chills through his body. In every direction, all that was visible were trees, the only noises those of his and his companions' boots and their animals' hooves crunching against shriveled grass and fallen leaves. Occasionally, crows—some of them genetically altered, their feathers stained a pinkish color—flapped from branch to branch, their harsh caws piercing the quiet.

Maybe it was because of the extensive amount of folklore he'd been reading, but these days, the dark played tricks on Gus's eyes, making him see monsters when nothing was there.

Nothing could be there, after all, as the stories he so loved weren't real.

And even if there was a chance that they *were* real (and he knew there wasn't), his compound was on the western side of a mountain range called the Black Hills, located within the fallen United States of America—far, far away from the places those magical tales took place.

Yet he still found himself imagining all manner of malevolent faeries prowling the woods at night. He saw them skulking in the shadows, waiting for the perfect moment to strike.

In masses of collapsed cottonwoods, he imagined there were redcaps hiding, plotting to slaughter any stray travelers passing by.

In murders of crows, he imagined there were sluagh flying, scouring the forest floor for the next unlucky fellow whose soul they might devour.

In fast-moving streams, he imagined there were kelpies biding their time, anticipating the moment a person came close enough to drown and eat.

Thankfully, the logical side of his brain knew he had nothing to worry about—even as far as nonfictional threats went. The worst anyone on scavenge-duty had encountered in the last year was a couple of mountain lions and some rattlesnakes, and although he and his teammates had never run into anything like that, they knew how to take care of it as easily as the other people of the compound had: with bullets.

*No one* left the compound without a loaded gun and extra ammo.

Gus and his team were safe.

The sun dipped below the horizon, and if it weren't for the smog blanketing the sky (a lingering effect of the Nuclear War, which the elders said should clear up any decade now), the moon and stars might have lit up the night. The temperature fell even further, clouds of breath filling the air in front of Gus's face and fogging up his glasses.

"Guess we should have packed our coats," Nancy remarked as she walked in front of Gus, guiding her pig along. She began to shiver. "I hate when the weather gets like this. Hot during the day, cold at night."

Twigs cracked to the left. Hand flying to his holster, Gus looked that way, his goat bleating, Nancy's pig squealing.

A flash of movement in the trees, there and gone in an instant.

"What the . . . ?" Oliver tossed his bundle of birds over his shoulder and retrieved his flashlight, his teeth chattering. He and Adam stood several feet to Gus's right. "Did you guys see that?"

Adam drew his handgun. "Probably a mountain lion. We're almost home, so just keep your eyes peeled and your weapons ready."

"Maybe speed it up a little too," Gus added, and he and Nancy pulled out their handguns. The team continued toward the compound.

Not five minutes had passed before more branches snapped behind them. Again, the goat bleated, and the pig squealed.

Everyone swung around, preparing to shoot. Oliver shined his flashlight into the trees.

The glow revealed a creature that made Gus's skin prickle with goose bumps.

Suspended in the air was some kind of moth, its brown-and-orange wings twitching, but it was far too large to be a natural-born insect. Gus couldn't see its head, thorax, abdomen, or even its antennae, but he had a clear view of the back of its outstretched forewings and hindwings, and they were huge. From one side to the other, they had to span well over two yards.

"Does that thing have fucking *feet*?" Adam cried out.

Gus gazed at the space below the giant moth wings, and sure enough, he saw a pair of human legs and feet. They were pale, with raised pink stitch scars wrapped—

A gunshot roared into the air from behind Gus. He staggered forward, his ears ringing.

Another gunshot, then another and another and another. The goat tried to run, and Gus's skin burned from the friction of the rope rubbing against it. Gritting his teeth, he tightened his hold on the cord. He looped it around his hand and wrist, but the goat was frantic. The animal careered into the trees, dragging him sideways. He dropped his handgun and slammed into the forest floor shoulder-first. The rope scraped out of his grasp, ripped his flesh raw.

Head throbbing, hand and wrist stinging, Gus scrambled to his feet. But before he could chase after the goat, someone seized him by the arm. He looked over. It was Nancy, her expression etched with horror. She didn't have her pig anymore.

She yelled something at him, though he couldn't hear what. Then she jerked him away, toward the compound, Oliver and Adam already sprinting in that direction. Oliver had dropped his birds, and Adam his guns.

*What happened? Didn't they shoot that thing?* Gus glanced over his shoulder, expecting to see the moth-creature dead on the ground after so many gunshots had gone off.

But instead of a lifeless heap, he saw four dark figures standing together, staring intently at him. They seemed to be human, seemed to have human faces and human bodies, but the silhouette of insect wings protruding from their backs gave them away. They fluttered their unnatural appendages and soared into the night sky.

Gus faced forward and ran as fast as he could, terror arcing through his veins.

# FOUR

By the time Gus and his team reached Wall One—a fifty-foot-tall corrugated barrier erected long ago with scavenged metal—the ringing in his ears had subsided, and he could hear his teammates a bit. But their voices were muffled, as if his ears were clogged with cotton.

Oliver stuffed his flashlight into his backpack, yanked out his walkie-talkie, and pounded his free fist against Wall One's door, which, like the compound's other three entrances, blended seamlessly with the rest of its wall due to the patchwork nature of the walls' construction. Unless someone saw where the doors were located from the inside, or saw where the scavenge-teams exited and entered the compound for scavenge-duty, they wouldn't be able to find the doors, wouldn't even know they were there.

"Let us in!" Oliver cried, beating on the entrance again. "Fucking let us in!"

"And get MP!" Adam yelled into the walkie-talkie. "There's something in the woods, and we couldn't kill it! We couldn't kill any of them!"

"Okay," a young man with a deep voice said on the other end of the walkie-talkie. "We're coming down from the tower. Just hold on."

Nancy released Gus, and pins and needles rushed through his wrist, palm, and fingers. She'd been holding onto him so tightly that she'd cut off circulation.

Heart still racing, he shook his tingling hand and tried to catch his breath. Had the moth-creatures or people or whatever they were followed him and his team to the compound?

If they had, and if their intentions were less than agreeable, would the military police be forced to use precious grenades and other hard-to-get weapons to keep the peace, since bullets apparently didn't work on them?

And what about the stitch scars on the legs and feet of the first moth-person they'd seen? Now that Gus had a moment to think, to breathe, he realized the marks were the same as the ones all over the woman from the library.

Had Saoirse been *real*?

Had she vanished from sight because she had the legitimate ability to disappear, not because she was a figment of Gus's imagination? Was she one of those freaky things in the woods, and had she somehow folded her wings behind her back so he couldn't see them? Was she—were all of them—a sort of science experiment, as he'd first suspected when he'd noticed her scars?

Why would scientists want to turn people into bulletproof moth-creatures with the power of invisibility, anyway? What did that accomplish? *Maybe it doesn't have to accomplish anything if the goal is to simply defy nature.*

He had to admit, if Saoirse turned out to be real, he'd be relieved. If she was real, that meant he wasn't seeing things.

Then again, if she was real, that could also mean she was one of the moth-people they'd encountered, and if she'd followed him from the city, it was his fault this had happened in the first place.

Not only that, but if she intended to harm the compound or its inhabitants, the military police would track her down and try to kill her.

Gus hoped it wouldn't come to that.

*It might not*, he thought. *Saoirse seemed harmless, maybe even nice. She could've attacked me twice now, but she didn't, and I wouldn't have stood a chance, considering she's bulletproof.*

*If she really is one of those moth-people, then maybe we misunderstood what they wanted. Were they following us because they need help or something?*

Metal creaked against metal as the pair on tonight's watch-duty of Wall One (it should be Evie and William, if Gus remembered correctly) undid the door's many deadbolts and opened it.

Gus and his teammates stumbled into the open area beyond Wall One's entrance, the long rectangular watchtower that was supported by tall beams and ladders high above their heads. Rows of LED bulbs, dim and flickering, hung from a mess of wires at the bottom of the tower's base, barely illuminating the dry dirt ground and Evie and William as the pair shut the door and fastened its bolts and latches.

"Where—is—MP?" Oliver asked between gasps.

Evie and William turned around to face Gus and the others. "They're on their way," William said, and crossed his umber arms over his chest. Gus stood relatively tall at five foot eleven, but William had a good five inches on him, not to mention at least a hundred pounds of pure muscle. "What happened out there?"

After catching his breath, Adam explained how the team had come across the moth-people, how they'd looked human but had insect wings. "When Nancy shot at the first one, the bullet veered off course," he said. "Almost like it was, I don't know, redirected or something?"

"Redirected by an unseen force," Oliver chimed in.

"Yes, that's it. Redirected by an unseen force," Adam agreed. "It hit the ground instead of the target, and then three more of the creatures showed up. Nancy and I shot at the others, but the redirection-thing kept happening, so we cut our losses and ran."

Gus's eyes went wide as he processed what Adam was saying. The moth-people weren't bulletproof, but they could *deflect* bullets? Somehow the latter was even more bizarre than the former.

"They can fly though, you guys," Adam went on. "When I looked back, I saw it."

"I saw it too," Gus said, and Nancy and Oliver added, "Uh-huh," in unison.

Evie cussed, brushing obsidian curls out of her tawny face. Since they'd all been children, she'd been tiny, and she'd grown up to be one of the shortest women in the compound. "I bet a lunatic scientist kidnapped some people and experimented on them, and now they've escaped the lab."

Gus nodded and replied, "That's what I think." He was starting to calm down, his hearing and heart rate returning to normal. "If that's the case, maybe medical can help them. Get them back to normal." His teammates gave him incredulous looks. "What?"

"They're freaks, Gus," Nancy said. "Monsters. There is no 'normal' for them anymore." He clenched his teeth, holding himself back from retorting that Saoirse had seemed pretty damn normal to him back when he first saw her in the library, that she could have rushed him but didn't. His teammates knew he'd gone into the city, but they had no idea why, had no idea whom he'd met or what he'd brought back. *And William and Evie don't even know as much as they do.*

*Better just keep my mouth shut.*

William chuckled. "Monsters? C'mon, Nancy, don't be dramatic."

"I'm not!" she protested.

Another chuckle. "It was dark, which makes everything more frightening. I'm sure they really are science experiments, but redirecting bullets? Flying? Be real."

Adam threw his hands in the air. "We *are* being real!"

"We wouldn't lie about something like this!" Oliver exclaimed.

Footsteps crunched in the dirt on Gus's right, and he looked that way. Two figures walked toward them, the dark, distant outlines of the Wall One MP and artillery quarters looming behind the approaching silhouettes.

The figures drew closer and stepped into the dim light, and Gus saw they were a pair of military police clad in chain mail and bulletproof vests, their faces concealed by helmets. They had tons of gear strapped all over them—Tasers, batons, machetes, guns, handcuffs. Gus was sure they had grenades stashed away as well.

"What seems to be the problem here?" the first officer asked, her voice stifled by her helmet.

Adam re-explained everything that had occurred, and for several moments, the military police were quiet. They glanced at each other, then at Gus and his teammates.

Then they burst into a fit of laughter.

"You've gotta be kiddin' me." The second officer slapped his knee in amusement. "I mean, it *is* one of the more creative stories we've been fed when a scavenge-team fails to bring back anything, so I'll give ya that, at least."

"It's not a story," Nancy insisted. "We're telling the truth. There's something out there, and you have to take care of it before tomorrow's team leaves for duty!"

The military police went silent again, and Gus bit his tongue, resisting the urge to suggest that perhaps this whole situation was a misunderstanding. Under no circumstances could he draw MP's attention and prompt them into asking him questions, especially when he was walking around with contraband in his backpack.

Eventually, the officers nodded at each other. The first raised her walkie-talkie to her helmet where her mouth should be. "This is Tamara. Let the sergeant know Paul and I are leaving. Just checking on an anomaly scavenge-team twenty-one claims to have seen. Should be back in a few hours. Over."

A woman on the other end of the device replied, "Copy."

"Go on home, team twenty-one." The second officer—Paul—shoved his way past Gus and the others. "And hope we find something out there. Otherwise, it'll be your asses." Tamara followed Paul's lead.

William and Evie unlocked the door and opened it to let the officers out of the compound, and an uneasy feeling settled in Gus's stomach as they disappeared into the night.

# FIVE

Saoirse soared across the dark sky with three of her fellow Children. The scent of foul, manufactured impurities polluted her nostrils, and the stitch scars covering her body throbbed with familiar pain.

Moving frequently and with insufficient rest—as she had today—often made her hurt like this, and the more she exerted herself, the worse it became.

Soon the Children arrived outside a crude human settlement. "Do you truly believe he's the one we're looking for?" Malachi asked, the deep bass of his voice as cold and cruel as always.

The four of them flew closer to the ground, hiding in the trees, and Saoirse recalled the young man Malachi was referring to. The one she'd come across in the ruined city, the one they'd been following.

*Gus Brandon.*

She thought of his lopsided smile. Of his wild hair and kind, curious brown eyes. Of his ruddy complexion and funny accent and the large spectacles that sat too far down on his nose. Of his big hands and feet, and of how inelegantly they moved with the rest of his lanky frame.

Most importantly, she thought of how, as he'd browsed the bookshelves in the library, bright-white magic had erupted all around his head in serpentine tendrils of smoke, warping until they'd formed the unmistakable characteristics of his lineage.

Within moments, he'd gone from human to faerie.

"Yes, I do," Saoirse answered.

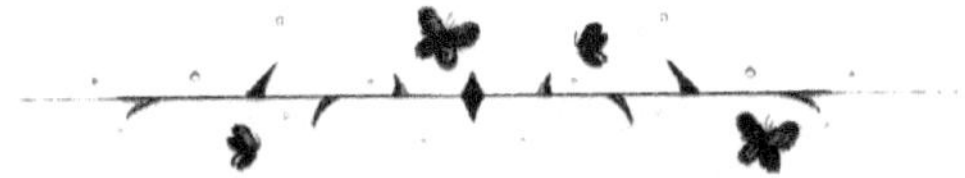

After Gus dumped out the contents of his backpack, careful to ensure Evie and William didn't discover the book within his bag's hidden sleeve, they questioned him about how he'd lost his rope and handgun and failed to bring anything back from duty. They'd finished interrogating his teammates before starting in on him, and Adam, Oliver, and Nancy had already exited the area.

"Sorry, Gus," Evie said as William scribbled on a notepad. "We just have to make sure the losses are properly reported to supply and artillery." William finished writing everything down and signed Gus back in, and finally, he was allowed to leave.

Eager for rest, he speed-walked south, the dingy lampposts attached to the buildings ahead guiding his path. He had at least a thirty-minute trek ahead of him; he needed to travel past the Wall One MP and artillery quarters and the plaza, both of which made up the northern section of the compound. Then he had to pass multiple apartment complexes before he reached the one he lived in.

He entered the Wall One MP and artillery quarters, a crammed cluster of buildings that housed about a fourth of those who worked in MP and artillery. Like the rest of the structures in the compound, they had solar panels attached to their roofs and were fashioned with pieces of buildings from the Golden Era, a hodgepodge of scraps smashed together to form something relatively functional.

Since Gus was assigned to construction, his job was to help maintain the mismatched establishments of the compound, and to (hopefully) assemble better ones when it was eventually expanded.

He reached the other side of the quarters and entered the more open space of the plaza, where the shops and recreational activities were located.

To his left, the familiar voice of a young man hissed, "Hey, Gus!" Muscles tensing, he stopped, turned that way, and peered into the faint light. His scavenge-teammates leaned against the back wall of an officer's quarters two buildings down, the three of them waving at him. "Can we talk to you?" Oliver went on. "Please?"

With a sigh, Gus made his way over. "What's up?" he asked when he reached them.

"We're gonna head to the bar for a beer," Nancy said. "Try to relax after what happened."

"Care to join us?" Adam added.

"Uhh, nah." Gus pushed up his glasses. "I'm way too tired. I've got an early morning at work too."

Adam shrugged. "Suit yourself. But one of these days, you really should come out with us."

"You know," Oliver whispered, "so you can find joy in something other than sneaking into relics, you risk-taking lunatic."

"Not that we haven't taken risks too," Adam said quickly. "Thank you. For not telling anyone, I mean."

"Sure," Gus replied. "No problem."

"We talked about it, and we think it's only fair we don't say anything about you either." Gus perked up a bit at Oliver's words. "Sorry for that, by the way," Oliver continued. "You were right about the forest being as dangerous as any relic."

*No need to tell them the whole thing might have been my fault, right? Wouldn't wanna ruin the moment . . . or make them change their minds.* "It's fine." He scratched the back of his neck. "I'm sorry too. For being an ass."

They smiled at him, and he allowed his body to relax. Perhaps, if he was feeling up to it, he'd go out to the bar with them the next time they asked.

"Um, anyway, I'm gonna go," he said. "See ya."

"See ya," the three of them replied, not quite at the

same time. They walked southwest through the plaza, toward the corner where the bar was at, while Gus let out another sigh—this time in relief—and continued south toward his apartment complex.

About half an hour later, he reached his building, a two-level structure that wasn't exactly pleasing to the eye. The team who'd constructed it had certainly done their best, but that didn't change the fact that the walls and floors and ceilings were a mess of incongruous woods and metals, the glass of the windows either permanently stained or riddled with cracks.

Body sagging from exhaustion, he opened the front door of the complex and walked through the lobby to the stairs, then trudged up to room forty-six located on the second level. He dug his key out of his backpack, unlocked the door, and stepped inside.

Unsurprisingly, Ronnie was still awake. Ronnie always waited up for Gus on the days he had scavenge- or watch-duty. He'd lived here with the old man for about a year—ever since his parents died from the virus that had infected so many in the compound. Their apartment had been fumigated, then given to a newly married couple expecting their first child.

The elders had welcomed Ronnie into the compound nearly two decades ago, and they'd placed him in construction, just as they had Gus's father, and later Gus. Ronnie had quickly befriended Dad at work, had looked out for Gus for as long as he could remember.

To be honest, Ronnie was the only person Gus

could call family.

Always had been.

Ronnie sat on a cushioned recliner in the living room, reading some sort of manual under the glow of his shaded floor lamp. Gus had no idea how even at the age of seventy, Ronnie stayed in great shape and maintained a full head of black hair.

"Hey." Ronnie closed the ring binder in his lap. "How was scavenge-duty?"

"Weird, man. Weird." Gus shut and locked the door and tossed his backpack aside, then shook off his boots, not wanting to dirty the various rugs that covered Ronnie's floors. "Are there any leftovers?"

"Yup. Saved 'em for ya."

Stomach growling, Gus shuffled into the kitchen and grabbed a plate out of one of the apartment's three cupboards, all of which were fashioned with jagged pieces of aluminum. He retrieved the noodles from the fridge (its paint was flaking, its top and bottom doors full of dents), then plopped the noodles onto his dish and threw the cold meal into the microwave (an appliance just as worn down as the fridge) for a minute.

"Why was duty weird?" Ronnie asked.

Gus explained everything that had occurred: from meeting Saoirse in the library, to his teammates calling him out for ditching them, to encountering four frightening science experiments in the woods . . . and how one of them might have been Saoirse.

"Huh." Ronnie leaned back in his chair, stroking his mustache. "You did have a peculiar day."

"Told you." Gus pulled his dinner out of the microwave. It was probably cold by now, but he didn't care enough to reheat it. He got a fork from the silverware drawer, sat down in a steel chair at Ronnie's round oak dining table, and started shoveling noodles into his mouth, which turned out to be lukewarm, not cold. They were bland, practically tasteless, and he wished he could afford fresh produce every day. He craved the sweet-and-sour burst of strawberries on his tongue, yearned for the watery crunch of cucumbers in his teeth.

"I wouldn't worry about it," Ronnie said. "Crazy stuff happens all the time out there, and we're none the wiser because *we're* in *here*. Well, most of the time." He paused. "Anyway, I'm sure MP will take care of whatever it is you saw. Let's just hope they leave the attractive young lady alone, eh?"

Gus almost choked on his noodles. "Besides the scars, I didn't mention her looks," he snapped, his mouth full of partially chewed food.

"You didn't have to. I can tell she's a stunner by the way you say her name. Maybe next time you're out scavenging, you can ask her to dinner."

Gus gulped down his bite. "C'mon, Ronnie. Beverly *just* broke things off with me, like, a couple of months ago. Would you knock it off?"

"All right, all right, I'm sorry. I didn't know you were still stewing over that." Ronnie stood up and walked over to Gus's backpack. "You manage to visit the library this time? You see that friendly squirrel?"

"Mm-hmm."

"He doing good?"

"Yup."

Ronnie unzipped the bag, unbuttoned the secret sleeve, and pulled out the book Gus had smuggled in. "Real-life encounters with changelings, huh? Sounds interesting. You going to start it tonight?"

"I dunno. I'm pretty tired."

"Good thing you're young and can stay up all night, unlike this old man."

Ronnie examined the cover art for a second, which featured an illustration Gus had seen a few times in other folkloric books. It was a stylized scene, the earth-tone watercolors nearly monochromatic, with a yellow-haired maiden trekking through forest between two trolls. It had been painted by John Bauer in the early 1910s, if he remembered correctly.

The old man strolled over to Gus, set the book on the table. "Start it. For me. Don't forget to let me know what you think tomorrow."

Sucking down the last of his noodles, Gus smiled a little. If it meant they'd be discussing the book the next day, then staying up to read wouldn't be so bad. After all, Ronnie was the one who'd gotten Gus interested in mythology and folklore over ten years ago, and other than Beverly, he was the only person who knew that Gus visited the city and stole books from the library during scavenge-duty.

His parents had had their suspicions—they'd constantly scolded Gus for his daydreaming. They'd also caught him reading a few times, and Dad had uncovered part of his book stash in his closet, but he'd never explicitly told them about the library. Why would he? They'd never cared about his interests, never cared about his happiness. In fact, they probably would have turned him in for the contraband they were aware of if it weren't for Ronnie's pleading on Gus's behalf, and if it weren't for the fact that they'd have been investigated for illegal activities as well.

"Will do," he said.

"Great! Hey, what happened to your hand?"

Gus looked down at his free hand resting on the table. "Oh, the rope. When my goat got away. I guess it did a number on me, huh?"

"It sure did. Let me get you something for it." Ronnie hastened to the bathroom and returned with a jar of ointment and a roll of bandages. He sat down at the table next to Gus and, ever so gently, rubbed some of the cool, clear, jellylike salve on the injury, then bandaged Gus's hand and stood up.

"Thanks, Ronnie."

Ronnie clapped Gus on the shoulder. "I'm headin' to bed. Early morning at the elementary school and all that. Need my beauty sleep for Mrs. Jones and Mrs. Morgan." With a wink, he started toward his bedroom.

Gus took his dishes to the rusty sink, rolling his eyes at the thought of Ronnie flirting with the widows who'd worked at the school for over forty years. "I'm stationed there tomorrow, too."

"In that case, we can walk together. Have our chat

in the morning. And hey, be sure to shut off the lamp before you turn in."

"Of course." They weren't supposed to keep lights on constantly because with all the smog, they needed to conserve what energy the solar panels produced.

The door to Ronnie's room creaked open and shut, and Gus washed his dishes and set them aside to dry. Then he grabbed the book about changelings, sat in the chair by the lamp, and dove into the stories.

# SIX

"C'mon, Gus. Time to get up."

Gus cracked open his eyes. He blinked a few times, cussing as he realized he'd fallen asleep in the recliner, the lamp still shining brightly, the book pages-down in his lap. *Great, that's gonna be a hefty fine.* To his right in the kitchen, Ronnie wrapped what appeared to be a sandwich with wax paper and placed it in a small metal lunch box.

"Sorry about the lamp," Gus said, and switched it off.

"It's fine." Ronnie sounded distracted. Had he woken up late? "Just get going. You've got twenty minutes before we need to leave." Gus nodded and set his book on Ronnie's wooden side table. He made himself some toast for breakfast, prepped his lunch and backpack, took a quick shower, and got dressed. Then he and Ronnie left, locking the apartment behind them and exiting the building.

As usual, hundreds of people dressed just like them—colorless T-shirts, cargo pants, and combat boots—were walking to their respective workplaces. It was a forest of nearly identical individuals teeming up and down the dirt paths, chatting with neighbors and congesting the alleyways.

Side by side, Gus and Ronnie weaved through the morning crowds, heading west toward the elementary school. It was within Wall Four, which was also where the other two schools, medical, and the Wall Four MP and artillery quarters were located.

"You must not have wanted to put the book down last night," Ronnie remarked as they walked.

"I really didn't," Gus said, and frowned. As interesting as the stories were, they tugged at his heartstrings in ways others had not. "I can't believe some folks back in the day *actually* believed their kids were switched out with faeries."

"Tragic, don't you think?"

"Yeah, I do. I guess it makes sense though, considering the times."

Ronnie hummed in agreement. "Absolutely. If the survival of a family depended on the parents and all the children working, and if one of the children was born different, the parents wouldn't have always been able to care for them."

"I guess it was probably easier for people to believe

that the 'changeling' wasn't their own. You know, if they decided to get rid of it."

"Exactly. Were there any stories where the family cared for the changeling, though? That happened too. Sometimes, parents believed that if they mistreated it, their real child would be harmed."

"I didn't read any of those cases yet, no. But I only got about a quarter of the way through the book before I passed out, so I'm sure there's at least one in there."

They continued their discussion until reaching the elementary school: a single-level rectangular structure with twenty classrooms inside. Gus vividly recalled reporting here every workday from preschool to fifth grade to learn how to read and how to do basic math. During that time, he'd also learned about how the compound had come to be. From sixth to eighth grade, he'd attended the middle school, where he'd been taught survival skills, had been assessed for a job, and had been sorted into construction. Then, from ninth to twelfth grade, he'd gone to the high school, where he'd continued his survival studies in the mornings and worked part-time for construction in the afternoons.

Up ahead, their foreman Hank stood outside the entrance of the school, scratching his bald liver-spotted scalp as he studied the paper attached to his clipboard. Either the rest of the crew hadn't arrived yet, or they'd already started their jobs for the day. "Morning, boys," Hank greeted as Gus and Ronnie approached, keeping his gaze trained on the clipboard.

"Morning," they replied in unison.

"Gus, I'm gonna have you take a look at some of the playground equipment, if you think you can manage it, and Ronnie, you're gonna be repairing a leak in the boys' bathroom. The principal's been nagging construction about it for weeks."

Ronnie raised a brow. "Am I a sub for plumbing today or something? Leaks fall under MEP."

Hank looked up from his paper. "Didn't someone tell you? Construction absorbed MEP a while back. They didn't have enough people—too many died last year, and they haven't been able to recuperate. We're all gonna have extra on our plates until the youngsters graduate and go full-time."

"Ah, okay." With that, Ronnie started toward the building's entrance. "Don't lose track of time, kiddo," he said to Gus over his shoulder. "I'll be out front for lunch."

"Sounds good." Gus headed around the side of the school toward the playground out back, children giggling and squealing as they played during their first recess.

As he reached the edge of the playground, kids running in all directions, he spotted which piece of equipment needed attention: half of the bars on the jungle gym had come loose and fallen to the gravel.

He was about to set off toward the jungle gym when a young woman called from behind him, "Gus! I didn't know you'd be here today!"

He cringed, slowly turned around. Beverly's friend Kathryn walked toward him from the building's side door, a thick packet of papers in her rich-brown hands. Two years older than him and Beverly, Kathryn was slim and pretty and about his height. Her raven coils were tied up in a puff, her amber eyes glittering with what appeared to be genuine delight at seeing him.

"Kathryn," he said, forcing a smile. "What are you doing here? Shouldn't you be in medical?" Like Beverly, Kathryn was a nurse, one of only thirty-nine in the entire compound. Thankfully, Hank would never trust Gus with projects as important as ones in medical often were, so Gus didn't have to worry about running into Beverly, Kathryn, or any of their other nurse friends—not unless there was an assembly or they happened to be shopping at the same time as him.

"We're here to give the kids their radiation vaccines." Kathryn held up her packet. "I was about to pull a few of them."

"Seriously? They're getting those already?"

"Well, summer *did* just end. It's that time again." She laughed. "We should be jabbing construction within the next week or so too."

Gus opened his mouth to reply, but the side door opened, and a painfully familiar young woman stepped outside.

As usual, Beverly was radiant, her cedar-brown tresses styled in a braid over her shoulder, her porcelain skin dewier than ever. She stood only a few inches shorter than Gus, her dainty frame exaggerated by her baggy T-shirt and cargo pants.

"Hey, Mr. Byrne wants—" Beverly stopped when

she noticed Gus, her gray eyes widening. Sunlight reflected off the silver band she wore on her slight left ring finger. "Hey, Gus."

"Hey, Bev." He reminded himself not to stare at her engagement ring.

"What are you doing here?"

"The same thing you are. Working."

She offered a teasing smile. "Construction must be desperate for help if they're trusting *you* with projects at the schools. There's nothing more important than our children. Can you actually focus on fixing their equipment with that overactive imagination of yours?"

Was she seriously bringing this up in front of Kathryn? And worse than that, out in public? She *was* just joking, but . . . When she broke things off with him, she'd promised to continue keeping his secrets about the library, the books.

"Uh, yeah, I think we're short-staffed all around." He jerked his head in the direction of the jungle gym and took a step that way. "Listen, I'm on the clock, so . . . I'd better go."

Beverly's smile fell. "Okay, then. Go."

"It was nice to see you, Gus," Kathryn said.

"You, too," he lied, then made his way onto the playground, trying to put the encounter out of his mind.

Soon the bell rang. The teachers who'd been supervising recess rounded up the children and ushered them inside, and Gus worked on repairing the jungle gym. He did his best to focus on the task, but even still, he couldn't keep his thoughts from wandering, couldn't stop daydreaming about the changeling stories he'd read last night.

As he located his tools, he thought of a mother who'd left her baby boy unattended for just a moment. She claimed that when she'd returned, the baby was gone, replaced with a new child dressed in the first's clothes.

She immediately threw out the unfamiliar baby and went in search of her son.

As he made his measurements, he thought of a father who said he'd come into his daughters' nursery to investigate suspicious noises, only to find the twin infants parading around their room and playing tin whistles more skillfully than even the most talented of musicians.

The father dragged the girls out into the forest and abandoned them there.

As he tightened his bolts, he thought of parents who'd asserted their son didn't look right, wasn't acting like himself, had eaten every last crumb of food in the house.

In the end, they set their little boy on fire.

The more Gus thought about it, the more the changeling stories reminded him of his own childhood. While Mom and Dad had never physically harmed him, had always fed and washed and clothed him, he'd never felt as if they'd truly cared for him, as if he'd truly belonged.

He remembered once—he'd been four, maybe five

years old—when he'd just been released from school and was walking home with Mom. He'd wanted to hold her hand, other kids held their parents' hands, but every time he reached for her, she yanked away.

There had been another time, back in the first grade, when he'd asked Dad a question at the dinner table, and all the man replied with was, *"Would you shut up and finish your potatoes already?"*

But the worst of it had been when, at around the age of seven or eight, he'd realized that he couldn't recall an instance in which his parents had told him they loved him. Honestly, he couldn't think of a single time they'd said, *"We love you, Gus."*

Maybe they'd thought that it was fine, that if he was technically cared for, it didn't matter how they otherwise treated him. But to him, it had mattered a great deal. It had given him pits in his stomach and stings in his eyes and a crushing loneliness that was always there, that never really went away.

At least he'd had Ronnie. At least every time he'd needed his parents—really needed them, dammit—and they hadn't been there, Ronnie *had* been there.

*Like in elementary school*, he thought with a smile. *How he studied with me for those super-hard math tests. Or how he helped me with ideas for my and Bev's first date. Or how he came to high school graduation.*

Gus made sure to check the time on his watch between tasks, and before he knew it, noon came. He returned his tools to his tool kit and locked it so the kids couldn't get into it, grabbed his lunch, and headed toward the front of the school to meet Ronnie.

As he neared his destination, he saw that Ronnie, Hank, and the rest of the ten-person crew stationed at the elementary school today had already arrived, but they weren't hanging out. They weren't eating and bullshitting as they did every other day. Instead, they were standing around a stocky military police officer. The officer seemed to be asking Ronnie questions, while the others listened to what was being discussed. *Oh boy. What happened?*

Gus pushed through his peers toward Ronnie, the other crew members side-eyeing him. He began to hear bits and pieces of what was being said.

"Would you mind if we brought you to quarters and questioned you further?" the officer asked. Gus thought he recognized the guy's voice but couldn't place his identity because of the helmet.

"Yes, I *would* mind," Ronnie replied tersely. "I have nothing else to say to you."

Brow knitting, Gus reached Ronnie's side. "What's going on?"

"Gus Brandon," the officer said, "I need you to come with me, please."

"Care to tell me why?"

The officer sighed, paused. A moment later, he removed his helmet, and Gus pressed his lips into a thin line. *I knew I recognized his voice.* It was Lewis Evans, the guy Beverly had started seeing after she broke things off with Gus.

The guy she'd be *marrying* in a few short weeks.

Gus didn't know Lewis well. With his black hair and taupe skin, he was a little over three years older than Gus and Beverly, and Gus had only seen him in passing. What Gus *did* know about him was that his twenty-fifth birthday was coming up this winter, and that that was part of why he and Beverly were rushing into wedlock.

"The MPs you and your scavenge-teammates sent out last night never came back," Lewis explained in a gentle tone. "We haven't heard a word from them, either. The elders decided that since the four of you asked them to go out, it's only fair you help retrieve them."

"But we—"

"All the departments are short-staffed," Lewis went on. "MP doesn't have the manpower to launch a proper search party right now. I know it's frustrating, but that's why the elders are calling on you and your teammates to help track down the missing officers. They appreciate your cooperation."

"Gus isn't stepping foot out of the compound," Ronnie asserted. "He's already finished his duties for this cycle. Besides, searching for missing persons isn't his job."

Wyatt—a man in his fifties—snorted. "You say that as if Brandon actually does his job."

Laughter from several members of construction. Ronnie shot Wyatt and the rest of them a threatening glare, and Gus shrugged. "At least I've never come in piss drunk and almost crushed someone with equipment. Remind me, Wyatt, how many lashings did you get for that? You had to pick up a bunch of extra duties for it too, right?" Wyatt's nostrils flared, but he stayed quiet.

"Speaking of duties, my brother was on watch last night," Jane chimed in. She was William's younger sister, and Gus had graduated with her. "He said Gus lost a gun and didn't bring back anything from the scavenge yesterday."

"That isn't the full st—"

"Exactly!" Logan exclaimed. He was another older man, a friend of Wyatt's. "It won't kill the little pest to chip in for MP. Less of a mess for us to clean up at the end of the day, too." More laughing, and Ronnie balled his fists, stomping toward Logan.

Gus reached out to stop Ronnie—their shit-talking wasn't worth getting in a physical altercation and, ultimately, getting a penalty over—but Lewis beat him to it. The officer grabbed Ronnie by the arm and pulled him back. "All right, all right. Everybody just calm down and quit with the bickering. Gus and I need to leave"—he gave Ronnie a pointed look—"*again*, at the request of the elders. I need to know that a fight won't break out after we go, and that this department will have a productive rest of the day."

Everyone in construction went silent. Ronnie continued scowling at the others, but eventually, his expression softened. "Can I at least go with him?" He turned to face Lewis. "Can I help search for the officers?"

Lewis released his hold on Ronnie. "No. You're too old to leave the compound, and the elders only want team twenty-one and a few officers to do it."

"But that's not—"

"It's okay." Gus placed a hand on Ronnie's shoulder. "I'll be okay. I'll have Nancy and Adam and Oliver and some MPs with me."

Ronnie looked over at Gus, genuine fear in his dark eyes. "I don't like this."

Where had this concern been last night when Gus initially told Ronnie about the weird moth-people in the woods? "Really, Ronnie, it's gonna be fine. There's nothing to worry about, all right?"

"All right," Ronnie replied, although he didn't sound convinced.

Lewis gestured at Gus. "Why don't you gather your things, and then we'll leave?"

# SEVEN

Saoirse had been sitting in the tree for hours, watching the crude human settlement, waiting for Gus Brandon to come out. To be honest, she didn't even know if he would. Each group of people she'd encountered behaved in such vastly different ways.

"Have you seen anything yet?" Malachi asked. He flew toward her; his wings had always reminded her of a death's-head hawk moth's, mottled with onyx and cocoa and ochre. As he sat down next to her, his hazel gaze roamed over her body, drinking her in. A halo shone around his auburn hair as the sun glared behind him, and his mark-less, peach-white cheeks flushed in the heat.

She scooted away from him and crossed her arms over her chest. *Why couldn't he have bothered Margaret or*

*Moira?* "Not yet," she answered.

"Too bad." He shifted his stare from Saoirse to the wall ahead. "I want out of here."

Saoirse nodded. She wanted to leave the Mortalworld too, wanted this whole ordeal to be over.

Then she could finally rest, could finally be free of her pain.

"Wait, is that him?" Malachi pointed, and sure enough, there he was. Even from a distance, she recognized Gus Brandon walking out of the settlement door with his three companions from yesterday and a fourth she didn't recognize.

"It is," she said. "We have to get the others."

Lewis hadn't been kidding when he'd said MP was short-staffed. To Gus's shock, the officers who'd gathered his teammates—the same ones who were supposed to participate in this search—were pulled at the last minute to deal with fights in the plaza. The search party only consisted of Lewis and scavenge-team twenty-one now.

Gus and his teammates were supplied with walkie-talkies, guns, knives, food, water, rope, flashlights, first aid kits, and other small essential items, which they stored in their backpacks, and Lewis was decked out in equipment. The officer clutched a locked and loaded shotgun, an extra-large bag filled to the brim with gear strapped to his shoulders. On top of wearing his regular helmet and armor, he had a Taser, a baton, and a machete dangling from his belt.

After exiting the compound through Wall One, the five of them quickly located the missing officers' tracks and began following the prints into the forest, the afternoon sun blazing high in the sky. The tracks led in the direction of the meeting point from yesterday—the edge of the ravine—presumably because the officers had followed Gus's and the others' tracks last night. Lewis was at the helm, and Gus and the others trailed behind him, their boots crunching against dry grass and leaves.

Adam, Nancy, and Oliver held their pocketknives, their hands trembling as they looked this way and that. Gus assumed they were watching out for the moth-people, but he wasn't worried about stumbling across the science experiments (as he'd concluded they meant no harm), so he'd opted to keep the gun in his holster and the knife in his backpack.

If anything, what Gus was most anxious about was being in Lewis's company. Not because the officer seemed to be an unpleasant person—on the contrary, he seemed kind, patient. But Gus and Beverly had been together for years. In middle school, she'd taken pity on him for his inability to make friends and had kept him company. By the time they'd turned seventeen, they'd started seeing each other (Gus had had a sneaking suspicion that Beverly enjoyed rebelling against her parents by being involved with the village freak), and they hadn't ended things until this last summer.

Basically, it was strange for Gus to be around the man who'd soon be marrying the woman he'd loved and lost. *Well,* he thought, *"lost" probably isn't the best word for it. In a way, I just . . . let her go. She wouldn't have broken things off if I'd have done what she wanted when she wanted me to.*

*"I can't wait for you anymore,"* she'd said on the night their relationship ended. They'd been sitting on his bed, in his room in Ronnie's apartment, when they had the talk. *"I wanna help the world get back to what it was. I wanna get married, start a family."*

Not that getting married and starting a family was an option for anyone in the compound. The elders put a lot of emphasis on wanting what they defined as "as many well-adjusted workers as possible," and to get that, they controlled every aspect of people's lives, including their family structures and reproductive choices. Once a single man reached the age of twenty-five, he was considered ineligible to choose his own spouse, and the elders bound him to whichever woman deemed capable of childbirth was available and closest to his age. Unless medical considered someone infertile, or unless the compound took in someone past the age of forty (like Ronnie), the elders required everyone have a spouse.

Then, after a couple was married, medical stopped administering their birth control shots. They were required to live together and to conceive four children—unless it became clear that giving birth so many times was a major health risk to the mother. But usually in those cases, she would have already lost her life as she brought another into the world, her husband married off to someone else before her body was in the ground.

*"What if we left the compound?"* he suggested. *"What if we escaped, started new lives together? You're a nurse. You could steal all the birth control shots we need, and—"*

*"Do you hear yourself right now? Even if I wanted to leave with you, where would we go? Realistically? How would we survive out there?"*

*"I . . . haven't thought of that yet."*

*"Of course you haven't. You're too busy with your head in the clouds."* She looked away from him, scoffed. *"Would you have even married me before you were considered ineligible? If I wasn't already forced to be with somebody else?"*

*"Why would you—why would you even* ask *me something like that?"*

*"Because I want your answer, Gus."*

He'd thought then, thought long and hard about whether he'd be ready to be a husband and a father by the age of twenty-five, whether he'd be ready to be a husband and a father *ever.*

Finally, he took a deep, shuddering breath and said, *"I can't give you one. My parents . . ."* He didn't have to finish. She knew exactly what he meant. Even still, she started crying, and for the first time since they were kids, he couldn't console her.

After that, she assured him that she'd keep his secrets about the books and the library and left the apartment. Five weeks later, he heard from Oliver that she'd been seen around the plaza with Lewis Evans. A month later, the pair were engaged. It stung, and Gus did what he could to avoid seeing her, to avoid thinking about it, but at the same time, he was . . . relieved. Because a part of him knew, even when she'd asked him, that he would've never married her. Plan or no plan for survival, he would've fled the compound before being forced to have children with anyone.

"Whoa." Lewis stopped between two yellowing aspen trees a short distance away from the ravine. He motioned for Gus and the others to halt, and they followed the order.

"Did you find something?" Adam asked.

Lewis examined the ground. He walked in a half circle, careful not to disturb whatever he was focusing on. "The tracks end, and . . ."

The fearful tone in Lewis's voice made Gus uneasy. He took a small, cautious step forward. "And?"

"And then it looks like there was a struggle. Judging by the impressions in the grass and dirt, I—I think Tamara and Paul were dragged away. By what, I'm not sure."

"Oh, shit." The color drained from Oliver's face. "It was those moth-monsters."

For the first time today, Lewis sounded annoyed. "Come on. We all know there aren't any 'monsters' out here."

Oliver opened his mouth to argue, but Gus interjected. "I really don't think they're monsters. I think they're science experiments."

"It doesn't matter what they are," Adam said. "They're terrifying, and they're dangerous."

"I'm actually not so sure they're dangerous either," Gus replied. "If they wanted to hurt us, don't you think they would have already? Considering they can deflect bullets and fly and everything?"

Lewis shook his head, returning his attention to the ground before him, and Adam adjusted his backpack straps with his free hand. "What?" Adam demanded. "You don't believe we saw those things? You think we're making them up?"

"I don't know." Lewis sighed tiredly. "What I *do* know is that we need to follow these impressions if we're going to find Tamara and Paul. Stay close to me." He raised his shotgun, preparing to fire at a moment's notice, and stalked alongside the trail.

"You'll want to put that gun away and use your machete or something," Oliver said as the four of them hurried after Lewis. "We really did see monsters, and they really did redirect bullets."

"If they can redirect bullets, I doubt a blade will do much against them," Lewis countered.

"Maybe not, but—"

Lewis shushed Oliver and pressed on.

Mere seconds of walking had passed when Oliver, who treaded on Gus's left, halted and gasped. "What is it?" Adam asked, stopping next to Oliver.

Oliver pointed at a cluster of birch trees farther up the trail of impressions. "Is that . . . blood?"

Everyone stopped in their tracks, looked toward the birch trees. "Blood?" Nancy said. "Where?"

"Close to the base of the tree up front," Oliver replied. He sounded exasperated. "Look at it—like, *actually* look at it."

Lewis crept toward the birches. "Oliver's right. There's blood. Dried blood."

Nancy and Adam edged up behind Lewis, and Gus narrowed his eyes and adjusted his glasses. He peered in the direction Oliver had indicated, near the front tree's base, and sure enough, there it was.

A streak of rust red smeared across the white bark.

"Sorry to say," Oliver started, "but I don't think Tamara and Paul made it. We should go back. *Before* the moth-monsters get us next."

"There's no way to be sure whether this is human blood," Lewis argued. "It could have come from anything that bleeds."

A pained moan drifted out of the woods farther down the trail, and Gus put his hand to his holster. Had the sound come from the missing officers? It made him think of ghosts, of wayward spirits refusing to cross over to the land of the dead.

"Tamara!" Lewis shouted. "Is that you?"

Another moan, and then a quiet, "*Help—me.*"

# EIGHT

Saoirse was glad that it didn't take long to reach Margaret and Moira. They'd been flying away from their post as well, weaving through the trees toward Saoirse and Malachi.

Though equally beautiful, the two didn't look alike. Margaret's scarless skin was ebony black while Moira's was bronze brown; Margaret's long hair was twisted in braids while Moira's cascaded in waves. Not only that, but Margaret's wings resembled a rosy maple moth's: fuzzy baby pink with thick, irregular bands of lemon yellow, while Moira's resembled a ghostly silk moth's: sharp Stygian strokes inked upon gossamer, a single kohl-lined, burnt-orange orb staring out from each forewing and hindwing.

"He just came out," Malachi told them. "Let's go

before we lose his trail."

Margaret shook her head. "We'll have to split up." For as long as Saoirse had known her, her voice had been high-pitched and bubbly, her sentences effervescent. "We spotted the other creature."

"Margaret has to bind it," Moira added. She couldn't have expressed herself any differently from Margaret, her voice a husky monotone. "She'll need our help."

"You're sure we can't just kill it?" Malachi asked.

"Absolutely not," Margaret said. "We can't risk its soul warning him before reincarnation."

Malachi turned to Saoirse. "Will you be all right handling him on your own?"

She nodded, grateful that it would only be her at first. Sure, it would be difficult, but her plan would work better that way. "Go," she said. "I'll signal you later."

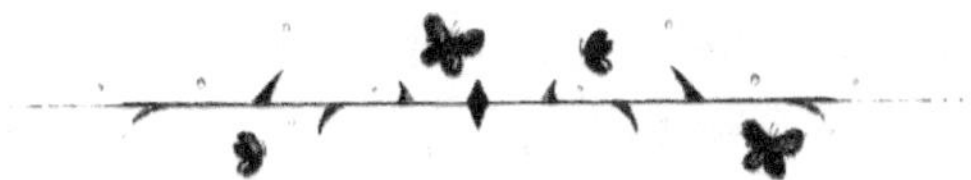

Gus dashed through the forest beside his scavenge-teammates, the four of them close behind Lewis.

Within seconds they burst from the woods.

Reached the edge of the ravine.

Stopped dead.

*I can't believe what I'm seeing.*

A middle-aged woman with ash-blonde hair—

Tamara, Gus deduced—lay on her back in a puddle of blood on the riverbank. She was nude, her arms and legs bent at unnatural angles, bones splashed with scarlet jutting from her cream-colored skin.

But what made the scene even more disturbing was the whole human skeleton resting in the grass beside her. It looked perfectly polished, its skull and all its bones gleaming in the sunlight as if something had licked them clean.

What, or who, could have done this?

"Holy shit." Lewis threw his slinged gun over his shoulder and sprinted over to Tamara. "That's not Paul, is it?" He jerked his head at the skeleton.

Tamara groaned, her gaze distant. "Y-yes. The— skeleton. The—skeleton . . ."

"Don't worry. We'll get you away from the skeleton." Lewis kicked the bones out of the way, knelt next to Tamara, and began digging through his bag. "We'll get you home."

Gus realized he'd been holding his breath. He let it out, hastened over to Lewis. "What do you need us to do?"

"Gus, call the compound," Lewis said. "Tell them what's going on and that they need to be ready for us. Oliver, take my stuff so I can carry Tamara. Adam and Nancy, keep watch for the sick fuck that did this, and have your guns ready. *Please.*"

He pulled out a syringe and a vial labeled "morphine" and started preparing to administer it. At the same time, Oliver ran over to get Lewis's bag,

Adam and Nancy put their knives away and retrieved their guns, and Gus grabbed his walkie-talkie and pushed the device's press-to-talk button.

"This is Gus Brandon," he said, the words spilling out in rapid succession, "calling from the ravine three miles north of the compound. We found the missing MPs, but Paul is dead. Tamara's arms and legs are broken. Lewis is administering morphine right now, and then we'll start the run back. We need people from medical to meet us at Wall One's entrance, and we need whoever's on watch-duty to be ready to let us in right away. I repeat, we need people from medical to meet us at Wall One's entrance, and we need whoever's on watch-duty to be ready to let us in right away. Over."

Static crackled on the other end. "Copy, Gus," said a woman. "This is the Wall One MP and artillery quarters. We'll contact medical and the pair on Wall One's duty for you in case they didn't hear your message. Can you bring Paul's body back? Over."

It was a morbid question, yet she had to ask it. The compound had had difficulties growing crops in the past, but they'd discovered that burying their dead in farming's soil helped tremendously. "No, there's nothing left of him. He's just bones. Over."

An uncomfortably long stretch of silence. More static. "How do you know it's Paul if all you've found is a skeleton?"

Before Gus could explain, before he could say that Tamara herself had confirmed the bones were Paul's, there was a swashing sound, as if a massive fish were swimming right at the surface of the river. Gus looked that way, his brow furrowing.

A pair of human hands was reaching out of the water. Pale and tinged with blue, deep-purple veins spiderwebbing across the flesh.

The rest of the person the hands belonged to—a chubby bearded man—erupted from the water, started splashing toward the riverbank. He appeared to be naked, and his whole body (what was visible of it, anyway) looked just as pale and veiny as his hands. His unmoving eyes and mouth gaped open, frozen in a soulless expression that Gus had only ever seen on the dead.

But this man wasn't dead. Dead people couldn't walk or swim. They couldn't even move.

So what was wrong with him?

"Paul?" Lewis called, positioning Tamara over his neck and shoulders; it appeared she'd fallen unconscious. Paul didn't answer Lewis, didn't make a sound, his expression unchanging as he waded through the shallow water.

Oliver dropped Lewis's bag and reached for his holster, and Nancy and Adam ran up next to him, their guns pointed at Paul. "Don't!" Lewis yelled, and the three of them stopped. "It's the other officer! He needs our help!"

Gus recalled the virus that had taken his parents. How it had made them cough so hard they vomited, so hard the veins popped out of their necks and temples. Was a new virus about to plague the compound, and had Paul gotten sick with it overnight? Did it, like the last virus, give its victims a fever high enough to cook their brains in their skulls? That would explain Paul's nudity and discoloration, and why he was in the cold water with a dull look on his face. Also why they'd found Tamara naked and with all her limbs broken. Maybe Paul had gone crazy and attacked her.

The problem was that theory didn't explain how the spotless skeleton lying on the riverbank had gotten there. Could it have been the work of a cult? Part of some sick, twisted human-sacrifice ritual? If so, where did Tamara and Paul fit into it?

"Gus?" the woman on the other end of the walkie-talkie said. "Are you there? Do I need to send backup?"

He didn't reply, couldn't.

It happened too fast.

Paul reached land and bolted for Lewis and Tamara. Nancy shot at him twice, one bullet tearing through his left shoulder, the other whizzing past his head. But he didn't fall to the ground or grimace in pain. He didn't react at all.

Expression blank as ever, Paul seized Tamara by the ankles and wrenched her from Lewis.

More gunshots, and Gus dropped his walkie-talkie and barreled toward Paul, his ears ringing, his heart in his throat. He didn't know what was going on, didn't have the slightest clue. He just knew he had to get Tamara back from Paul.

He collided with the man, tried to grab Tamara, to get her away, but Paul hurled Tamara toward the river.

*No!* She went flying and landed face-first in the shallows with a sickening *craaack*. Fresh blood seeped out of her, clouding the water with red. *Shit! That didn't kill her, did it?*

Paul clawed for Gus next. Gus ducked under the man's arms and rushed down the bank after Tamara—*please be alive, please be alive*—but he froze mid-run, transfixed, when he saw more hands, more people, burst from the surface of the water.

Except they weren't really people, not anymore.

They were skeletons.

# NINE

Gus tried to make sense of what was happening as he stood at the riverbank, his pulse quickening, his breaths coming out faster and faster.

How was this possible? He counted six of them—six whole skeletons, their bones glistening with river water in the sunlight—walking toward land. Bullets thundered through the air, put holes in the things' skulls, but still they strode forward.

Were they the result of more experiments? Had they been worked on by mad scientists, as he suspected Saoirse had? Were scientists the ones who'd attacked Paul and Tamara?

*Tamara. You were going to help Tamara.*

*Get her and run.*

He vaulted to the woman's side and rolled her over.

Her nose was crushed in, but to his relief, she coughed up water, gulped in air. He put his hands under her armpits, readying himself to carry her as Lewis had.

Shouts and more gunshots behind him, and he glanced over his shoulder. Paul had wrestled Lewis to the ground, Adam and Oliver desperately trying to pull the crazed man off him. All the while, Nancy kept shooting at the skeletons, the gunshots so loud Gus could barely hear himself think.

The stench of death, of rot, assaulted his nostrils, and he gagged. Ivory appeared in his peripheral, and he looked that way, a shiver snaking down his spine. A skeleton had stopped a few feet in front of him and Tamara.

"*Fuck!*" With Tamara in his arms, he clambered to his feet, but something seized him by the neck—something behind him, something hard and cold and wet on his skin. It jerked him backward through the shallows, and he lost grip of Tamara. She splashed into the water once more.

He wrestled against whatever had grabbed him, tried to get back to Tamara, to help her, but it was too late.

The skeleton that had stopped before her and Gus knelt over her. It took her head in its hands as though she were its lover, then gashed open her throat with its teeth.

Gus stopped struggling, fell limp as he watched the skeleton devour Tamara. Chunks of chewed-up gore spilled down its "throat," accumulated in its "stomach." It even slurped down her blood with its—

*Wait a second. How does that thing have a* tongue?

Gus's head grew light. He hadn't noticed it before, but a faint white mist circulated around the skeleton's bones like blood pumping through a body. The haze seemed to be what animated the bones, what kept gore suspended in the stomach area, and it became more concentrated, opaquer, as it streamed through the hole at the base of the skull, as it oozed out of the mouth in the shape of a long pointy tongue and lapped up Tamara's bodily fluids.

The thing holding him turned him around, the putrid scent from before intensifying. Suddenly he found himself staring into the fog-filled eye sockets of a skull, a skeleton.

The skeleton lifted him out of the water with one "hand," grabbed his left arm with the other. It opened its mouth wide, bit hard into his biceps.

Burning, blinding pain.

Gus screamed, realized with horrifying clarity as the skeleton chewed on the bloody chunk of his flesh, as his skin and muscle turned to pulp in its teeth, that he was about to die.

The skeleton swallowed, leaned in to continue its feast, but powerful wind whooshed from the right. It blasted past Gus, blowing his hair about wildly, and roared through the skeleton, carrying away the circulating mist and the rancid smell.

In an instant the skeleton released Gus. It collapsed, its bones scattering every which way, and he tumbled into the shallow water, sand swirling around him as he hit the riverbed.

*I'm alive.* Relief flooded him, though the wound in his arm seared with pain. *Hurt, but alive.* He scrambled to his feet, his injured arm hanging limply at his side. Water had seeped into the fibers of his pants and shirt, making them heavy.

He glanced in the direction the gust had come from. When he saw who stood there, his breath caught.

It was a barefoot young woman with round green eyes. Wet platinum-blonde wisps framed her pretty face, raised pink stitch scars wrapping around her visible skin. Huge brown-and-orange moth wings stretched out behind her back, and for a moment, she reminded Gus of the winged faeries he'd seen paintings of in books. Had illustrations like those at all inspired the mad scientists who'd experimented on her?

"Saoirse?" His ears still rang. He almost couldn't hear himself speaking. "You just—you just *saved* me."

Her wings folded downward, disappearing behind her, and if he hadn't just been attacked by a bloodthirsty skeleton, his jaw probably would have dropped in marvel at her. She dashed to his side, grabbed his good arm, and pulled him farther into the water. "Hopefully, that was all of them," she said. "Now come on. I thought I saw a gate nearby. I have to take you to it."

"But those things are—"

"I already dealt with them. All the ones I saw, anyway."

"But—but my teammates . . ." He planted his boots against the riverbed. The water was up to his waist now.

She stopped too, giving him an expectant look. "What are you waiting for? This is important."

Was she crazy? There had been walking skeletons on the loose—one that bit out a chunk of his arm, and another that brutally murdered Tamara—and she wanted him to forget about it, to ditch everyone else and swim to who knows where?

No, absolutely not.

He tried to tug away from her but couldn't. Was he already weak from adrenaline dump? "Listen, thank you for saving my life, but I have to—"

"Don't thank me," she interjected. "Don't thank anyone anymore."

What the hell? He tried to pull away once more, but Saoirse held firm. "I need to get back to the others," he insisted. "I need to make sure they're okay and get them medical help and . . ."

He trailed off again, captivated as her wings extended into view and began to flutter. Droplets sprayed in all directions, showering him as she floated up into the air. "You know you'll have to let go of this place, don't you, Gus Brandon?"

That snapped him out of his trance. "Huh?"

She flew down to him and cupped his cheeks with her palms. They were warm—soft and smooth, save for the bumps of her scars. He found himself allowing her to draw his face closer to hers.

"Let go, Gus," she said, and before he could come

to his senses, before he could shove her away and flee, she dragged him down, into the river.

# TEN

Bubbles whirled from Gus's lips as he struggled against Saoirse, as she heaved him farther out into the water. Despite her short, curvy figure, she was *strong*. He kicked and scratched, thrust his right palm into her eyes, her nose, her mouth. But she only dug her nails into his cheeks and towed him along, blood ribboning from his face and arm.

The ledge they stood on dropped off abruptly, revealing a cavernous section of river. She dove into the cavity, and he kept on thrashing.

Why was she doing this? Why was she trying to drown him? She'd just saved him from being devoured by the skeleton. Why go to the trouble of killing him when she could have simply left him for dead?

Seconds passed, although it felt like minutes, and

suddenly the sun seemed far away. His movements grew heavy, clumsy. His lungs were on fire, and his vision faded in and out. How much longer would it be before he drowned?

His boots hit something hard. He looked down, saw that he and Saoirse were at the brink of a tunnel on the side of a shelf of sand and rock. The diameter of the tunnel wasn't big, maybe the size of Ronnie's dining table, but it was dark inside, and Gus couldn't see the end of it. How far did it go? Were there any pockets of air in it?

Saoirse pulled him into the tunnel, plunging them both into black. There was a rumbling noise, a current of water pushing them forward. The force sent them somersaulting through the water, slammed them against the walls of the tunnel, and when they stopped, Saoirse did something Gus could have never expected.

She let him go.

Pulse pounding in his ears, he paddled back the way they came. He kicked hard, swimming to the tunnel's entrance, then propelled himself back into the open water, toward the surface.

The river was dark, so dark he could barely see the sun. It was little more than a sliver now, a shard of white alight in the sky. Had the smog thickened while he was in the tunnel? And was it just him, or was the water suddenly a whole lot colder than before?

In no time he burst out of the river. He could have sworn he was farther from the surface than that, that Saoirse had dragged him much deeper into the river, but he wasn't about to complain about reaching the surface so soon. Closing his eyes, he gasped for air, relishing the fact that his heart was still beating, that he was still breathing.

"Glad you—made it," Saoirse said between labored breaths.

At the sound of her voice—crystal clear, his ears no longer ringing—he nearly jumped out of his skin. He opened his eyes and scowled at her, his glasses dripping with water. "What did you do *that* for?"

"You'll—see."

What was that supposed to mean? And why was it so dark out here? This went beyond the sun disappearing behind smog. It was almost as if . . .

He looked up. A crescent moon shone through the cloudy indigo sky, dozens of stars twinkling like flashlights turning on and off in a shadowy forest.

"What the . . . ?" He whirled around in the water, glanced in every direction, searching for his companions, for any familiar landmarks. But he recognized nothing, because he was no longer in the river at the edge of the ravine three miles north of the compound.

He was in a pond, a small one, in the middle of lush woodland illuminated by the moon and stars. Blue bioluminescent bugs flitted about its dense woods, casting cerulean glares on sprawling oaks and worn paths.

"Welcome—home," Saoirse said, still gasping.

He turned to her. Her chest heaved, her droopy eyes

creasing from strain. Was she tired because she'd dragged him into the river? *Good. After that trick, she had it coming.* "'Welcome home'?" He splashed backward, farther from her. "What are you talking about? Where am I, and what the hell is going on?"

Heavy breaths. "You don't—feel the pull—to this place?"

"Of course I don't!"

She opened her mouth to reply. A weak cry escaped her instead, and she floundered in the water for a moment. Then her eyes rolled into the back of her head, the rest of her going limp, and she sank beneath the surface of the pond.

"Saoirse!" He dove into the water, swam after her. Despite the limited light, he could see her as she floated down, down, down, and he reached for her with both hands and—

*Wait, how am I using my left arm?*

His heart almost stopped as he looked at and brushed his biceps. There was no blood, no wound, not even a mark where the skeleton had bitten him.

He touched his cheeks next, didn't feel any evidence that Saoirse had dug her nails into them. The skin was perfectly smooth.

With a shake of his head, he returned his focus to Saoirse. Yes, the stunt she'd pulled was ridiculous, but he couldn't let her drown. He'd figure out where he was and how his injuries had healed later.

He reached her, scooped her up in his arms, and paddled to the surface, then held her head above water and swam to land. Once on solid ground, he lifted her into a bridal carry and walked a few yards to the top of a small incline with plenty of grass. He laid her down, but she wasn't breathing, so he shifted her into a sitting position.

She broke out into a fit of coughing, water spewing from her lips, and he held her in place, waiting for her to spit it all up.

Giggles echoed in the trees up ahead. The laughter was childlike, reminding Gus of kids at school during recess. But it was also mischievous, as if said kids were plotting a prank on their teacher.

He turned his head that way, peered into the woods. He was close enough to the forest to see that the glowing blue bugs were butterflies. How had they become so brightly bioluminescent? Was it the result of fallout? More experiments?

A humanoid shadow crept out from behind one of the oaks. It was about the size of a toddler, its limbs gaunt and elongated. The shadow ducked behind the tree once again, whispered something. More giggles rang through the air like jingling bells.

"Piskies," Saoirse said, her voice scratchy and pained. "There must be a moor nearby."

He laughed a bit, relieved to see her awake. She seemed stable enough to sit on her own, so he let her go, her wings like wet velvet as his fingers brushed against them. "Piskies?" he asked with another chuckle. "Like, the Cornish faeries? From old folklore?"

"Piskies aren't only from 'old folklore.' They're as

real as you and me."

"Ohh-kay." Had he hit his head? Was he dreaming? Or was he still drowning in that river, his brain conjuring up a few last images as it died?

"It was kind of you to rescue me when I fell unconscious. Especially after the way I startled you to bring you here." If this were a dream, it would be a vivid one, because he was starting to pick up more of how she spoke. Whenever she used the long *i*, it sounded more like "oi" rather than "ie," and instead of blending her *t*'s and *h*'s in words like "the" and "they're," she pronounced the consonants separately, but the separation wasn't harsh. In fact, he wouldn't have described anything she uttered as harsh. Her words had a light, almost sighing type of quality, harmonious as a lullaby. "If for some reason you felt a debt was owed," she went on, "consider it repaid."

"Yeah, no. This isn't happening. It isn't real." He pinched his forearm hard. Nothing happened, nothing changed.

Saoirse giggled, yesterday's genuine smile returning, and Gus found his breath hitching as it had before, in the library. Suddenly he found himself keenly aware of her dress, of soaked-through folds of fabric clinging to her breasts and hips. He made himself focus on her face.

"I think you'll soon find that this is all very real, Gus Brandon," she said, and as she finished her sentence, her smile disappeared. She clamped her eyes shut and grunted in pain.

"What's wrong?" Instinctively, he reached for her. Drew his hand back to his side when he realized what he was doing.

"My—scars." More gasping. Was she going to pass out again? "I've done—too much. They—*hurt*." She took several long, deep breaths, then lay back in the grass.

A minute later, her breaths grew even. Had her pain improved? "Listen, Gus," she said slowly, her eyes still closed. "Now that you've seen this place, it will be easier to let go. I never wanted to just whisk you away, to rip you from your life without warning. I only wanted to show you where you're meant to be. So go back for a little while, say your goodbyes, come to terms with everything. It hasn't been long, and even if anything moved, you shouldn't end up far from where we came from. But know this: The other Children and I will be back for you. That's why we came. To get *you*. The realm is in trouble, and you're the only one who can save it."

"You want me to . . . to go back?"

"Yes. Through the gate."

"The gate?"

"The tunnel. Swim through it, and hurry."

Perhaps this was his brain's way of waking him up. The dream was over, and it was time for him to return to reality. That, or he was about to die.

He needed to find out either way, and so, without another word, he walked back to the pond and stepped into the water. He sucked in a breath, held it, and dove beneath the surface, plunging toward the tunnel at the bottom.

Soon he reached the tunnel and flung himself into black. A current pushed him forward again, sent him banging against the tunnel walls.

Then he made it to the other side, and he didn't find himself in bed, awake from a dream, nor did he enter the dark nothingness of death. He didn't even wind up in the river from earlier.

Instead, he tumbled onto the fractured floor of the library in the destroyed city.

# PART TWO

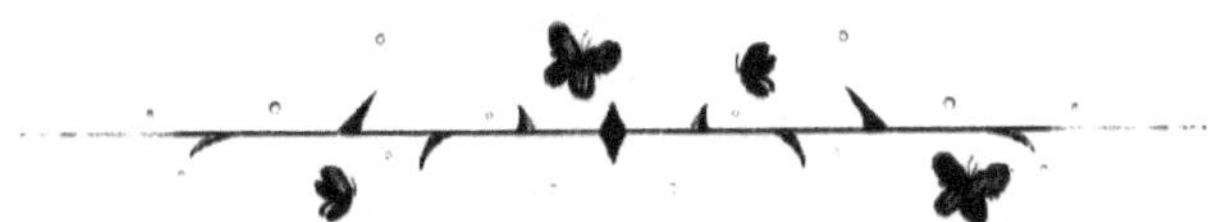

# THE GATES

# ELEVEN

Gus landed on his face, his nose bouncing off a stray piece of wood uprooted from the floor. The force sent his glasses launching into the air, clattering to the ground. Pain shot through his skull, and he let out a long groan.

When the hurt finally ebbed, he retrieved his glasses and put them back on, then glanced around, taking in his surroundings. He was at the far edge of his favorite section in the library, bookshelves in front of him, the oak tree behind him.

Except . . .

He did a double take. Was that a *hole* in the trunk of the tree?

He whirled around to get a better look.

Yes, there *was* a hole in the tree, one about the size

of the tunnel he'd just swum through. The wood was jagged at the edges, as though the trunk had a mouth lined with serrated teeth. *It can't be the same tunnel, right?*

Rumbling within the tree, its branches above jerking and snapping, and then the hole began to shrink. Cracking, the cavity grew smaller and smaller, until finally it closed altogether.

Gus put his face in his hands, every inch of him sopping wet, water pooling beneath him on the floor. Had all of that—the pond and forest, the butterflies and healing, the piskies and Saoirse—been real?

He checked his arm.

Nothing.

No pain, no wound to be seen.

And he could move it.

Had what just occurred *not* been a hallucination, a dream, a figment of his imagination as he drowned? If it hadn't been, that meant Saoirse truly had taken him to a world beyond this one, just as she'd implied.

And judging by the fact that she'd called the giggling creatures in the woods "piskies," he had reason to believe that the world she'd taken him to was indeed a fantastical one, a world he'd read about time and time again. Sometimes it was called Annwn, sometimes Elphame, sometimes Tír na nÓg, sometimes the Land of Faerie. It had many names, but Gus and Ronnie usually referred to it as the "Otherworld" while talking books. It was the realm of the gods and the fair folk and, in many stories, the realm of the dead as well. It was said to mirror Earth, acting as a sort of parallel dimension to the real world.

Gus recalled a book he'd read a while ago that documented the various protagonists populating the mythologies of the Celtic nations. Several of them entered the Otherworld, usually through portals. Some of the gates were located within trees or water, some within mushroom rings or hill forts, some within clouds of mist.

If the Otherworld was somehow real, and if that's where he'd truly been taken, it would explain how his wounds had healed—Tír na nÓg meant "land of the young." In the stories, the supernatural beings who lived in the Otherworld were thought to be blessed with eternal youth and good health. It made sense that visiting such a place, even for a short time, could heal one's injuries.

But then, if Saoirse had indeed taken Gus to the real-life Otherworld, that meant he might have been wrong about her. She might not be a science experiment, but a creature pulled straight from folklore.

A faerie.

There were multiple theories about what faeries were, where they'd come from. Some folklorists speculated that they were fallen angels cast out of heaven by the Abrahamic god. Others suggested that they could be spirits of nature or of the dead, or that they could be related to or an evolution of the pagan deities.

No matter the theory, they were always mysterious

and supernatural, and there were many different "species" of them, some humanoid, some not.

What had those flying faeries been called? The ones Saoirse reminded him of when he saw her with wings? Artists began depicting them in eighteenth-century illustrations, popularizing the idea that faeries were winged beings. Some folklorists had even speculated that flying faeries had power over the air . . .

"Sylph," he whispered in disbelief. "Saoirse is a—a sylph?"

It was then that he recalled some of what she'd said while the two of them were in the pond.

*"Welcome—home."*

*"You don't—feel the pull—to this place?"*

*"I only wanted to show you where you're meant to be."*

Gus's head spun. Had he heard her correctly? Because if he had, then it seemed as if she was suggesting that *he* was from the Otherworld. As if she was suggesting that *he* was a faerie living among humankind, a changeling.

But that couldn't be true, right?

*I mean, if I'm not really Mom and Dad's kid, it could explain why they never liked me. It could explain why I was never part of the family, why—*

He stopped himself. It felt ludicrous to entertain this idea, and the rational side of his brain took over. "I'm *not* a changeling," he whispered for his own benefit, "and Saoirse's not a sylph. She didn't take me to the Otherworld, because it doesn't exist. None of that stuff does."

The words of the elders repeated in his mind. *"There are no gods, no afterlife, no reincarnation. We know these things to be false because they cannot be seen or touched."*

Except Gus had seen *something*, hadn't he? Touched it too? The pond, the grass, the girl. He might not be a changeling, but that didn't change the fact that in the blink of an eye, he had witnessed day turn to night, had seen Cornish piskies and magically illuminated butterflies in the woods.

And he *wasn't* going crazy, *wasn't* imagining things. Even before Saoirse dragged him through that tunnel, he'd been attacked by walking, man-eating skeletons. At first, he'd tried to rationalize the situation, tried to come up with a logical explanation for it, but maybe there wasn't one.

Maybe the elders were wrong, and the stories of old were right. Maybe there was magic in the world, things people couldn't explain.

He'd have to ask the others what they thought. After all, he hadn't been alone when the skeletons attacked. His teammates and Lewis had been there with him, could confirm that they'd seen the same—

*Shit! My teammates! Lewis!* He clambered to his feet, his soaked hair and clothes sticking to his skin. What if they'd ended up like Tamara? What if they hadn't gotten away before Saoirse showed up?

Chittering sounded to the left. He turned and found Remington perched atop a bookshelf. "Hey, Rem," he said, gaining his bearings. "Sorry, but I have to go." Swiftly, he petted the black squirrel behind the ears and started running out of the library.

Paws pitter-pattering, and then a weight hit his shoulder, little claws digging through his shirt, into his skin. "Sure," he said with a grimace. "Why not? You can come with. But when I head back to the compound, you have to go home. They'll wanna eat you." Remington merely let out a contented chirp in response.

Out of the library and through the ruins Gus hurried, into the forest, toward the edge of the ravine. The whole way there, Remington held onto his shoulder. The squirrel offered occasional squeaks, nuzzling his neck and cheek and tickling his jaw with prickly whiskers.

It wasn't long before he reached his destination, the river a short way ahead, supplies and human bones scattered everywhere.

Far worse than that, however, were the corpses.

Tamara lay on the riverbank just as he remembered her. Nude and drenched with red, her throat ripped open like a canyon.

But she wasn't the only one.

A short distance from her was Lewis. He was clearly dead, not breathing, not moving. His unblinking eyes were foggy, glazed over, and his armor had been stripped away, innards leaking from a laceration in his gut.

Gus's chest tightened, his stomach lurching. He hadn't known Lewis well, but he knew Beverly. No, she wasn't his anymore, but he still wanted her to be happy.

He still hated to see her cry.

Imprints in the dirt—tracks resembling the soles of combat boots—trailed past Lewis's body toward the woods ahead of Gus, and in front of the trees were more human bones dispersed around a mess of bloody organs and entrails.

Gus stared hard at the gore, bile rising in his throat. Remington nuzzled his neck as if to console him.

With one step, two steps, three steps, he crept toward the pile of innards. Who was it? Which of his teammates had been massacred? Or had all of them been?

As he got closer, he caught sight of a head lying on its cheek in the mush. A head separated from its body, a head with ginger curls and freckled, sunburnt skin.

*Adam.*

Wires of muscle and tendon frayed out from Adam's severed neck, his face contorted with terror.

Gus couldn't keep himself from retching. He keeled over, sour chunks of vomit spewing from his mouth, his nose.

The hurling didn't stop until his stomach had been emptied of its contents, and even then, he continued to heave and gag. *This can't be happening. It can't, it can't.*

Leaves cracked from somewhere in the woods. Remington shrieked, leapt off Gus's shoulder and out of sight, and a man said, "Almost there. I think I see something."

Out of the trees stepped five military police officers. They stopped in their tracks, looking at the gore, then at Gus.

"Oh, thank fuck." Gus wiped his mouth with the back of his hand and stumbled toward the officers. "Are Nancy and Oliver back at—"

"Freeze, Brandon!" one of the officers shouted, pointing his shotgun at Gus. "Don't move!" The other officers aimed their weapons at Gus too, and he froze. Two officers kept their guns trained on him, while the other three circled the scene, examining what was left behind.

One of the officers investigating the area paused a bit farther down the bank. He picked up what looked like a torn-up net, its golden threads glimmering as though they'd been twisted from sunlight. Had it belonged to Saoirse, or had someone else come through here? "What the . . . ?" He packed it away safely with the rest of his things in his bag.

It wasn't long before the three of them finished their search, and the guy who'd found the net seized Gus by the wrists and handcuffed him. "Gus Brandon," he began, "you're under arrest for the murders of Tamara Wilcox, Lewis Evans, and Adam Conway."

# TWELVE

Saoirse didn't know how long she lay on the grass by the pond, a gaggle of piskies dancing behind her in the woods. She only knew that she needed the pain to stop.

She'd been far too active today. Flying everywhere. Finding Gus. Stopping the shard-raised. Dragging Gus through a gate.

How much more of this could she take? She wasn't like the other Children. They hadn't been torn to pieces and sewn back together. When they used their magic or were especially active, they didn't burn all over, didn't feel as though they'd been set ablaze.

At least if everything went according to plan, it should be over soon.

The others wouldn't appreciate her sending Gus back. If it were up to them, they would have never let him go. When they found out what she'd done, they would call her sensitive, scold her for caring about strangers. *"Little moth,"* Malachi would say, *"you're too emotional. If you want to survive this world, you need to learn not to feel so much."*

But she hadn't only released Gus for his benefit. She knew that if this was going to work in her favor, he had to trust her, and why would he do that if she never allowed him to come to grips with the situation?

"The sylph is dead! The sylph is dead! The sylph is dead!" the piskies sang, and Saoirse cracked open an eye to glare at the small faeries. She had an upside-down view of them as they twirled hand in hand around a tree, a kaleidoscope of glowing silver-studded blues dusting their mischievous faces with color. Like her, they had pointed ears, but they were much smaller than her, their clothes barely more than rags.

Groaning, and with a great deal of effort, Saoirse rolled over and began climbing to her feet. "I most certainly am *not* dead. Not yet."

The piskies squealed in fright, stopped their singing and dancing, and scampered into the forest where she couldn't see them. Apparently, they weren't in the mood for a fight today, which was good, because she had more important matters to tend to.

Body still aching, throbbing, she dove back into the pond and swam toward the gate. No matter how much she hurt, she couldn't give up. She had to ensure Gus stayed safe, had to finish convincing him to join her.

She had to put a stop to this, once and for all.

When she tumbled to the other side of the gate, she landed hard on her hip and shoulder, and as she struggled to her feet, she found herself surrounded by a cloud of mist so thick she couldn't discern her location, couldn't even see the ground.

She walked forward blindly, water dripping from her hair and dress. Every few steps, pinpricks nicked at the bottoms of her feet as if sharp, fragmented material littered the ground. But the sensations were nothing compared to the persisting pain of her scars, so she pressed on with relative ease.

A minute later, she emerged from the fog, saw the remnants of glass cylinders all around the large building, and realized where she was.

A torture chamber.

At least, it *had* been a torture chamber, before the thinning veil ripped open a new gate in the middle of it, before Saoirse and the other Children arrived here by accident and demolished it.

She remembered that day clearly. The cylinders had been filled to the brim with some kind of solution, bubbling and green, dismembered human remains floating through the gurgling liquid. There had been live humans too, some wearing shiny white coats and goggles and holding sharp silver instruments, others naked and strapped down to tables, their screams more guttural than a banshee's as they were sliced into.

Malachi had attacked first. He'd summoned wind, sent gales crashing through the closest cylinders. The humans had erupted with cries, fluid and glass and body parts raining down on them.

Margaret and Moira struck next. Using powerful gusts, they'd smashed people in coats against the walls and ceiling. Cracks sounded from the humans as their bones fractured, their blood and insides splattering about.

While the other Children continued destroying the chamber, Saoirse had flown over to an old man being held captive. She'd begun working him out of his bonds, telling him that it was going to be all right, that he'd be just fine.

Before she could free him, Malachi shoved her away and pressed his palms against the old man's chest. The veins in Malachi's arms and hands had flashed a rotten brown, the spoiled color seeping through his skin like noxious gas, and then the old man had taken his last breath.

Saoirse had wanted to save the other humans that day, the ones strapped to tables. But Malachi had killed them too. *"You know it's no use,"* he'd shouted at her. *"They're all going to die anyway."*

He wasn't wrong. The humans were killing themselves, killing everything in their realm, and so she hadn't fought back. She'd gathered her winds and shattered the remaining cylinders and tried to ignore the people crying for help. *This way is more merciful in the end*, she'd told herself, over and over.

The memory felt faint, distant, as if it had occurred a lifetime ago. But the state of the bodies suggested that only a few months had passed since. The corpses' stench had faded, their bloat gone, their drying, shriveled tendons stretched taut over bone. It would take a bit more time for them to fully skeletonize, and only then could the Skeleton Faerie take control of them.

Saoirse hastened around the brittle husks toward the building's entrance, avoiding their empty stares. She couldn't shake the feeling that the hollow eye sockets were somehow watching her as she passed, boring into her, and she shivered, the hairs on her neck and arms and legs standing on end.

She reached the entrance of the building, which had initially possessed doors made of metal that hadn't matched the rest of the structure. Margaret and Moira had blown the doors off their dilapidated hinges, leaving only the rectangular rock awning at the building's threshold. The English words on the front of the awning read "Rapid City Regional Airport," and it overlooked hills of barren land.

Much of the Mortalworld was like this now, unable to sustain life. The only habitable places were close to gates, mostly the old ones.

But if the veil continued to thin, if it ripped entirely, *all* would be lost.

Saoirse took a few deep breaths, steeling herself for more hurt, more exhaustion. *It won't be much longer. I can do it.*

She fluttered her wings and leapt into the air, then signaled the other Children and soared toward Gus's settlement.

# THIRTEEN

"I already told you, I didn't murder anyone," Gus said. "We were attacked. By Paul and . . ." He gulped. How was he supposed to explain that human skeletons had burst from the river, splashed to land, and started eating people? With each passing minute, the memory of this afternoon's events felt more like a bad dream rather than something that had actually happened.

"We already told you that all that's left of Paul are his bones," Officer Agnes said. "Medical matched his skull to his dental records after they brought back the bodies. He couldn't have attacked you." A dim light bulb buzzed on the ceiling above the older woman's head, and she clasped her tanned hands atop the table bolted to the floor between her and Gus. She'd removed her armor earlier, and underneath all the gear, she looked as ordinary as everyone else in the compound.

Behind her, Officer Reece paced the chipped concrete floor of the hot, windowless holding cell in the Wall One MP and artillery quarters. Like Agnes, he'd stripped down to his T-shirt, cargo pants, and combat boots, the pungent scent of sweat wafting from his body.

"Please, Gus," Agnes went on, "I need you to make this easier on yourself and everyone else involved. I need you to tell us the truth. If you didn't attack your comrades, who did?"

Gus opened and closed his mouth. What was he supposed to say? Even if he told them the truth, they wouldn't believe him.

"This is a waste of time," Reece said as he stopped pacing. "Let's just build a case without a confession. What happened is obvious. The kid's a nutjob, and the elders'll see that."

Gus slammed his left hand against the table; his right was cuffed to the chair he sat in, also bolted to the floor. "I'm not crazy, you asshole! I didn't do anything wrong!"

The balding man turned toward Gus and scowled, the expression wrinkling his face. "You want me to add 'disrespect of authority' to your file? You want a lashing?"

What did it matter? He'd already been arrested for triple murder. Being whipped for disrespect of authority was nothing, comparatively speaking. "If that'll make you feel better, then go on. Go right ahead."

He glared at Reece, daring the officer to follow through with the threat, and Reece's nostrils flared, his skin turning red with rage as he reached for the whip at his belt. He stomped around the table toward Gus. "You son of a bitch, I'm gonna—"

"That's enough!" Agnes jumped out of her chair. She reached over the table, seized Reece by the collar, and yanked him in close. "We were told to talk to him, not beat the crap out of him."

"You really think *talking* keeps sickos in line? You think it gets them to confess to crimes?"

Gus shook his head. "I'm not 'confessing' to anything. I didn't *do* anything. How can you think . . . Do you honestly believe I'm capable of doing something like that to Lewis? To *Adam?*" He swallowed down bile as he thought of their gory remains, their final expressions. "You still haven't even told me if Nancy and Oliver are okay."

Reece rolled his eyes. "Wow. This guy."

"What?" Gus shouted. "What the hell is your problem with me?" Reece jerked out of Agnes's grasp. In an instant he was upon Gus, clenching his hands around Gus's throat.

Gus punched him in the face, tried kicking him in the groin. Nothing fazed him. He squeezed harder, and Gus saw stars. Agnes ran around the table to get Reece off Gus but couldn't separate them.

"You really wanna know what my problem is with

you, Brandon?" Reece snarled. "I thought you were harmless. Lazy and weird, a loner with his head in the clouds, but harmless. I never imagined you to be the violent type, never imagined you to be the 'revenge' type either, yet here we are."

Spittle flew from Gus's lips as he choked for air. *Revenge?* he wanted to shout. *What are you talking about? Are you insane?* But then he recalled how Beverly and Lewis had been engaged, realized what Reece must have inferred when he and the other officers found Lewis's body.

"We don't know what happened for sure yet, Reece!" Agnes yelled. "Or whether he was working with people from the outside! If you kill him, we'll have no way of finding out anything! *Stop!*"

Just as Gus's vision began to fade in and out, Reece's grip on his throat loosened. The officer pulled away, stepped back, and Gus burst into a fit of violent coughing. "I—didn't—want—revenge," he croaked. "I—swear."

The cell door was thrown open, and the other three officers who'd brought Gus back to the compound stormed inside. They each held their own duffel bags full of . . . well, *something.*

"We've got it," one of them said while the other two shut and locked the door. "We've got what we need."

"You found the contraband?" Agnes asked.

"Yes." The officer stopped in front of the table and raised her duffel bag. As she dumped out its contents, Gus tensed.

*My book stash.*

# FOURTEEN

The walls of the cell seemed to rotate, Gus's mind reeling as the five military police officers sifted through his beloved books. Had they confiscated all thirty-four publications? It appeared they very well could have, but it was hard to know without counting.

"Look at this." Agnes held up a book that Gus had smuggled in months ago. "This section references human sacrifice. This 'god' forced his people to kill their firstborn children in his name."

"This one talks about human sacrifice too," another officer said.

They continued examining the passages in question, and Reece sneered at Gus. "I can't believe you were telling the truth about something, Brandon. This *wasn't* all about revenge. You got yourself mixed up in a cult."

"That would explain the depravity of the crimes," yet another officer chimed in, "and the golden net. It's definitely not ours—it must belong to them. I'm so glad Bev told us about these. Otherwise, we wouldn't have known to look."

The mention of Beverly made the room stop spinning. Gus cleared his throat, his mouth dry. "Beverly . . . she told you about my books?"

"She sure did, sicko. Right after we told her about Lewis." Reece chuckled. "She said you tried to get her to leave the compound with you, too. Is Ronnie in on this?"

When Gus didn't reply, dumbstruck at the betrayal, one of them said, "Most likely. That guy's always given me the creeps. We were going to arrest him as well— there's no way he didn't know about these. The first one we found was out in the open, on the living room table. But he's not at work, and he wasn't in the apartment. I'm guessing he heard about Brandon's arrest and hid. We'll find him by tomorrow, I'm sure."

"Tell me, Brandon, was Ronnie working for the cult all along?" Reece asked. "Did they send him here to spy on the compound? Is he the one who let them know the five of you were outside the walls—far enough from the folks on watch-duty—so they could attack?"

Snapping out of his daze, Gus shook his head. "What? *No.*" He started to stand, remembered that they'd cuffed him to the chair.

Agnes set the book she'd been looking at on the table. "Is he at least the one who got you interested in this stuff? Be honest, and maybe we can negotiate a lighter sentence for you."

"You've got it all wrong," Gus said. "There is no 'cult.' I'm not working with a cult. Ronnie's not working with a cult. I've never even *met* someone from a cult. These books, they have nothing to do with what happened today. The stuff they talk about isn't real, and they—"

He paused. Thought of Saoirse, of where she'd taken him. Did he honestly still believe what he was saying? Did he honestly still believe that folklore and mythology, that fair folk and the Otherworld, weren't real? After everything he'd seen?

A sound like gunshots popped outside, followed by people screaming. Gus flinched at the noises. "What the hell!" Reece cried. He and Agnes grabbed their armor and started shoving it back on.

"Thomas, Harry, Isla, go check on that," Agnes ordered. "We're right behind you." The three officers nodded at Agnes, readied their weapons, and ran toward the door.

But they never reached it.

Despite the door's numerous locks, someone from outside threw it open, nearly ripping it off its hinges, and Gus caught a glimpse of a green dress and moth wings.

Violent gales, earsplitting gunfire.

Gus ducked under the table as best he could. He tried to curl into the fetal position and shield his head.

Long, agonizing seconds ticked by before the wind

and bullets stopped.

Movement in his peripheral vision.

A pair of pale legs covered in raised pink stitch scars trudged up beside him.

"Saoirse!" he exclaimed, his ears ringing. "What are you doing here?" No reply. Were her knees buckling? "Saoirse?"

She collapsed. He tried to catch her, but she was just out of reach, and she hit the floor sideways. He winced as her head bounced off the concrete. *Not again.*

He thought he heard more yelling outside, more gunshots. What was going on out there? *"The other Children and I will be back for you,"* he remembered Saoirse saying. *"That's why we came. To get* you.*"*

That had to be what'd happened. Saoirse and her companions had tracked him here, flown into the compound. The pair on watch-duty had tried to shoot them, and when that didn't work and the people in the compound saw them, panic overtook everyone, the situation spiraling out of control.

*I just need to find a way out of these handcuffs, hide Saoirse so no one shoots her, and calm everything down before somebody gets killed.*

*Okay, key for the cuffs. Maybe one of the officers has one?*

He glanced around the room and found that Saoirse must have knocked them all unconscious. Thomas, Harry, and Isla were crumpled on the floor at least ten feet ahead of him, and Agnes lay far enough to the left that he couldn't reach her either.

But Reece was on his right, and the man didn't seem

too far away. Gus could probably grab him by the foot and drag him over.

Gus positioned himself as closely as possible to Reece. He stretched his arm, his abdomen. The tips of his fingers brushed against the heel of Reece's boot.

He stretched himself more, as much as he could. His hand shook from strain, but he managed to curl his middle and index fingers around the dangling loop of the boot's laces, started tugging Reece this way.

Ivory in the corner of his vision.

His stomach plunged to the ground.

Three human skeletons, with white mist swirling around their bones, entered the holding cell from the open doorway.

Gus's pulse skyrocketed as he watched the skeletons walk toward Thomas, Harry, and Isla. Where had they come from, and how had they gotten into the compound? Had a door been compromised? Had they scaled the walls?

"Saoirse," he whispered, glancing over his shoulder at her, but she was still out cold, her chest rising and falling with shallow breaths. *Shit.*

Moving as quietly as he could so as to not alert the skeletons (could they hear anything without ears? They seemed to have a sense of sight, and they didn't have eyes, so better safe than sorry) he continued pulling Reece toward himself. All the while, the skeletons stripped the three officers of their armor and clothes. *Please wake up, Saoirse. Please, please wake up.*

Soon Reece was close enough that Gus could search

for a key. He tried the man's belt first, but it only held weapons.

A muffled yelp of horror, of pain. He turned his head that way; a skeleton had bitten a chunk out of one of the officers. Blood spurted from a bite in the man's stomach, and he let out a wail. He writhed under the skeleton, trying to escape its grasp. The thing held him down and tore out another mouthful of flesh.

Swallowing hard, Gus dug through Reece's pockets next, but it was no use. They were empty.

A woman screamed behind him. He looked back. It was Agnes, scrambling to her feet, pointing her gun at the skeletons as they feasted on her peers.

Gus opened his mouth to tell her not to shoot them, that it was no use, but before he could get out a word, she fired at the closest skeleton.

The bullet missed, hit a wall. She shot again. This time, the bullet went straight through a skeleton's temple. The force jerked its skull to the side, but it ignored Agnes, continued grinding innards with its teeth.

Movement at the entrance of the holding cell, and two more skeletons appeared. They came inside, the first heading in Agnes's direction, the second in Saoirse's.

Gus couldn't worry about being quiet or drawing attention to himself anymore. *"Unlock my handcuffs!"* he bellowed at Agnes. Could she hear him after all the gunfire? *"These are the things that killed Adam and Lewis and Tamara! I didn't tell you about them because I knew you wouldn't believe me!*"

Agnes faced him with wide eyes. She seemed to have heard him, and better yet, she seemed to have realized he was telling the truth. She nodded, snatched a set of keys from her pocket, and lunged for him.

The first skeleton seized her by the hair. It jerked her backward, and the keys went soaring. *Fuck. Fuck fuck fuck!*

The keys clattered to the floor in front of Saoirse, who still lay unconscious.

Agnes howled, the sound shrinking into a choking, gurgling noise as the skeleton sank its teeth into her throat.

"*SAOIRSE!*" Gus screamed at the top of his lungs.

The second skeleton was walking straight toward her. She stirred.

"*IT'S ME, GUS!*"

The skeleton stopped in front of her, reached down for her. Her eyes twitched behind the lids.

"*YOU HAVE TO WAKE UP AND STOP THIS THING, OR IT'S GONNA KILL YOU!*"

The skeleton grabbed her by the arm and picked her up.

"*IT'S GONNA KILL US BOTH!*"

The thing unhinged its jaw like a gaping snake. It stood up straight, lifted Saoirse toward its mouth.

"*SAOIRSE!*"

Her eyes snapped open.

A swift wave of her arm, and a gust ripped through the skeleton.

Its mist dispersed, its bones scattering. Saoirse tumbled to the floor. She shot Gus a quick glance, as if checking on him, as if ensuring he was okay, then leapt to her feet. She summoned more wind and propelled it at the skeleton devouring Agnes.

The thing fell apart, and Saoirse pivoted toward the other skeletons. But instead of attacking them, she froze, her expression falling. Gus followed her gaze to see what was wrong.

Just like before, the officers were being eaten by the skeletons. But the skeletons . . . they had *changed*. They weren't even skeletons anymore. Thick cords of muscle concealed their bones, and as they gorged themselves, threads of veins and other stringy matter wormed out of the tissue like maggots emerging from carrion. The ropes of flesh wrapped round and round each other, melding and fusing together until, at last, the live musculoskeletal systems transformed into people.

Yes, *people*. Naked people. And from what Gus could tell, they looked eerily similar to the military police officers they were devouring, save for the deep-purple veins spiderwebbing all over their pale, blue-tinged skin.

He remembered the skeleton next to Tamara when he and the others had found her, remembered "Paul" when the man had emerged from the river.

The realization sent chills down his spine.

*What* are *these things?*

Saoirse grabbed a fistful of hair at the back of her head and pulled the hair out. No, wait—she didn't pull out her hair, she pulled out something *from* her hair. It looked like a ball of shiny golden yarn.

She pitched the ball at the closest "person," and it came apart midair, the strings of yarn unraveling within milliseconds. Then, in the blink of an eye, the threads came back together, tying themselves into dozens of knots, forming a net that glimmered like the sun's rays.

The net hit and wrapped around its target. Saoirse grabbed another ball from her hair and tossed it at the second closest "person," then did the same to the third, enveloping all of them in the golden mesh. None of them reacted; they just kept gnawing on the bones of their victims, sucking down what sparse flesh clung to the remains.

Saoirse swung around and seized the set of keys Agnes had dropped. She hurried to Gus's side, started trying different keys in the lock cylinder on the handcuffs.

"Why didn't you use your wind-power thing on them?" Gus asked, although he feared he already knew the answer.

"Because it's—pointless," she said between gasps. She jammed the seventh key into the cylinder and twisted, and the cuffs came free. "There's nothing—I can do to—stop them now."

"Besides trap them for a little while, right?" He shook off the cuffs and stood, and she straightened herself, still catching her breath. "You must've trapped the one that turned into Paul. I saw the net, but not him."

"Yes, even the—tools of the gods—don't last forever—against the shard-raised."

"Tools of the *gods*?"

Gunfire outside, followed by a thunderous *boom*.

The holding cell shuddered violently.

Saoirse staggered forward, straight into Gus. He threw his arms around her and crushed her to his chest.

Cracks appeared at the entrance, on the ceiling. "The room!" she cried. "It's—"

Gus hurled himself and Saoirse to the floor, shielding her with his body.

A roaring, deafening, shattering crash.

# FIFTEEN

Gus's ears were ringing again, his pounding skull heavier than a brick of lead. He was vaguely aware of a throbbing ache in his foot, his ankle. Vaguely aware that something hard was pressing into his stomach, and of the fact that he was bobbing up and down, up and down, up and down.

He blinked hard. He wasn't sure what he was looking at, what was in front of him. It appeared to be some kind of fabric, a deep-brown shade.

He lifted his head. Someone with closed insect wings (not Saoirse's, these wings were yellow and brown and black) carried him over their shoulder as they ran. They wore a brown shirt and beige pants, and their feet were bare.

Grunting in effort, Gus raised his head a bit more,

saw what was happening.

He was in the compound, in the Wall One MP and artillery quarters.

And it was chaos.

Buildings were toppled over, wreckage blocking the paths. Officers were running, many of them without helmets, their eyes frightened, their mouths split wide open in screams. Skeletons chased them, grabbed them, ate them.

Booming like before. It sounded as though it were in the distance, but it cut through the ringing in Gus's ears when the shrieks of others had not.

The ground tremored. Whoever was carrying him stumbled to the side, fell to the dirt.

Something sharp at the back of his head, and he succumbed to darkness.

Gus was hurt. His skull was bashed in, his foot mangled.

There was blood, so much blood. It was warm and sticky on Saoirse's hands.

She yelled his name as he convulsed, couldn't even hear herself over the violence around them.

Why had he done that? Before, in the building? Why had he shielded her from the cave-in? That wasn't what he was supposed to do. That wasn't how this was supposed to go. It was *her* job to keep *him* from harm in moments such as these, not the other way around.

*She* should have protected him. *She* should have been knocked unconscious. *She* should have had her foot crushed under wreckage, should have been carried out of there by Malachi and struck in the skull with debris.

Because of the damage to Gus's head, he might not make it out of the Mortalworld alive. And if he didn't, all of this would have been for nothing. She wouldn't be free of her scars for decades to come.

As he continued to twitch and quiver, someone picked him up. Malachi. Bruises and scrapes marred the visible skin of the faerie with the auburn hair, his clothes practically slashed to shreds. He fluttered his wings and leapt toward the early evening sky.

Saoirse struggled to her feet, struggled to spread her wings, struggled to breathe. There was no way she could keep up with Malachi, but that was all right. What mattered was that they got Gus home before his heart stopped.

Something hard and cold clamped around her wrist, and a sickening stench she knew all too well hit her nostrils.

A shard-raised—still only bones—gazed down at her. It opened its jaw, ready to sink its teeth into her flesh. *Oh no, you don't.* With a furious snarl, she conjured her magic and gutted the shard-raised of its own.

As the monster fell apart, her head grew light, her knees wobbling. *Not now, not now!*

A resounding explosion. The force sent the earth spasming and flung Saoirse sideways. She crashed into a pile of rubble, her body erupting with fresh pain.

Groaning, she wondered: How many explosions had that been now? Eight, nine? When would it end? When would the humans realize their efforts against the shard-raised were futile? That fighting back only made things worse?

Hands on her right arm, her left arm, and then she was in the air. Margaret and Moira carried her, soaring after Malachi. With stoic expressions the pair stared forward, didn't glance at the crumbling settlement below them even once.

Saoirse should have done the same.

"Gus?" Saoirse's whisper echoed through the void, through the great expanse of nothingness. She sounded anxious and far away. "Gus, have you finished healing yet?"

He forced his eyes open and found her. Her face was fuzzy, her edges blurred. A striking tapestry of yellows and oranges and pinks and purples stretched out across the sky behind her.

But wait . . .

It wasn't just her. No, it was *two* of her, both of them leaning over him as he lay in coarse sand. The pair of

Saoirses tilted back and forth, their heads crisscrossing.

He blinked several times, and the two Saoirses merged into one. "Are you there?" she asked. He tried to say *barely* but grumbled out nonsense instead, and her hazy features started to grow sharper, her brow creased with worry. Gently, she brushed the pads of her fingers against his cheek, his jaw. "Go back to sleep, then," she said. "You have plenty of time to rest. The other Children are out looking for our next gate."

He had no idea what that meant, but he didn't care. Saoirse's fingertips felt good, tingly on his skin, and he leaned into her touch and closed his eyes, drifting back to the void.

# SIXTEEN

There was rushing water somewhere, tons of it. Gus could hear it clearly. It hissed and splashed, never a break in its constant movement, its hypnotic sound. Was it a waterfall? A river?

As he listened to the running liquid, he noticed a powerful, distinctly vegetal scent—like the forest he'd traversed countless times, but stronger, damp and lush. It permeated his nose, flooding his nasal passages as if he'd stuffed them with spinach.

He blinked open his eyes. He lay on his back in the sand, the sky straight above him, which wasn't strange; what *was* strange was the sky's appearance. It was perfectly clear, no smog, not even a cloud in sight, and it was the most striking shade of cobalt blue he'd ever seen.

Except, no ... the sky wasn't *just* blue. Undercurrents of violet and magenta bled into the hue like watercolor, sunlight radiating through the painted atmosphere in streams.

What on earth had happened? What was this place, and how had he gotten here? The last thing he remembered was the military police arresting him, interrogating him, dumping out bags of his books. They'd said Beverly had told them about the stash, and then ... black. He clawed through his memories, dug into the deep recesses of his mind, but he couldn't recall escaping the officers, leaving the compound, ending up here.

*I still can't believe Bev didn't keep my secret. She promised. She must really love him.*

An ache in his chest as he thought of Lewis's corpse by the river. Another ache as he thought of Adam's remains and Oliver and Nancy. *Please be alive.*

A woman's familiar giggling to his right, and he looked that way. Saoirse twirled on the sand about ten feet from him, her arms stretched toward the sky as dozens of insects with red-and-black wings—moths, they had to be moths, their bodies and antennae fuzzy, stocky—flittered all about her. Still spinning, she made billowing motions with her arms, and the moths followed her movements with perfect precision. *It's like they're dancing with her*, he thought, unable to keep himself from smiling.

She laughed again, louder and more animated this time. In response, the moths seemed to light up from the inside. Scarlet shone from their wings, and as Gus squinted at them, he was almost certain he saw paths of delicate little stars sweeping behind them, the trails twinkling a brilliant white.

He grunted, started pulling himself into a seated position. Saoirse stopped her twirling, and the moths scattered. "Gus!" She rushed to his side.

"Sorry." He propped himself up on his elbows. "I didn't mean to interrupt."

"Interrupt?"

"Uhh, you know. You and the moths, or whatever they are."

She sat down on her knees beside him and grinned, her usual melancholy nowhere to be seen. Out of the couple of times he'd interacted with her, this had to be the happiest, most vibrant she'd appeared, and it made him forget about all his problems for a few moments. "'Cinnabar moths' is what they're called, and it was a whole eclipse of them. They're so pretty!"

"Yeah," he agreed, though he wasn't thinking of the insects. His stare was stuck on her.

Surprise skittered across her expression before she smiled shyly at the sand, and he kicked himself, realizing he shouldn't have let that slip out. After all, he'd only just met her. He looked away and cleared his throat, absentmindedly lifting his wrist to check the time.

Shock and dismay battered through him when he saw that the glass covering his watch's clockface had been smashed, the clock arms stuck on a quarter to five—that must be when it had broken. But how had it happened? Had the military police officers done it to punish him, or had it been an accident? He couldn't remember.

He briefly considered taking off the watch but decided not to. It was special because Ronnie had given it to him. *Maybe I can have it fixed.*

"How did you get me out of the compound?" he asked Saoirse, wanting to change the subject, to get to the bottom of things. "Not that I'm complaining. The last thing I remember was being handcuffed to a chair." A warm breeze, followed by a light spray of water, tickled the side of his arm, neck, and face. Did he smell . . . fish?

She faced him once more, her joy growing quivery, fracturing at the edges. Hints of sadness slipped through the cracks, and Gus found himself wondering why. She didn't seem to be in pain, so it couldn't be her scars. What had changed? "O-oh, you look healed up," she said, "but your brain hasn't finished mending itself yet. If it had, you'd have all your memories. Don't worry, it shouldn't be much longer. You heal quick, you know. Faster than most."

"That's good, I guess." He paused. How had he gotten hurt, anyway? Had Reece and the other officers beat him senseless? "So . . . how did you get me out of there, exactly? You didn't say."

"I suppose I didn't, did I?" She tucked her hair behind her ears—her *pointed* ears—and Gus's jaw dropped, his other thoughts falling by the wayside.

How hadn't he noticed *those* before? Had she concealed them with glamour? Was that how she'd disappeared back in the library, by utilizing glamour? He'd read that faeries sometimes used magic to change their appearances or to hide themselves. *Is that the conclusion I've come to? That faeries are real, and that Saoirse is one of them?*

*Is there any other conclusion to come to at this point?*

"I was too weak to break you out myself," she explained. "The other Children had to help us. They flew us over the walls."

Apparently, she wasn't willing to give many details, which was fine, he supposed. He'd remember more when he finished healing and his memories returned. "The other Children?"

"I've mentioned them before. My companions."

"Oh right, right . . . And where did you guys take me?"

"A place called Tír na nÓg."

"Tír na nÓg? We're in the—the Otherworld?"

"Oh, not Tír na nÓg the *realm*. Tír na nÓg the *island*. Which I suppose is still in the Otherworld, so you're not technically wrong."

"We're on an *island?*" He'd never visited an island before (impossible to do when landlocked and unable to travel). Scrambling to his feet, he looked around, could hardly believe his eyes. "Holy shit," he said, breathless. "Holy shit, holy shit, *holy shit.*" Less than thirty feet away, waves crashed against the beach he stood on, yellow sand and rocky terrain stretching left and right for miles. There were low cliffs beyond the shore, and behind the bluffs, green. Nothing but green. "Wait, where're the different colored leaves? It's autumn."

"Seasons in the Otherworld are opposite to the Mortalworld's now. It's spring here, but you'll love it when autumn comes around. There's nothing better than autumn in the Otherworld."

"*Wow.*"

She stood up beside him as he stared at the cliffs and trees. "How do you know so much about all this, anyway? First the piskies, now Tír na nÓg. I thought you said you hadn't felt a pull to the realm? But if that were true, you'd know a lot less than you seem to." Water splashed from somewhere behind them. "Not again," she grumbled, turning around. "Hey, what did I tell you before? Get out of here! If you even try touching him, I'll send you straight to the Mortalworld!" Another splash. Gus pivoted to find the source, met a startling sight.

Four women, perhaps the most stunning he'd ever seen, were lounging in the shallows. Each of them had a different shade of gray skin, their hair the color of moss. Gus couldn't see their legs, couldn't see much below their ribs because of the water. What he *could* see, however, were their bare breasts as they leered at him, desire blazing in their eyes.

Cheeks heating, Gus tried not to stare. It wasn't that he'd never been with a woman before—he'd been with Beverly countless times—but these women were strangers, Saoirse was *right there*, and the whole situation felt incredibly awkward. To make matters worse, the women grinned at him with sharp teeth, the look in their eyes changing from lust to something wicked, something villainous, and all the warmth rushed from his body.

"How could we possibly resist him?" one of them drawled. She started to crawl forward through the water. "He's even prettier now that his head is fixed."

Another slithered this way too, hissing, "I positively adore the spectacles you've given him, and just look at the magic swirling around his skull. He must be someone interesting."

He shuddered and stepped back as the other two women followed suit, creeping through the shallows toward shore. Yes, they were beautiful, but right now, his instincts were screaming, *Stay away!*

Saoirse's nostrils flared. "I'm warning you. Get back! You can't have him. I found him, so he belongs to me."

He shot her an incredulous look. "Wait, what?"

"Play along," she whispered with a side-eye. "Unless you'd rather live at the bottom of the sea as the subservient lover of a merrow for the rest of your days?"

Blinking in surprise, he glanced at the gray-skinned women, then at Saoirse, then at the gray-skinned women again. Could they really be merrows? The half-humanoid, half-fish faeries of Irish folklore?

"This is the last time I'll say it!" Saoirse barked.

"He's *mine*. You can go search elsewhere for your next great romance." She offered them a little wave of her fingers. "Bye-bye, now!"

Not knowing exactly what to do but quite certain he didn't want to be made a merrow's lover, Gus followed Saoirse's lead and waved at the women. "That's right! Not interested, ladies! See you never!"

They stopped and scowled at him, let out a volley of hisses and earsplitting shrieks, then spun around and splashed back toward where they came from. Soon they reached a deeper section of water, and as they dove headfirst beneath the frothy surface, Gus swore he saw four scaly silver fish tails where their legs should have been.

With a heavy exhale, he plopped himself back onto the beach, pushed his glasses up to his forehead, and rubbed his eyes. "Saoirse, be honest with me. Am I hallucinating? Am I dreaming? Am I dead? This can't be real, right?"

"Oh, we're back to that now, are we?" She sounded as if she was smirking, her tone sarcastic and teasing.

He opened one eye to look at her, allowing his glasses to fall into place. She was, indeed, smirking at him. "Back to what now?"

"'This isn't happening,'" she said in a mocking voice. "'It isn't real.'" She must have overcome whatever was troubling her before, because she'd returned to her happier self.

"Is that supposed to be me?"

"Of course. Who else would it be?" Giggling, a

genuine smile, and Gus found himself opening his other eye, his gaze locked on Saoirse for that fleeting moment.

As quickly as her laughter began it faded, and she perched herself next to him and gave his forearm a light pinch. "Ow!" he protested, although it hadn't hurt. "What was that for?"

"You're not hallucinating. You're not dreaming. You're not dead. This *is* real."

He sighed again. "So, we're really on the island of Tír na nÓg in the Otherworld, and those women were really merrows? Genuine, in-the-flesh merrows?"

"You know what merrows are." It wasn't a question. She crossed her arms, playful suspicion on her face.

"Sure do."

"Tell me why they were after you, then."

It was his turn to smirk. "Didn't you hear what they said? I'm pretty, apparently. So pretty they couldn't resist me." She snorted and rolled her eyes, and he continued, "In all seriousness though, I'm guessing they were after me because they don't like to take male merrows as mates. From what I understand, the males are, um—let's just say they're not the most attractive, while the females are insanely gorgeous."

Saoirse cocked her head at him. "How do you know all these things?"

"Books, mostly. I was on the hunt for more when we met in the library. Which definitely wasn't where I was supposed to be, by the way."

"A bit of a rebel, are you?"

"Probably, yeah, but I never really thought about it like that. I was just desperate to read stories about old superstitions and fair folk."

"The pull." She spoke in barely more than a whisper. "You *did* feel the pull to this place. Through its stories."

"Maybe, but if it weren't for Ronnie, I never would have—"

A sudden flood of memories.

Saoirse entering the holding cell, the skeletons arriving after her, the violence that ensued.

Saoirse unlocking his cuffs, the building caving in.

Him falling unconscious, and when he awoke, skeletons attacking, bombs exploding.

Sharp pain at the back of his head.

Him passing out once more.

The memories ended, thrusting him back to the present. He leapt to his feet and snarled out a series of curses.

"What is it?" Saoirse jumped up after him. "Did more of your memories come back?"

He put his head in his hands. "Yes. You didn't happen to stop all those skeletons attacking the compound, did you?"

"Not all of them, no."

"... *Why?*"

"Because your head was split open, and you were on the brink of death? If we hadn't brought you here as fast as we did, you'd be gone. Besides, there were too many shard-raised for me to handle. I would have fainted and been eaten before I could push the magic out of all of them."

"No, no, no." He let his hands fall to his sides and started pacing. "There's Ronnie, and if they survived the attack at the river, there's Oliver and Nancy, and Beverly and . . ." *Everyone else in the compound, everyone I've ever known.* Yes, plenty of them had treated him like shit, but that didn't mean they deserved to be torn apart, eaten alive.

Well . . . maybe the elders did. Some of the military police did too. But everybody else?

"We have to go back!" He stopped and turned to Saoirse again. There was no trace of joy left in her, a somber, almost guilty expression on her face.

This must be why she hadn't given him many details regarding how she'd gotten him out of the compound. She'd wanted to avoid the subject for as long as possible, dance around it until she couldn't anymore.

"What is it?" he cried. "Tell me!"

Excruciating silence, and then, "We can't go back."

His stomach dropped. "What do you mean, we can't go back? Like, it's impossible?"

"It's not that it's impossible. It's just that—"

"If it's not impossible, then we need to do it, and we need to do it *now*. Didn't you see what was happening to all those people?"

"Unfortunately, yes, I did."

"Okay, well, you have the power to end it. Maybe you couldn't before, since your scars were hurting you and whatnot, but you must've had time to rest, and you seem fine now. You're not out of breath anymore. If we go back, you can stop those skeletons, just like you stopped the ones by the river and the ones in the holding cell. You can save everyone that's still alive."

Her top lash line drooped even more than before. "I can stop the skeletons with my powers, but I can't stop the corpses that way. Sure, I can temporarily trap them with my sunlight-nets, but I only have a couple dozen of those left, and all the shard-raised are likely to have transformed by now. I can't do what you're asking of me."

He grunted in frustration. She was telling the truth, because faeries didn't lie, at least not in the stories. Whether that was because they were incapable of outright lying or because they despised outright lying, he couldn't be sure, but the most they ever did was twist the truth by using clever wordplay, and it wasn't as though she were speaking in vague terms.

"Are you absolutely certain that *all* the skeletons have turned into corpses?" he asked. "That you wouldn't be able to stop even one of them from killing another person?"

"I'm not 'absolutely certain,' but . . ." She hugged her sides, avoiding his stare. "Gus, really. It's best we don't try to go back."

"But what if there are innocent people in the compound fighting to stay alive? What if we do nothing to help them, and they die because of us?"

"I know this is hard to hear, but those people aren't

our responsibility. The Otherworld is, and it needs you. Desperately. You have to save it."

Sucking in a sharp breath, he turned away from her. "So what if they're not our responsibility? That doesn't mean we should just leave them to die. And about the Otherworld . . . that doesn't make any sense. I've lived my whole life with people, as a *person*. Faeries living with humans, pretending to be humans, are usually changelings."

"Yes, and that's what you are. A changeling. You were born a faerie, to faerie parents, and they traded you for a human baby when you were only a few days old."

"No . . ." He pressed a hand to his forehead, his palm slick with sweat. "I don't . . ."

"Let me guess. Throughout your whole life, you never felt like your parents really cared about you?" His heart almost stopped at her words. He faced her again, and their eyes met. "That's because they didn't. Because you weren't their kin, their blood."

He thought of Ronnie, of the bond they'd shared for as long as Gus could remember. "You don't have to be blood-related to someone to care about them."

"Maybe not. But from what I understand, that's what happens to changelings. Their sham parents always reject them, one way or another."

"All right, fine," he said, throwing his hands in the air. "Say I'm a changeling. Say I was banished from the Otherworld and switched out for a human. If this place needs me so badly, if I'm the only one who can 'save' it, why was I ever sent away in the first place? And why was I left in the compound? It's in *North America*. A whole *ocean* away from where changeling lore comes from."

"You were sent away because your parents knew that you'd be stolen from them, that your power would fall into the wrong hands. And the compound is closer to where 'changeling lore' comes from than you might think."

He blinked in surprise. What did she mean by that? Was the Otherworld *not* a mirror of the real world, as he'd initially thought?

For now, he couldn't worry about it, as there were more important issues at hand. He put the question out of his mind. "But how could my 'power' fall into the wrong hands if I don't have any powers? Because I *don't* have any! Also, from what I've read, faeries don't lie, but I lie all the time. I've lied to my parents, my teammates, my superiors . . ."

"Your powers haven't manifested yet and you can lie because you've lived as a human for so long," she explained. "When a faerie lives as a human, they take on the non-magical characteristics of the humans around them. They essentially *become* a human. The same goes for a human when they live as a faerie. They take on the magical traits of the faeries around them and, in a sense, *become* a faerie."

"Is that why I don't look like you? I've been living with humans, so I look human? By that logic, it'll be no time before I have the pointy ears, the wings, the—"

"Usually only sylphs have wings, and you're not a sylph. The physical characteristics you develop will reflect your lineage."

"Well, what's my lineage? Who're my real parents? What's the name they gave me? And why—" He closed his mouth, opened it again, then pinched the bridge of his nose. "You know what? Don't answer any of that. Forget we ever had this conversation. I don't care if I'm a changeling. I don't care where I came from. Compared to all the fucked-up shit going on with the skeletons, none of it matters." He lowered his hand and breathed deeply. "I have to get back to the compound, okay? And you don't have to come with me, but I'd really appreciate it if you did. Now *please*, tell me where the gate you brought me through is."

A new voice, deep and masculine, yelled from the cliffs, "I can tell you where a gate is." Gus pivoted toward the bluffs. A man and two women, all of them barefoot and with differently colored insect wings, bounded off a precipice near Gus and Saoirse and soared down toward them. "It most likely won't take you where you want it to," the man went on, "but it will take you to the Mortalworld nonetheless."

"You won't want to use that first gate again, anyway," chirped one of the women. As she moved through the air, her pearlescent dress shimmered with hints of color that complemented her fuzzy pink-and-yellow wings, her braided locks so long they fell past her waist. "Unless you'd like the merrows to try stealing you again."

In a flat tone, the other woman added, "The gate we came here through is in their element, and it was difficult enough to fight them off *one* time underwater." She had long hair too, but hers tumbled in waves, her black lace top and skirt matching the lines in her snowy wings.

Back in the forest when Gus and his teammates had encountered the "moth-people," it'd been so dark and he'd been so startled that he hadn't gotten the best look at any of them except Saoirse, so based on appearances alone, he wasn't sure if these three were the faeries she'd been with before. But because they had accents like her, had pointed ears like her, and because she wasn't at all startled by their arrival, he figured that it was safe to assume they were her companions.

Still, as they landed on the beach in front of her and Gus, she shrank in on herself, lowering her head and crossing her arms as though in discomfort.

It was a strange reaction, but Gus couldn't get hung up on it. People's lives were at stake. *Ronnie's* life was at stake. He had no idea whether these three would take him where he needed to go—if they really were faeries, they'd probably try to mess with him rather than help him—but he had to see.

Setting his jaw, he stepped toward the newcomers. The women were about Beverly's size, and the man stood one or two inches taller than Gus. The man ran a hand through his shoulder-length auburn hair as though to ensure it lay perfectly; he wore a brown shirt and beige pants that clung to the bulging muscles of his frame, a dagger in a leather sheath hanging from his belt. "Where is it?" Gus demanded. "This other gate? I need to get back to my compound."

The man let out an almost sinister chuckle. The utterance dripped with contempt, oozed with malice, and Gus wondered what or who the hatred was directed at, or if this was just the man's general disposition. "Did you mishear us, or are you dull? The gate likely doesn't lead where you want it to."

"Does it at least lead somewhere close, like the last one I went through did? I can walk the rest of the way."

"There's really no way of knowing what's on the other side of any of the gates, unless one can see through the veil, so why don't I just take you to it? We can go through it together." The man beckoned Gus forward, a sneer on his lips. "Come on, follow me."

"I don't even know your name. Why would I follow you anywhere?"

"The ignorance of one who's been living among humans for far too long," the man scoffed. "No one here knows my True Name, and no one ever will. Names hold a great deal of power. If someone possessed mine, they'd have dominion over me."

"You can let up on the condescension. I already knew that faer—" Gus stopped himself. In the stories, faeries didn't like to be called "faeries," they liked to be called euphemisms such as the "fair folk," the "good people," or the "people of the mounds." Saoirse used "faerie" a lot, and she didn't seem to mind Gus using it, but that didn't mean everyone else in the Otherworld would be okay with it. *If I want their help, I need to try and play by their rules.* "That the *fair folk* go by aliases," he continued. "When I said I don't know your name, I meant I don't know what to call you. I don't know who you are."

Narrowing his eyes at Gus, the man flexed his arms and pecs, his jaw ticking. Was that supposed to be intimidating? Gus stood his ground, holding the man's threatening stare.

As if to break the tension, Saoirse stepped between them. "Gus, meet Malachi. Malachi, Gus."

Malachi glared at Gus for a second longer before turning his attention to Saoirse. "My little moth, always so sensitive. Always such a peacekeeper."

Involuntarily, Gus's nose scrunched up in disgust. His "little moth"? Was that a pet name? Were they together or something? If he hadn't liked this guy before, he definitely didn't like him now.

"I told you to stop calling me that," Saoirse said, frowning at Malachi.

Malachi faced Gus again, this time with a snicker. "Old habits die hard, I suppose."

Okay, yeah, this guy was an ass, and before Gus could think better of it, he said, "Maybe you should let them die a little easier."

Saoirse's lips parted in surprise, and Malachi opened his mouth to snap back. But before he could, the woman with the pearlescent dress pushed past him and Saoirse and looked Gus up and down. "It's nice to finally see you in the light, all awake and healed. To really put a face to the name, you know? Call me Margaret, 'Gus Brandon.'"

"Moira," said the woman in black, raising a hand in greeting.

Gus clapped once. "Awesome, great. Nice to meet you. Now, what about that gate you mentioned? Where is it?"

"Like I said, I'll take you to it." Malachi leapt into the air and soared toward the cliffs. "It's not far from here, but we can't have you getting lost now, can we?"

# SEVENTEEN

Gus probably shouldn't have followed these people (or fair folk, or sylphs, or whatever they wanted to be called) into the forest of the island called Tír na nÓg. Even so, he'd found himself allowing Saoirse to use her wind-powers to carry him up from the beach to the bluffs, and then they'd all headed into the woods, the damp vegetal smell growing ever stronger.

As they trekked through dense greenery, Saoirse stayed beside Gus, while Margaret, Moira, and Malachi walked up ahead. Birds sang in the trees and flew through the sky. Hares leapt across the forest floor, diving into the safety of flowery shrubs that buzzed with bees. Every so often, Gus even thought he saw flashes of rippling brown-red fur, of tined antlers that could have been mistaken for branches, moving in the woods.

Something interesting happened twice as well. A couple of moths flittered by, the insects drawn to Saoirse as if she were the moon and stars. When she saw them, the sorrow in her eyes melted away. She waved at them and said hello, and they glowed in reply, those strange sparkles trailing after them as they disappeared into the woods. *I guess if I ever wanna cheer her up, all I need to do is find some moths.*

Not that he was concerned with cheering her up right now. As they traveled deeper into the woods, he couldn't help but wonder whether he'd made a mistake in trusting her, in following her and her companions. *What if she tricks me? What if they all trick me?*

*I should tell them to piss off unless they're willing to actually help me.*

Except what good would that do? What other choice did he have? He needed to get back to Ronnie and everyone else. And to do that, he needed to get out of here. He needed to go through the gate they were leading him to.

The last time he'd traveled through a portal—after seeing a type of faerie native to the Celtic nation of *Cornwall*, no less—he'd wound up mere miles from home. Because of that, and because of what Saoirse had said earlier (*"the compound is closer to where 'changeling lore' comes from than you might think"*), he wasn't sure whether the Otherworld was a mirror of the real world anymore.

He wasn't sure how the gates worked either; he'd

have to ask about it at some point. But he'd arrived close to home the last time he traveled through one, so this next time shouldn't be much different, right? Maybe he'd end up south, east, or west of the compound instead of north, but he'd find his way back from any direction, so long as he could identify familiar landmarks.

Except how much time did he have before the skeletons finished massacring his compound? A day, an hour? Or had every person he knew already been slaughtered? Bullets didn't work on the skeletons, and he had no idea whether explosives could keep them at bay. Not to mention the fact that Saoirse might not come back with him—might not agree to stop those things—for some asinine reason. She'd claimed it was because she couldn't incapacitate the corpses, didn't have enough nets for all of them, but why couldn't she go back and simply trap as many of the monsters as possible? Surely that would at least save *some* lives, right? Give *some* people a chance to escape?

Yes, it would, he was sure of it, and there had to be a way to convince her to do it. Because if there wasn't . . .

His stomach clenched. If he couldn't persuade her, it would be hopeless. Ronnie and so many others would be killed.

The thought of Beverly, of Nancy and Oliver, of the thousands of other innocent people in the compound all dying like Adam and Lewis and the other officers had made him sick, made his chest tight and his eyes hot and watery.

But the thought of losing *Ronnie* that way? No, no . . . He had to force himself to not think about it. He couldn't fathom it.

He remembered the day he'd first realized that Ronnie was his family, that Ronnie had *always* been his family, so clearly. He'd been thirteen, and they'd been walking through the plaza together, hauling bags of food and other household supplies to Ronnie's apartment. They'd done that sometimes, when Ronnie needed help and Dad couldn't do it.

*"Why don't my parents love me?"* Gus had asked out of nowhere. The thought had popped into his head, and since his parents weren't around, it was safe to vocalize. *"Bev's parents love her. My other classmates' parents love them. What's wrong with me?"*

Ronnie had halted right in the middle of the path. Gus stopped too, gazed over at the old man as he hung his head. *"There's nothing wrong with you,"* he'd eventually said. *"Joel and Sofia never wanted children, but they didn't have a choice. It's good they haven't had anymore."*

The reply made tears spring into Gus's eyes. He'd hoped for reassurance, for Ronnie to tell him that he was mistaken, that his parents did, in fact, love him.

He removed his glasses and wiped his face on his shirt. Maybe that way the huffing, muttering people maneuvering around them wouldn't see him cry.

Ronnie set down his bags, and a strong hand clasped Gus's shoulder. He let go of his shirt, put his glasses back on. *"But I gotta tell ya, I'm so, so glad your parents had* you." Ronnie gave Gus's shoulder a comforting squeeze. *"A world without you isn't a world I wanna live in, kiddo."*

In that moment, everything made sense. Everything clicked into place. Maybe Gus's parents didn't care for him, but Ronnie did, and that was more than enough.

Without another word, Gus had dropped what he was carrying, thrown his arms around Ronnie, and hugged the old man tight.

Hopefully, the military police had been correct in presuming that Ronnie was hiding. Hopefully, he stayed there, and hopefully, it was somewhere the skeletons couldn't reach him. *Just hold on, man. I'm coming for you. You're gonna be okay.*

*You have to be.*

"You *are* aware that they won't take you where you want to go?" Saoirse suddenly whispered to him.

"I gathered that, but I don't care," he whispered back. "So long as I'm in the 'Mortalworld,' I can find my way to the compound."

"Maybe . . . if you manage to escape."

"Escape from what?"

She didn't respond with words, but with a dark expression that gave Gus goose bumps. *I'm their captive, aren't I?*

For whole minutes the pair were quiet, as were Moira and Margaret and Malachi, the only sound that of wet grass squelching beneath boots and bare feet.

It wasn't long before Gus couldn't take it anymore. He decided now was as good a time as ever to ask

Saoirse the dozens of questions nagging at his mind, starting with: "Do you know how the skeletons invaded the compound?"

"When I got there to wait for you, the entrance was open," she said, her tone despondent. "They were— they were *piling* in, a whole horde of them."

"Shit. I bet the scavenge-team finished early, and those things followed them back." He sighed. "Do bombs work against them, at least?"

"What do you mean 'work against'?"

"You know, do bombs blow the skeletons up? Bullets don't affect them of course, like how bullets don't affect any of you, but what about explosives?"

"Explosives scatter parts of the shard-raised for a while, but the enchantment that reanimates them will always piece them back together. As for bullets not affecting us . . . They can harm us, even kill us, just like any other weapon. But if we're quick enough, we can deflect them."

He stopped, and she did too. "All four of you have wind-powers, huh? It isn't only you."

She made a quiet noise of exasperation. "Gus . . ."

"Why didn't one of you, just *one* of you, stay behind to stop the skeletons?"

"I already told you. You were severely injured, and we were most concerned with your safety. With your *life*."

"So you don't care about those people's safety? Their lives?"

"It's not that!"

"What is it, then? Because that's what it seems like."

"Stopping the shard-raised before coming here wouldn't have changed anything in the end. It wouldn't have changed any of their fates." Without so much as a backward glance, she stomped ahead of him.

He chased after her. Reached out to grab her hand, thought better of it. "I'm sure you honestly believe that, but it can't be the reality. Stopping those things before coming here *would* have changed things. It would have saved lives, and we wouldn't have to go back now."

"We're not going back now," she replied tersely.

"So you're just gonna let thousands of people die?" Against his better judgment, he reached out for her again. Took her hand in his, pulled her back toward him. He thought she'd snap at him, thought she'd yank away, but her expression softened, her shoulders relaxing as she focused on their tangled fingers.

Standing so close to her—only a few inches between them—he noticed just how short she was. She wasn't as small as Evie, but she'd have to tilt up her face if she were to look at him, her forehead at his chin. On impulse, his gaze fell to her lips, lush and pink, and for the briefest of moments he wondered what it would be like to kiss her. How would she feel, how would she taste?

*Dammit, Gus. Stop it.*

"Listen," he began, shaking off his inappropriately timed thoughts, "my *family* is back there, the only one I've got. That man . . . he *can't* die. I *can't* lose him. If I'm really as important as you say, then please, help me save him and whoever else is still alive. After that, I'll do whatever you want, no questions asked."

She looked up, and their gazes locked. "You don't understand." There was a tremor in her voice.

"What don't I understand?"

"I don't have a choice, and . . ." She glanced off to the side, tore her hand from his.

He turned his head that way and found the other three watching them. Moira and Margaret wore curious expressions, their attention shifting slowly between him and Saoirse, while Malachi was all hostility and detestation, glaring daggers at him.

"The two of you coming?" Moira called.

Saoirse nodded. "Y-yes. We are. We were just talking. Gus was asking about the shard-raised."

"Of course he was, the poor thing." Margaret shared a glance with Moira, then Malachi. Then they jumped into the air and flew back toward Gus and Saoirse. "Let's walk together, talk together," Margaret went on, the trio landing before the pair, "and help our long-lost changeling understand more about the monsters that dragged him here."

# EIGHTEEN

Gus considered Margaret's words, piecing them together with the details he'd gathered thus far. "The skeletons—or corpses, or whatever—are the reason you all brought me here," he said. "They're not just terrorizing the compound. They're terrorizing the Otherworld, and you think I can stop them."

Margaret sashayed between him and Saoirse. "My, my, aren't you perceptive? You've nearly figured it out on your own."

"Don't stroke his ego," Moira said. "That's only part of what's going on." She walked over next, stood between him and Saoirse as well. "It's not as if the shard-raised are acting of their own accord. They have no desires, no motives. They're merely instruments."

Malachi positioned himself beside Saoirse, blocking

her from view, and instructed the group to keep moving. As they trudged on, Gus tried to steer back to her side, but Margaret and Moira kept intercepting him by either speeding up or slowing down, and Malachi even glared at him periodically.

Was it just him, or was the way they treated her *strange?* It made him uneasy, made him feel like something was wrong. Were they holding her hostage? She'd said she didn't "have a choice." Had she meant she didn't have a choice about being here? With them? Were she and Gus both prisoners?

An appalling thought hit him then. He knew now that Saoirse probably hadn't gotten her scars from mad scientists, but the marks couldn't have appeared out of nowhere. And the wounds that caused them would have had to be severe enough that the Otherworld couldn't fully heal them . . .

*Iron*, he thought. *Maybe they cut her up with an iron weapon, and she couldn't completely recover.* In the stories, iron was a weakness of the faeries. It could repel, burn, or even kill them, depending on their strength. *That would explain it.*

Margaret stuck out her tongue at him. "I thought you had questions about the shard-raised."

"I—I do." *I need to get Saoirse alone later and ask more questions.* "You said they're instruments? Instruments for what?"

"Not for what, but for whom," Moira replied.

"For whom, then?"

"The Skeleton Faerie," Malachi said.

The title sent shivers down Gus's spine, though he wasn't sure why. "And who is that, exactly?"

"You've read a lot of books, haven't you?" Saoirse asked, Malachi still blocking her from view.

"Yeah?"

"Did any of the books you read contain the story about the cauldron that revived the dead?"

Despite the circumstances, Gus couldn't help but perk up a bit. Of course he knew that story! It was "Branwen, Daughter of Llyr." It made up the second branch of the *Mabinogi* and was one of his favorite tales from Welsh—no, *all* of Celtic—mythology, mainly because of the enchanted cauldron she was talking about. The Cauldron of Rebirth.

But wait . . . Since Saoirse had brought up the story, did that mean it was real? That it was historical fact rather than medieval literature? It felt strange thinking about the Four Branches as if they'd actually happened, but if sylphs and piskies and merrows and changelings and Tír na nÓg were real, why would the *Mabinogi*— and all other mythology and folklore from around the world, for that matter—not be?

"We're close." Malachi broke off from everyone else and placed himself up front again. "It won't be long now."

Saoirse, back in view, shifted closer to Gus and the others as they continued walking. "The story I mentioned," she said. "Do you know it, Gus?"

"I do," he replied. "But what does the Cauldron of Rebirth have to do with this Skeleton Faerie person?"

"Everything," Malachi practically growled. "The Skeleton Faerie has *everything* to do with the Pair Dadeni."

"Ohh-kay. Care to elaborate?"

Margaret flashed him a mischievous grin. "How does the cauldron's story go, changeling? Relay it for us. We love a good story, even if we've heard it before."

Gus knit his brow. He'd never discussed this stuff with anyone other than Ronnie. While Beverly had (for a time) kept his secrets, she hadn't shared his interests. "Well . . ."

"Just start from the beginning," Moira said. "You obviously know it."

"Right. Sure." He cleared his throat. This was going to be awkward. "The Cauldron of Rebirth wasn't any normal cauldron. It was a magical cauldron that could bring people back from the dead. To reanimate a corpse with it, you just put the body into it, and poof, you're done. The only issue is that the reanimated corpse wouldn't be able to speak. It'd be completely silent."

He paused to think about how to phrase the next part, but he must have taken too long, because Moira said, "Who owned the cauldron?"

He swallowed, coughed. "Uhh, the cauldron had all sorts of owners over the years. First it belonged to some giants under a lake, and then Bran the Blessed, King of Britain got it, and then Bran gave it to Matholwch, King of Ireland as compensation for an offense."

"An offense?" Margaret sang, feigning curiosity.

"Yeah, umm—basically, Bran and his sister Branwen's half-brother Efnysien was mad because no one thought to ask his permission for Branwen to marry Matholwch. So during Branwen and Matholwch's wedding, Efnysien mutilated Matholwch's horses. To make up for what happened, Bran replaced the horses, and he also gave Matholwch silver rods and golden plates." Okay, maybe this wasn't as bad as he thought. He was starting to get into it, was even using his hands as he spoke.

"And was Matholwch satisfied with that compensation?" Moira asked.

Gus shook his head. "No, so Bran went ahead and gifted him the Cauldron of Rebirth on top of everything else. After the wedding festivities ended, Matholwch and Branwen went home to Ireland, and you'd think everything would've been okay, but it wasn't. Some of Matholwch's people started talking about what'd happened to his horses and criticized him for not doing more about it, and instead of ignoring them, he punished Branwen, banishing her to the castle kitchens. Branwen trained a starling to deliver a message to Bran, which told all about how Matholwch was treating her, and after Bran got the message, a war between Britain and Ireland started. Long story short, Matholwch used the cauldron to reanimate the corpses of his fallen soldiers during the war. But Efnysien figured out what Matholwch was doing, and he jumped into the cauldron and destroyed it from the inside, killing himself in the process."

Up ahead, Malachi let out a low chuckle. "Efnysien *destroyed* the Pair Dadeni? As in, there was nothing left of it?"

"No, there was something left of it," Gus replied. "It was broken into four pieces. It just couldn't be used any . . ." The realization hit him like a bullet to the chest. He stopped dead. "Oh."

"You figure it out yet?" Margaret paused before him. The others halted too, giving him expectant looks.

"That wasn't the end of the cauldron's story," he began. "Everyone thought that because it was broken, it couldn't be used anymore. But it *is* being used. By the Skeleton Faerie. Its magic is what's reanimating the skeletons and transforming them into the people they eat. That's why you call them the 'shard-raised.'"

Saoirse offered him a gloomy smile, and Margaret slow-clapped for him. "Maybe you're smarter than I thought," Moira said.

"Tha—" He stopped himself. *"Don't thank anyone anymore,"* Saoirse had told him back at the river. He'd thought she was being strange, but now he knew she was trying to protect him. One wasn't supposed to directly thank a faerie unless one wanted to be indebted to them. "I appreciate you saying so," he decided on instead. "I'm just confused about a few things. Like, how is the Skeleton Faerie utilizing the shards' power? And why? What's the motive? What are they getting out of it?"

Malachi motioned once more for everyone to keep

going, and they did. "We believe the Skeleton Faerie could have resurrected the shard-raised to wipe out humanity, but now they're out of control and killing our kind too."

"Hold on, *what?* Why would the Skeleton Faerie wanna wipe out humanity? What did humans do to piss them off so badly?"

Moira snorted. "How about damaging the veil between realms beyond repair?"

"That'll do it." Margaret threw her head back and laughed.

"The veil between . . . Oh, you mean the invisible barrier between my world and your world. So, wait, humans damaged that?" They all nodded. "But I thought the veil got thinner naturally," he continued. "On Samhain in the autumn and then again on Bealtaine in the spring."

"That's right," Saoirse said. "The veil *does* thin during Samhain and Bealtaine. But the atrocities humans have committed against their own realm have damaged its magic, whittling away its strength over the years."

"You're talking about the Nuclear War, aren't you?" He bit his bottom lip, thinking. "It wiped out entire countries, ended millions of lives. My elders say there are still large chunks of the planet that are uninhabitable."

Saoirse kept her focus on the grass. "Your elders are right about that. The only habitable places in the Mortalworld are close to gates. The old ones, the ancient ones. And yes—it was humanity's nuclear warfare that thinned the veil so much."

"Why are the only habitable places close to the gates? Wouldn't any area that remained virtually untouched by bombs be okay to live in?"

Margaret waggled a finger at him, tsk-tsking. "You fail to understand the gravity of the war's devastation. If it weren't for the Mortalworld leeching magic from the Otherworld, most life in the Mortalworld would be extinct because of it."

Gus ran a hand through his hair. "Wow, that's—Wow."

"We're here," Malachi cut in, and Gus turned his attention from Saoirse and the others to his surroundings and what stood before them.

Several hundred feet ahead, past the thinning forest, a huge misty clearing with an imposing castle on a hill beckoned. Fog billowed from the doorways and windows of the fortress, floating out onto the hill and into the rest of the clearing.

Gus shivered as the five of them crept forward in silence. He couldn't stop studying the castle; it reminded him of illustrated castles in the books he read, except parts of it were ruined, appearing as though war or natural disaster had ravaged them. Some of the towers had collapsed, causing the chambers beneath them to cave in, and even from here, he spotted plant life twisting up the walls, through the debris. It was as if the spirit of the land were reclaiming the hill for itself.

They stepped out of the forest, the haze that rolled along the grass so thick Gus could barely see his boots, the air so damp his hair started curling up.

For a long time, no one said a word. No one made a sound. The air was heavy with reverence, and Gus knew, deep in his gut, that something awful had happened here.

"The castle of the Tuatha Dé Danann," Malachi said as they approached the bottom of the hill, his tone grave.

Gus adjusted his glasses, gazing up at the castle. "Aren't they gods? Irish ones? Where are they living now?"

"They're long dead," Moira replied.

Gus bowed his head, and they started up the hill. He had so many new questions—for instance, how on earth had *gods* died? Weren't gods supposed to be immortal?—but he didn't have the heart to ask them right now.

They reached the top of the hill and stepped through the closest archway into the castle. It was even darker inside, the mist denser. Gus couldn't see the pattern of the floor, but he could hear the soles of his boots padding against its rocks. He tasted dew on his lips, felt his hair growing wild.

A glimmer of gold in the corner of his eye. He looked over. Saoirse held up one of her sunlight-nets, the tool still wrapped in a ball. It beamed against the shadows. "It'll work for now," she said.

They pressed on, slipping down long halls,

hastening through cavernous chambers, climbing up winding staircases. Mushrooms poked out from the gaps between the stones in the walls and ceilings, tendrils of vines hugging the moth-eaten, mildew-covered furniture spread erratically throughout the fortress.

It was quiet, with no signs of anyone else around, but every so often Gus glanced over his shoulder. He couldn't help but feel as though someone were watching them.

At last, they arrived at the highest level of the castle (other than the towers) and started down another hall. They reached the end of it, turned right, and approached what must be the gate.

The portal didn't feel like part of the castle; it felt like a location all its own. It was nothing but mist and murk, shrouds of fog swirling where there should have been structure.

"Look at that. One step closer to reaching the isle." Malachi vanished into the haze. Margaret followed him, then Moira.

Gus faced Saoirse. She'd managed to slip back to his side earlier, was already staring up at him. "You won't want to go through this alone," she said, offering him a hand.

"Why?"

"Because I have no idea what's on the other side."

After everything he'd seen—the skeletons, the corpses, the carnage—he was certain he could handle whatever they faced next.

Even so, he took Saoirse's hand, and together, they walked into the mist.

# NINETEEN

Gates never used to be this way, so unstable. Saoirse had been told of a time, years ago, when one could pass through a gate in the Otherworld and arrive at its parallel location in the Mortalworld, but that wasn't the case anymore.

This was a troubling era indeed.

She tightened her grip on Gus's hand as the fog swallowed them whole. She didn't want to lose him, for him to experience this alone, so she'd gone against her companions by staying back and offering him her hand.

She'd seen the looks on their faces when Gus grabbed her in the forest, when she didn't pull away. The confusion from Margaret and Moira, the outrage from Malachi. What did they want from her?

*To not let myself get attached to him*, she answered herself. *To not let him get attached to me.*

*It will only make this harder in the end.*

Easier said than done. How could she not care for him when he'd saved her life not once, but twice? When he was so concerned with the welfare of beings he wasn't responsible for? When he seemed to love reading as much as she did?

No matter what, this was going to be difficult . . . for everyone involved.

The fog began to clear, and rather than stone beneath Saoirse's bare feet, there was bark. The mist finished dispersing, revealed a gaping hole in the tree they now stood in, and she and Gus stepped out of the tree and onto the grass of autumnal woodland that smelled of smoke and cooking meat, the night sky above concealed by smog.

"Is it night in my world when it's day in your world?" Gus asked, looking at the sky.

"Generally," she answered.

"Okay, I thought so." Behind them, the gate closed for now, and a low grumbling noise came from Gus. He let go of her hand to clutch his stomach. "Man . . ."

She laughed a bit. "Should I have fed you earlier?"

"That would've been nice."

"I'll try to remember for next time."

"Appreciate it." He gave her a lopsided smile.

Heart skipping, she looked away quickly. "Malachi?" she called, and glanced around for the others. "Moira? Margaret?" No sign of them, no reply.

She rolled her eyes. "Great."

"We were transported to a different location than them, weren't we?" He didn't sound the least bit bothered by it. "Is there *any* rhyme or reason to how the gates work?"

She sighed, already tired from all the walking they'd done today. Surely, her scars would begin hurting soon. Perhaps she should have conserved her strength and *not* danced with that eclipse of cinnabars, but they were so pretty. She couldn't help herself. "Things have . . . changed," she said, hoping Gus didn't hear the fatigue in her voice. "The gates used to be static, the Otherworld and the Mortalworld perfectly aligned."

"Because the realms mirror each other," he replied matter-of-factly.

"As far as most of the geography goes, you're not wrong. But I think the best way of describing it would be that they exist in the same place and, at the same time, are located within different dimensions. The veil separates them; if it didn't, they'd be right on top of each other. And when the—" She stopped, thinking for a moment. Without a visual, it would be difficult to explain how humanity's bombs changed the realms' alignment. "Here, let me show you."

She scanned the trees to ensure there was no one around and guided Gus to a patch of dirt. Sitting before it, she positioned her legs like a merrow's tail, folding them to the right, then motioned for Gus to get comfortable too. He gave her a curious expression but sat beside her, and as he crossed his legs and adjusted himself, his shoulder brushed hers.

She sucked in a sharp breath. *For the love of the Good God, stop acting as if you've never been touched before.*

Holding up the sunlight-net, she cleared her throat and drew a circle in the soil with her free hand. "Think of this as your realm."

"Mm-hmm."

"Now"—she drew a second circle around the first, ensuring their lines were so close they almost touched—"think of this as my realm."

"All right."

Scribbling down a crude map of the continents within the circles, she went on. "Like I said, the realms used to be perfectly aligned. So if I was in Ireland of the Otherworld, if I went through a gate there, I would arrive at its parallel location in Ireland of the Mortalworld, and vice versa."

"And that went for all the gates everywhere? No exceptions?"

"Not until humanity's Nuclear War, which permanently shifted the Otherworld's placement, while the Mortalworld's placement stayed the same. The disruption rotated the Otherworld"—she drew a line from her makeshift Europe to her makeshift North America—"*this* way."

"There's something I still don't understand," he said. "Why would the Otherworld's placement cause the gates to shift the way they do? You mentioned that they used to be static, but they definitely aren't now. It seems like every time somebody goes through one, it takes them to a different location. Case in point: how the gate in the castle separated us from the others."

"That's just because the realms aren't aligned anymore, so the gates within regions bounce around, searching for their old counterparts. They don't usually move so quickly, though. We must have caught the last one right as it was shifting."

"Is that why the gate types don't always match?" His eyes brightened as he began to understand, the excitement in his expression and voice so infectious they gave her the energy to smile. "Like, the first one you took me through was underwater on both sides, but when I traveled back, I came through an oak tree. Something similar happened when we went through the gate in the castle. It was made of fog when we went in, but when we came out the other side, it was a tree."

"Yes, that's right. If the realms were aligned, that wouldn't happen. The gates would be the same on both sides."

"You mentioned that gates move 'within regions'— what does that mean?"

"It's a good thing," she assured him. "Over the years, the faeries that study the realms' new alignment and the gates' movement have found that a gate won't connect to another gate unless the two are relatively close. At most, they've only been recorded as several hundred miles away from each other. But thankfully for us, their distance is usually quite a bit less. Especially if not much time has passed between when you come out of a gate and go back in."

"Then the others can't be far."

"Exactly. I'll just use my flare-wand to signal them once I know we're far enough away from anyone who might see it and come after us, and we should find them fairly quickly."

"I doubt the folks having a cookout would chase us down if they saw your signal," Gus said. "If they're anything like the people of my . . ." He trailed off, his expression falling.

Guilt stabbed at Saoirse's chest. He was the only creature capable of saving the Otherworld from the Skeleton Faerie and, ultimately, complete ruin, but he was still a changeling. He'd still been raised in this realm, still had loved ones here. Leaving them to die would take an irreversible toll on him, but there was no other way. Their fates had been sealed since the moment humanity bombed itself into oblivion.

"Let's go." She climbed to her feet, stifling the pained sound that tried to escape her throat. "We'll keep moving as planned, and I'll only signal the others once I'm sure there's no one nearby."

He thought for a second, set his jaw, and stood up. "No. We're here. We're back. This might be the only time we can escape and save my compound."

"I already told you I can't go back there."

"But you can. We just have to hurry and leave before the others find us. They're holding you against your will, right? You're their prisoner."

She stepped back. "Excuse me? I am *not* their prisoner. What in the world gave you that impression?"

He tapped his chin, feigning contemplation. "Hmm, where to start . . . How about the way you were acting earlier? How you said you 'don't have a choice'? How you're cov—" He stopped. Seemed to reconsider his words.

*He was about to mention my scars, wasn't he?* Suddenly she felt self-conscious, wished that she was strong enough to use glamour on them all the time, or that Margaret's power of transformation didn't hurt them so much.

"How about when I touched you, and Malachi looked at me like he wanted to skin me alive?" Gus continued. "After that, he and Margaret and Moira didn't want us next to each other. It was like they were monitoring us or something. What was that about?"

"Malachi was jealous," she said. "And Margaret and Moira didn't want him to start a fight with you." That was only half of it, but Gus didn't have the full story yet. So long as he was bargaining for his compound, he wasn't ready for it.

"Jealous? Of what?"

"He and I . . . we were involved for a long time."

Gus nodded once, as though he'd suspected as much. "Okay, so you're not their hostage. Why would you *have* to go along with what they want, then? Why don't you have a choice?"

"Have you already forgotten everything we told you about the shard-raised? About the Skeleton Faerie?"

"Nope, and I'd be more apt to help with that if, you know, everyone I've ever known wasn't at risk of being eaten alive by walking skeletons."

She passed the sunlight-net between her hands. Should she give in? Tell him about humanity's destiny? She thought that if she were him, such a hard truth wouldn't help—at least not until she'd had more than a day to digest everything else first. But maybe she was wrong. He'd been taking most of this quite well, relatively speaking. Maybe a last bit of truth was what he needed to accept facts and do what must be done.

Before she could decide whether to tell him, something whizzed through the air toward them, and a wet, fleshy *thwack* sounded.

Gus's eyes went wide, rolled to the back of his head. Saoirse dropped the sunlight-net, cried his name as he slumped forward into her arms.

Another whizzing noise, another *thwack*, and there was sharp shooting pain in her shoulder. Tingling across her skin, her eyes closing against her will. For a moment, she was weightless, like a moth riding a breeze.

And then she fell senseless.


Masculine voices spoke in whispers she couldn't make out. Groggily, she opened her eyes.

It was still nighttime, and she still appeared to be in the forest from earlier. Treetops swayed high above her, although the sight of them was hindered by the thick woven ropes covering her face. *What happened? Where's Gus?*

She lifted her head to search for him, to make sense of the situation. But rather than finding answers, she found a nightmare.

She was sprawled out on the forest floor, trapped in a net, two men so malnourished they could have been mistaken for walking bones dragging her along. They muttered something to the taller, slightly stouter pair of men to their right, who were also hauling a net . . . which held Gus.

Panic gripped her, stealing her breath. She tried waving an arm to conjure winds but could barely move. Her limbs—no, *all* of her—felt heavy. Because of the sedatives, she guessed.

Visions of human torture chambers, of sleek white goggles and coats, of people being strapped down and hacked into, flashed through her mind.

She began to tremble. Her scars throbbed, echoing the tortures of her past. *Get away! I have to get away!*

Mustering all her strength, her willpower, she forced her hand into her hair, disabled the flare-wand's packing spell, and pulled out the crooked wooden stick. She pointed it upward, its tapered tip slipping easily through the gaps in the netting, and focused on her magic shooting out of it, erupting high in the sky where the others would see her location.

A feeling like vines slithering under her skin, curling around her bones, and orange light that could have been mistaken for flames burst from the wand and exploded into the smoggy atmosphere.

Shouts of surprise from the men. Something shot

into her thigh, and she fell unconscious again.

The next time she came to, it was still dark, but they weren't in the forest anymore. They were in a clearing, approaching a yard populated by wooden shacks and log pens that looked as though they were meant to hold farm animals. The yard was lined with two lofty mesh fenccs, and beyond it all stood a large stone structure, bars fastened vertically in the building's windows.

Saoirse bit back a groan, feeling even weaker than before, her body drained of its lifeblood. Her scars ached with exhaustion, and her wrists and ankles stung as if fire licked at the skin. She raised her head as best she could, looked down. *That explains it.* They'd bound her hands and feet with iron shackles.

Had the gods still been alive, she would have prayed.

The men reached the first fence, and four gaunt women, each of them with a gun, came shuffling down the fence line and unlocked and opened the barrier's door. The men stepped in, lugging Saoirse and Gus along. The women secured the door behind them, then opened the second fence's door and let the men into the yard.

The eight humans started talking, but Saoirse didn't register a word. Pulse pounding in her ears, she was trying to pull her hands and feet apart to break the shackles. All faeries possessed great strength—greater than humans, at least—but iron weakened their abilities, so her strength might not do her any good now.

Still, she couldn't sit and do nothing. She needed to escape. She needed to save both herself and Gus.

Keeping as quiet as possible, she continued struggling against the bonds, and the men dragged her and Gus across the yard, past shacks and pens, toward the stone building.

As a breeze picked up, sweeping through the yard, a scent hit her nostrils, a familiar one. It was the smell of smoke and cooking meat that had made Gus's stomach growl so loudly earlier.

She glanced around, spotted where she thought the smell could be coming from, and froze.

To the right beside a shack, there was a table of metal bars suspended by two poles over a firepit. Innocent enough, until she saw what lay in the smoldering ashes beneath.

Bones. Charred human bones.

Gus awoke on his side in a cramped, dimly lit room, the walls made of cracked concrete, the suffocating stench of must heavy in the air.

Heart rate spiking, he flung himself into a seated position. The side of his head banged against metal and started pounding upon impact. He shut his eyes and lay back down, spitting out a slew of curses.

When the hurt finally ebbed to a dull throb, he opened his eyes so he could inspect his surroundings. He was on a hard, bare mattress and there was a second bunk directly above him, held up by steel bars attached to his bedposts. Across from the bunks stood a rusty toilet and a sink, but other than that, the room appeared to be empty.

He sat up, keeping his head low so he wouldn't hit it again. As he crawled out of the bed, he noticed a barred window on the left wall, thin slices of sunrise shining in from outside. On the right wall stood a barred door, a second concrete room visible on the other side of it.

"Hello?" He checked the top bed. Empty.

He rushed to the door and pushed it. It didn't budge, so he tried pulling it, then sliding it. Nothing.

"Hey, let me outta here!" His shouts echoed into the next room, which he now saw was less of a room and more of a long concrete hallway. Across the way, rooms identical to the one he was trapped in lined the wall, except those rooms didn't have bars on their doors, didn't have doors at all. They didn't have people in them either, just some blankets and boxes of ammo.

*This is a repurposed prison from the Golden Era*, he realized. *What the hell happened?* He remembered exiting the gate with Saoirse. She'd told him how the gates worked, and they'd argued a bit. Then something sharp pierced him in the thigh, and the next thing he knew, he was here. *Someone must have seen us in the woods, shot me with a sleeping dart, and locked me in here.*

*But what about Saoirse? Did she escape? Is she all right?*

*She'd have already taken me to the next gate if they hadn't captured her too. She must be here, somewhere.*

*Unless they did something to her . . .*

He curled his fists around the bars of the door. *They'd better not have done something to her.* "The young woman I was with, where is she?"

"Gus?" Saoirse rasped from somewhere behind him.

He whipped around to find her, but the room was empty. "Saoirse! Where are you?"

"Down here on the floor. By the left corner at the back of your cell."

Had she used glamour to make herself invisible? He couldn't see her anywhere. Tentatively, he made his way toward the area she'd indicated.

"The crack," she said slowly, her voice strained. *What had they done to her?* "There's a crack between my wall and yours."

Okay, so she was in a cell of her own. He knelt, lowered himself onto his stomach, and as his cheek touched the cold concrete floor, he spotted the crack. It couldn't be more than a couple of inches tall and wide, but it was big enough that he could see one of Saoirse's eyes through it. The eye's top lash line drooped more than usual, red veins in its whites and a dark purple bag forming on the skin beneath it.

"Are you all right?" he asked.

"It's just the iron. I woke up while we were being dragged here and sent a signal to the others, and those maniacs bound me with it. I'm sure I don't need to explain to you how iron affects us."

"No, you don't. But how would they have known to use iron on you? Unless . . ."

"Uh-huh. I suspect it was a monumental stroke of luck. For them, anyway."

He cussed, rolling onto his back. "What if the others didn't see your signal?"

"If not, they'll still be looking for us. They'll track our location eventually."

"But what if they find us too late?"

"I don't—I don't know. So long as I'm in these, I can't use my powers."

"Maybe I could use your wand to send another signal?" he suggested. "Just in case. Will it fit through the crack?"

"Wouldn't matter if it did. I lost it when the men knocked me out a second time. Besides, until your powers have manifested, you won't be able to use magical items effectively."

He pinched the bridge of his nose, and neither of them said anything for the next several minutes.

Finally, he asked, "What kind of powers do you think I'll have? And how long do you think it'll take for them to show up? If there's a way to speed it up, maybe I can break us out myself. Maybe I can save the compound, too."

"No . . . no. Gus, there's—there's something I need to tell you. I wanted to wait until you'd had more time to process everything else, but . . ."

He turned to face her again. He didn't like how sad she sounded, or the way tears welled in her eye. "What is it?"

"All the humans you know, all the humans in the Mortalworld . . . they're not meant to live much longer."

"What do you mean?"

A long pause, a shaky sigh. "I mean that their species is fated for extinction."

# TWENTY

Gus thought for sure that Saoirse had misspoken, or that he'd misheard her. "Wait, what?" he blurted. "Did you just say that . . . that humanity is 'fated for extinction'?"

"Yes," she replied, her tears falling. "The humans will die, every last one. Their species will cease to exist. Nothing can be done to save them, but the faeries— the faeries can still be saved."

The room spun. Was he going to pass out again? "No, that can't be true."

"It is." A noise as if she was choking back a sob. "I can't tell a lie, remember?"

"How will it happen?"

"Nobody knows for sure. There are talks of more wars, more bombings, and if that's how humanity dies, they'll take the faeries with them. The Mortalworld will suck out the last of the Otherworld's magic, tearing the veil completely open and destroying us all."

"Hey, wait . . ." He furrowed his brow, cold understanding setting in. It was difficult not to raise his voice as he went on. "You and the others are on the Skeleton Faerie's side, aren't you? You *wanted* the skeletons to take out my compound, because you want humanity gone."

"I do *not* want humanity gone!" she exclaimed in her frail rasp. "I've never wanted the shard-raised to attack anyone! But I was weakened from exerting so much energy, and you were dying. We had to take you through a gate to save your life. Without you, the Otherworld is lost to the shard-raised, and the Skeleton Faerie can never be defeated."

"You keep saying that I'm important, that my parents hid me away, that I have to save your world. But *why*? What's so special about me?"

"Your lineage, Gus. That's what makes you special. Faeries are descendants—or 'Children,' as we sometimes say—of the gods. That's why we have powers, because we inherit the magic of our divine ancestors, and you're a Child of the god with the branch of death-magic that can properly harness the power of the cauldron's shards and, in turn, control the shard-raised in all their forms."

Death-magic? He racked his brain for the names of death gods he'd read about, but none came to mind. If only he'd taken and read that illustrated encyclopedia of Celtic deities instead of the book on changelings. "Who's the god that I'm descended from?"

"You're the last living descendant of the Lord of Corpses," she said. "Also known as Arawn, King of Annwn."

"Arawn," he repeated.

"Have you read about him?"

"Yeah, actually." He remembered the character clearly: Arawn was a king of the Otherworld in Welsh mythology, his story part of the first branch of the *Mabinogi*. Pwyll, Prince of Dyfed offended him by chasing his hunting hounds away from a stag. The prince and the king then traded places for a year, with the prince defeating the king's nemesis to atone for his offense. "I didn't realize he was a death god, though. You said he has the right branch of death-magic for controlling the shard-raised?"

"As the Lord of Corpses, Arawn could easily contain the Cauldron of Rebirth's power. Legends tell of his hunts through the wilds of Annwn, where he was flanked by his spectral hounds and an army of the dead."

"If he's so perfect for this job, why hasn't he stepped up and done it already? Why's he having his 'last living descendant' do it?" He paused. "He's not gone like the Tuatha Dé Danann are, is he?"

"Every god I know of is gone."

"But they're *gods*. How could they all have died, just like that?"

"Some were slaughtered in battle," she explained.

"But others, already tired from age, grew even frailer as the Mortalworld leeched magic from the Otherworld. It's said that eventually, their hearts just stopped beating."

"Oh boy." He ran a hand through his hair. "If the magic-leeching affects gods like that, then what about faeries? We've gotta be affected by it too, right?"

"That's right, we are. It used to take millennia for faeries to grow old and die, because back then, time in the Otherworld passed differently from time in the Mortalworld. Centuries would go by, but if you lived with the faeries, it would only feel like months to your body. Now, with the damage humans have done, time in the realms passes at the same rate, so faeries and humans age at the same rate. For instance, I was born a little over twenty years ago. If the realm were as it once was, I'd still be an infant, but I grew as quickly as human children do, so I'm your age."

"Oh yeah, I can't believe I didn't think to ask about the time-difference thing already," he said. "I read a lot of stories where regular people lived with the faeries for a while, and when they came home, they aged rapidly, died, even turned to dust. I always wondered why faeries didn't seem to age when they hopped between worlds."

"Back then, faeries *did* age more quickly while in your realm, but there were ways of slowing down the process or pausing it completely. But access to those methods is almost nonexistent these days—again, because of the Mortalworld leeching magic from the

Otherworld."

"Wow. Mankind really screwed everything up, didn't they?"

"Sadly."

Cupping his chin, Gus thought for a moment. "Maybe there's a way to fix it, or at least to keep it from getting worse. Maybe there's a way to save the innocent people of my world, not just the faeries."

"I promise you there isn't. Humanity's extinction has been prophesied, and there's no changing destiny."

"That doesn't mean I can't try."

". . . You can't be serious. What do you think you're going to do?"

"All faeries have powers, right? I'm descended from the 'Lord of Corpses,' so I'll be able to raise people from the dead. I'll basically have my own army that can't be killed. With that kind of help, I *could* stop the compound from being destroyed further, despite what you say. I could stop bombs and wars and warn people about what's happening to the veil, about how if they continue down this path, it'll destroy everyone and everything."

"To be clear, you won't be able to raise invincible corpses like those of the shard-raised by yourself. Arawn's corpses were never known to be invulnerable. They could be cut down by a blade—they certainly would have been torn apart by bullets and bombs—so yours will be too."

"If the bodies I reanimate aren't unstoppable like the Skeleton Faerie's are, then how am I supposed to beat the shard-raised? Control them?"

"You'll need a bit of help, just as the Skeleton Faerie does."

"Help . . . ?" He thought for a moment. "Oh, that's right. The cauldron's shards are what make the shard-raised invincible. Is that why Malachi mentioned an isle? Is that where the shards are?"

"Yes, the Isle of Bone and Blood. That's where we mean to take you. The last two cauldron shards are located there; the Skeleton Faerie only managed to take half of them."

The sound of metal creaking against metal echoed from somewhere outside the cell. Footfalls pounded, and Gus sat up. "Did you hear about the girl with the wings and the scars?" a man said. Rummaging noises, as if he was sifting through a box of supplies. "The one Mikey and Otis caught?"

A woman replied, "Hell, I *saw* her. I was on watch when they brought her in."

"Considering all the chemicals that've been pumped into her, all the surgeries she's had, do you think she'll be edible?" the man asked, and Gus inched backward, his spine against the wall. Had he heard that correctly? Was that man wondering whether Saoirse would be *edible?*

"It'll be fine," the woman asserted. "We just have to make sure she's cooked all the way through."

*Cooked all the way through?* Gus pressed a palm to his forehead. Their captors went on talking, but he wasn't listening, his mind reeling with comprehension. *These people are cannibals.*

*And we're their next meal.*

Soon the cannibals left, and before Gus had the chance to gather his wits, a familiar chittering sounded from the window. He looked that way, his jaw dropping when he saw what stood on its hind legs on the window ledge.

It was a little black furball, front paws clutching one of the metal bars, cheek pouches so swollen with gathered food they looked ready to burst.

"*Rem!*" Gus stood up and rushed to the window, and the squirrel hopped off the ledge and into his arms. He hugged Remington, and Remington chirped in excitement, nuzzling his neck.

"Who's this?" Saoirse croaked.

Still holding the squirrel, he returned to the opening in the wall and sat down. "Remington is the name I gave him, Rem for short. I see him in the library sometimes. I don't know how he found me . . . Maybe we're not far from the city."

"Maybe."

Another chirp, and Remington scampered out of Gus's arms to empty his pouches. "You don't happen to have keys for the doors and Saoirse's shackles in there, do you, little guy?" Gus joked as fat black walnuts and chokecherries tumbled from Remington's cheeks to the floor. "Seriously, though, why aren't you out burying this?"

As though in reply to Gus's questions, Remington offered a squeak. Then he scuttled back to the window, sprang off the ledge, and disappeared from sight.

"Well," Gus started, turning from the window, "that was weird."

"You think so?"

"Yeah, don't you?"

She didn't respond.

"Listen," he said. "There's no guarantee that the others will find us before . . ."

"I know."

"Maybe there's something in our cells that we can use to wear down the shackles?"

"If I can't break them, then whatever we have access to can't either."

A pause in conversation as he mulled over everything they'd discussed, and finally, an idea came to him. "What about my powers? Not the 'raising the dead' ones, but the other ones? You can fly and control wind, and I'm pretty sure you've been using glamour here and there. Will I be able to do more than one thing, like you?"

She hummed in confirmation. "No faerie has just one single ability. Like all the gods before us, we have greater strength than humans, can use glamour, and can cast spells. But our unique powers—flying, conjuring winds, raising the dead—those didn't belong to every god."

"Okay, so all faeries possess the same kind of 'baseline' magic, but as far as *unique* powers go, they inherit the abilities that the god they descended from had?"

"They *can*, but that doesn't mean they always do. Children of Lugh aren't guaranteed to be master craftsmen, great warriors, skilled artists, and everything else he was. They might be one of those things, two or three if they're lucky. In the past, some Children of Arawn have been exceptional hunters, some masters of the wild, so you might inherit those abilities as well, but again, there's no guarantee."

"If it's not a sure thing that Children inherit even one of the unique powers that their divine ancestor had, how do you know I'll have the raising-corpses power that Arawn had?"

"Because just as humanity's extinction was foretold, so was your ability to control the dead," she said. "And you can't change destiny, Gus Brandon."

"We'll see about that. But back to where I was going with this: You never told me whether we could speed up the process of my powers' development. Didn't you say they'll start showing up as long as I'm spending time with other faeries as a faerie?"

"Yes, that's true."

"Well, here I am, spending time with you, a faerie, and I'm pretty sure I'm well on my way to accepting that I might be a faerie too. That's got to count for something, right? That's got to mean I'll start changing soon. So, my question is . . . is there anything we can do to speed it up? So I can get us out of here?"

She fell silent, and he started to doubt his logic. Did he sound crazy? Was he talking nonsense, hungry and exhausted and desperate to escape this? It had really begun to seem that way, until she said, "I think you're onto something."

"You do?"

"I do. Want to pass me some of those nuts and berries? I need all the strength I can get before we try this."

"Wait, before we try what?"

"Channeling my magic into you." Now that she'd said it, it seemed obvious. "I've never done it before, but maybe it'll accelerate the appearance of your powers. Now pass me a bit of food, will you?"

"Are you sure? You know it was in his—"

"Why do you think he left food in the first place? It's no coincidence. What with all your knowledge, I thought you'd have figured it out by now."

He forced a laugh. "No way. You're not saying that—"

"I *am* saying it. Your parents wouldn't have sent you away without a guide, without someone to watch over you."

"Rem's a *squirrel.*"

"That creature is no ordinary squirrel. There's magic all around him. You'll see for yourself soon enough."

"All right." He glanced at the sink. "At least let me wash these first." He gathered the nuts and berries and carried them over, but when he turned the faucet, nothing came out. "No water. You'll have to eat them as is."

"That's fine."

He began rolling them to her through the crack in

the wall.

"Keep some for yourself," she said, her mouth already full. "You need strength too."

He did just that, popping his share of the chokecherries into his mouth, and as their tart juice showered his tongue, he began breaking open the nuts. He probably should have been more worried about bacteria or disease, considering he couldn't wash the food, but he was starving, and like Saoirse had said, they needed strength. "This isn't going to hurt you, is it? With the shackles draining your energy?"

"It might. But I imagine that being eaten by the maniacs who kidnapped us would hurt much, much more."

"Fair enough." He didn't press the issue further, just finished eating. Though the portions were meager, his stomach already felt better.

When Saoirse was done, she asked, "Ready?"

"Yes," he replied without hesitation, and he meant it, wholeheartedly. If his magical abilities manifested, even just the baseline ones, he could get himself and Saoirse out of here. He could travel to that isle and collect the remaining shards of the cauldron. He could make his own shard-raised and save whatever was left of the compound. He could defeat the Skeleton Faerie and stop humanity from destroying itself.

She shoved her index finger through the crack. "Wrap one of your fingers around mine," she said, and he followed the instruction. "If this works, I have no idea how it will feel, so just do your best to relax."

"Got it."

She took a deep breath, and a feeling like worms or snakes or *something* burrowed into his finger, through his hand, through his arm and shoulder and chest, through the rest of his body. It stole his breath, squirming deep within his flesh and twisting tight around his bones.

White light appeared in the corners of his eyes, consumed his vision. But when it faded and his sight returned, a new shock overcame him.

He was no longer alone in his cell.

# PART THREE

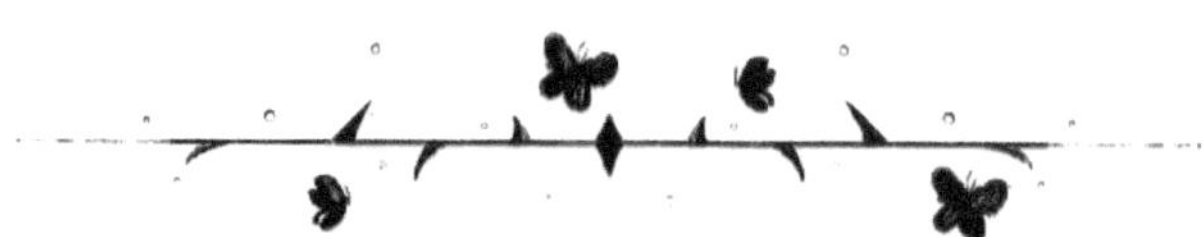

# THE GUIDE

# TWENTY-ONE

Was this how it felt to suffocate?

Moments ago, there'd been nothing but the aftertaste of nuts and berries in his mouth. Yet now he was choking on long, thin dead plants—vines, brittle and blackened—that were forcing themselves inside him. They tasted of earth, and they had little needlelike thorns that pricked and drew blood.

He wanted to reach up and grab the vegetation, to rip it out of his body, but he couldn't move. Other vines had encircled his torso, his limbs.

Gaze darting back and forth, up and down, he realized that the whole cell was infested with the writhing plants. They covered every inch of the furniture, walls, and ceiling, and they almost seemed to be multiplying, closing in on him as if to encase him here, as if to make this his grave. *Do they have Saoirse too?*

He jerked his head to the side, toward the crack, trying to see her, and the vines inside him forced themselves farther down. Reflexively, he gagged, sour bile and coppery blood mixing on his tongue, his lungs burning and his—

"*Gus!*" Saoirse sounded frantic. "*Gus, say something!*"

He blinked once, twice, three times.

The vines were gone.

Sitting in the cell in the prison from the Golden Era, he had his index finger entwined with Saoirse's. He moved his tongue around in his mouth, over his lips, and the taste of earth and bile and blood faded.

Saoirse released his finger, her breaths shallow. "Gus?"

"Yeah?"

"Are you—all right?"

"I think so," he lied, and wondered how much longer he'd be able to do that.

"Thank the—Good God. I thought something— horrible was—happening to—you."

"Me, too." Not a lie this time, because what the hell was that? It couldn't have been Saoirse's magic, right? *She's a sylph*, he thought. *She flies and controls the air. What does that have to do with murderous vines?*

*At least it's over and it wasn't real. It was just a vision.*

Only a second of solace before sharp shooting pain exploded above his temples, and he doubled over, clutching his head in his hands.

"What—is it?" Saoirse asked.

"My head *hurts*."

"Which part—of your head—hurts?"

"Above the temples."

"I think it—might have worked! I think your magic—might be trying to—break through!"

"Oh boy." He gritted his teeth.

"Just—rest. Try to—sleep. We'll see how—you're feeling and—what you can do—when you wake up."

"What if someone comes and tries to take you while I'm sleeping?"

"Stop worrying—about me. I'll be—fine."

"Are you sure?"

"*Yes.* Now—rest."

Despite his worry for Saoirse, he knew he needed to sleep this off, and she seemed firm in her stance about being all right without him, so he didn't question her further. Instead, he crawled over to the bunk and lay down, then set his glasses aside and shut his eyes.


The next time he awoke, his headache was gone, and the cell was dim, but it was still light outside. *Must be the afternoon? Maybe sometime in the evening?* If only his watch weren't broken.

He grabbed his glasses and put them on, crept over to the opening in the wall. "Saoirse?" he whispered.

No reply, and he couldn't see her. Was she in bed, sleeping? Or had the cannibals come to collect her?

"Hey," he said, louder this time. "Hey, are you okay? Are you there?"

Silence.

Worst-case scenarios began flooding his mind. "Saoirse!"

Rattling on the other side of the crack. A shadow swept over it, and a fingertip stroked his cheek. "Shh, it's okay," Saoirse said. Her breathing had returned to normal since their channeling session, but she still sounded awful. "I'm here. I was asleep."

Frantically, he reached up and hooked his index finger with hers, and for what felt like whole minutes, they held onto each other that way, though he wanted to do more, so much more. If it weren't for this wall, he would have pulled her close and wrapped his arms around her and—

*Stop*, he told himself. *Slow down. You barely know her.* Too bad that didn't change the way his heart was hammering in his chest.

In the end, Saoirse broke the quiet, let go of Gus. "I wanted to wait for you to wake up before I slept, but the iron was killing me. I had to rest. How are you feeling?"

"A lot better, now that you're awake. I thought—I thought that—"

"I meant your headache, Gus." Despite everything, it sounded as if she was smiling. "Is your headache any better?"

"Oh . . . Yeah, it's gone." He cleared his throat, in desperate need of water. He couldn't imagine how bad she must be feeling. "Should we get back to it then? The magic-channeling?"

"I'm not sure if we have to. Have they broken the skin yet?"

"Broken the— What are you talking about?"

"Oh, that's right. We never discussed the antlers."

"The antlers?"

"In my defense, I thought that you'd have known about it."

"Known about *what*?"

"Have you seen iconography of the Lord of Corpses?"

"Uhh, no? There weren't pictures in my edition of the *Mabinogi*." Again, he wished he'd taken and read that illustrated encyclopedia of Celtic deities. "Did Arawn have antlers or something?"

"When he wanted to."

He recalled something she'd said while they were on Tír na nÓg: *"You'll develop physical characteristics that reflect your lineage."* *Shit.* "I'm gonna grow antlers, aren't I?"

"All Children of Arawn with your ability do. They'll house your death-magic; they're a physical manifestation of it, just as a sylph's wings are a physical manifestation of her wind-magic. When we met— when you were looking at all those books—I saw the ghost of them swirling around your head. It was there in Tír na nÓg too. I think they're eager to appear."

"So the antlers growing means that my powers have shown up? That I can use them?"

"Their appearance means that your *death-magic* is present."

"What about my baseline abilities? Enhanced

strength, glamour usage, spell casting? That's what's gonna get us out of here."

"By the time your death-magic develops, everything else will have too. You might not be able to use it all, but it'll be there."

He reached up to touch the space above his right temple, his left. He had no new appendages, no breaks in the skin or even bumps. "There's nothing there yet."

"Do you at least feel stronger?"

"I'm not really sure what that's supposed to feel like."

"Maybe 'feel' isn't the right word for it. Hmm . . . Why don't you try bending the bars of your window?"

He raised a brow at her suggestion but climbed to his feet and walked to the window anyway. Outside there was a fenced-in yard, dozens of wooden shacks and pens standing in the brown grass. The structures were crude, makeshift in nature, planks hanging unevenly and nails jutting out.

What were they supposed to hold? They looked empty, and they couldn't be for people the cannibals planned on eating. Anyone with half a brain could have escaped from them. Besides, there were perfectly good cells inside the prison.

Then it hit him.

*The virus. It killed a ton of our people, a ton of our animals. How far did it spread?*

He shook his head, forcing the thought from his mind. Until they were out of this, he couldn't focus on anything but escape.

He wrapped his hands around two of the metal bars and tried pulling them apart.

Movement under his skin. Magic? Maybe, except it didn't feel like the magic from before, didn't feel like vines burrowing inside him. It felt cold and featherlight, like ghosts gliding through his blood, but it was so weak, so faint . . .

He looked at the bars.

Nothing.

"I can't do it," he said, and returned to where he'd been sitting.

"But you had a headache after the channeling?"

"Yup. And I felt something just now, under my skin."

She poked her index finger through the crack. "We'll have to keep doing this until it sticks."

"Are you positive it won't weaken you? Hurt you more? You don't sound good."

"Again, it can't be worse than being eaten," she reiterated. "Now come on. I really think this will work if we keep at it."

Reluctantly, he linked his finger with hers, hoping he wouldn't have another strange vision, hoping she'd be okay when this was over.

Like before, the strange sensation slithered through him. Light overtook his vision. Then he was suffocating again, vines in his nose and mouth and throat. They trapped him in place, wriggled all around him.

He didn't struggle this time. Even as he tasted dirt,

even as thorns drew blood that coated his tongue and flooded his esophagus, he didn't try to break free. It would be over any moment now.

Except the seconds kept ticking by, and the vision still wasn't over. He attempted a cough, a gasp for breath, but the vines didn't relent. They wormed down, deeper inside him, as though rooting themselves within the soft tissues of his organs.

*What does this have to do with Saoirse's magic?* he wondered again. *Probably nothing, right?* Sure, she was channeling energy into him, but that didn't mean the visions were related to her. Could they be related to Arawn, to the god's power over the wild and the dead?

Ivory emerged from the vines above him, beside him, and as he narrowed his eyes, he swore he saw human skulls surrounding him, wrapped in the plants like prey in a spider's silk.

"*Gus?*"

He blinked hard.

The vines and skulls disappeared.

He was in the cell once more.

"What the hell"—he let go of Saoirse—"is up with the vines?"

"Oh—no," she said between gasps. "You saw—vines?"

"I didn't just *see* them. They were *inside* me, Saoirse. All around me, too. And there were skulls everywhere, and—" Agony erupted above his temples. He hissed through his teeth.

"Was that—it? Was that—all you—saw?"

*"Yeah."*

She said something else, her tone laced with distress. But the pain in his head was so intense he couldn't make out her words. It forced him down, his head smacking against the floor.

She might have gone on talking, but he couldn't be sure. He was drifting away, body numb as his senses faded, and before long, he knew no more.

*Vines, skulls?* Saoirse thought. Tears welled in her eyes, burning them, blurring her sight. *Why would he have seen that?*

But a part of her already knew, didn't need to wonder. Magic was in the body, and body in the magic. The two were intrinsically connected.

And after what her body had endured . . .

It only made sense that Gus would see flashes of it as her magic coursed through him. She kicked herself for not realizing the possibility sooner.

The sobs escaped her then, wretched and shuddering.

She was grateful Gus wasn't awake to hear them.

# TWENTY-TWO

Something tickled Gus's nose, scratchy and fine as hairs. That was when he realized he lay on concrete, the space above his temples throbbing. How long had he been out this time?

He opened his eyes, found himself in the cell. It was a bit darker than before, and a smell like pork sizzling over a fire permeated the air. Under normal circumstances it would have made his mouth water, but right now it just made his stomach churn.

The furry face of a black squirrel hovered in his peripheral. Gus shifted to look at Remington, the creature's dark eyes wide as he stared at Gus, his cheek pouches (once again) so full they looked ready to burst.

"Hey there," Gus rasped. He *really* needed a drink. "Sorry we ate your food. I swear it was for a good reason." Remington merely chirped, emptied his pouches of more nuts and berries, and scurried over to and out the window. *Guess I'd better tell Saoirse she was definitely right about him.*

As if on cue, a sniffle came from her cell.

"Hey, you okay?" he said.

More sniffling. "Does it matter?"

"Of course it does."

It took her a while to speak again. "Remington brought more food, then?"

"Y-yeah." Had the magic-channeling drained more of her energy than she'd expected? Had he said or done something wrong?

"How are you feeling?" she asked. "How's your head?"

He winced, the throbbing in his skull growing especially strong. He rubbed the space above his temples, felt bumps where it had previously been smooth. "I think my antlers might be coming in."

"Good. Maybe we don't need to do anymore magic-channeling." That had to be it—she was beyond drained. She sounded downcast, defeated.

"Seriously, are you okay? Would food help you feel better?"

"No, it wouldn't. Why don't you try bending the bars again?"

". . . Okay." He climbed to his feet, made his way to the window, and strained against the metal. The cold sensation passed through him, but it was no use. The bars wouldn't budge. "I can't do it."

She muttered a slew of curses and sniffled some more.

"Saoirse, what is it?" He walked back over and knelt before the opening in the wall. "Did I do something to upset you?"

"No, not at all."

What was going on with her then? Thinking it over, he bit his lip.

Wait . . .

Could it be related to the vision he'd had? The one with the vines and skulls? Initially, he thought it'd had nothing to do with her. But she'd been fine before he mentioned it, and now . . .

"Listen," he began, "I get that we haven't known each other for very long, but I'm here. You can talk to me."

"I . . . I . . ." It seemed she wanted to say more.
But she didn't.

Noises started up from outside their cells—a door opening, boots pounding, someone talking—and Gus grabbed the food Remington had brought them and shoved it into the corner, hoping no one would see.

Soon a brunette woman who looked to be in her thirties appeared. She was alarmingly emaciated and dressed similarly to the residents of his compound. She went into the cell across from Gus, her white flesh hanging flaccid from her bones.

When she looked over at them and spotted him watching her, she quit muttering to herself but didn't say anything to him, just dropped her head and gathered ammo from a box in the cell.

Was that . . . *guilt?* That expression on her face? If he played this right, would she let them go?

"You know this is wrong," he said, and she stopped. "I can see it on your face. You don't wanna do this. You don't wanna kill us."

She shot him a quick glance.

Returned to stuffing her backpack.

He climbed to his feet and edged toward the door. "I'm right, aren't I?"

No reply.

"If you let us go, we'll help you, we'll—"

"*Shut up!*" she screeched, swinging around to face him. "*Shut the fuck up!*" Her resounding screams stunned him into silence. "If we had any other options," she went on, "we wouldn't be doing this. But we don't, all right? We don't."

"What about farming, growing your own food? Scavenging and hunting? My compound does all those things, and we've never had to resort to eating people."

With a scoff, she shook her head. "You don't get it. We can't grow a damn thing around here anymore, and there aren't any animals left to hunt. They're all dead, along with the ones we had in the yard and—and most of our people, too."

He grasped the bars of the door. "What happened to them?"

"They died. From sickness. Then our crops went bad, and there wasn't enough outside our fences to sustain us. If that first group hadn't passed by, we would've starved that winter."

"You could leave this place," Saoirse cut in weakly. "You could come with us. We'll take you to where there's more to eat."

"And risk being captured by some other group?" She let out a laugh, cold and cruel. "No. I'm safe here, behind the fences. I'm not going anywhere. Besides, the two of you should be enough to get us by for at least a couple of months. There's only fifteen of us left."

"You won't be able to keep us alive for that long without extra food," Gus countered.

"We don't have to," she said. "We found a freezer and the tools to power it in a demolished lab a few weeks ago. It broke down yesterday—which is why you're still alive—but with any luck, it should be back up and running by tonight."

# TWENTY-THREE

The cannibal left the same way she came, and Gus hurried back to the opening in the wall, dread festering within him as he processed the fact that by tonight, he could very well be slaughtered, could very well be stored in a freezer.

"Pass me some food," Saoirse said.

"Already on it," he replied, gathering the nuts and berries from the corner. He split the provisions roughly in half, making sure that Saoirse would have more, then rolled her portion over.

They scarfed down the food, and after they finished, Saoirse shoved her finger through the crack, Gus primed to loop it with his own.

White light, and he was surrounded by the vines, wrapped in the vines, choked with the vines. There were skulls everywhere too, the plants making the bones dance in circles around him.

Suddenly his arms and legs smarted with pain, his neck and face smarted with pain, his joints and muscles and flesh and bones and *his whole body* smarted with pain. All at once, it was as if he were being cut open and set on fire.

And just when he thought it couldn't get worse, there were tearing noises.

The sounds came from *him*.

He was being shredded like wet paper, the vines smothering his efforts at a scream.

He thought of Saoirse then, of the stitch scars wrapping around her flesh. *This is why she's upset, isn't it? This vision . . . this is what happened to her.*

*This is how she got her scars.*

If only there were time to figure out why he'd be seeing her memories in the first place.

He blinked, *hard*, and a second later he was back in his cell. His breaths came in ragged gasps, as did Saoirse's.

He gulped, opened his mouth to ask her if she was all right, but before he could speak, the sharp shooting agony above his temples knocked him into numb oblivion.


Yells woke him.

He sat up, but the throbbing in his head almost took him down again, the shadowy outlines of his dark room tilting back and forth.

Gingerly, he touched the space above his temples. There was blood, sticky and warm, but there was something else too. Something hard and with sharp edges protruding from his skull.

*My antlers.*

The shrieks persisted. They sounded close, and there was no mistaking who they came from.

Saoirse.

"No, no! Let me go!"

Head spinning, Gus clambered into a standing position, stumbled to the door.

"Give it a rest, you ugly bitch," said a man, "before I slit your throat myself."

Gus seized the bars and focused on heaving the door open, on breaking the locks holding it in place.

"Don't!" cried another man. "She has to be bled out properly. It helps with spoilage."

Chills beneath Gus's skin, and this time it was stronger. This time, metal squealed as the locks fractured.

"What was that?" the first man asked.

Gus wrenched open the door and leapt into the hall.

The beam of a flashlight to his right. He turned that way, found four men. One pointed the flashlight at him. Two others had Saoirse by the arms as they dragged her across the concrete.

"What the hell!"

"How'd he get out?"

"When'd he grow antlers?"

"He's one'uh them experiments!"

Calling on his new strength, Gus barreled toward them.

Yellow in his eyes and hands in his face. With clenched fists he swung blindly, the flashlight clattering to the ground. Hot blood splashed across his knuckles, and the cannibal he'd hit howled. Then they were on the floor, Gus straddling the cannibal, pinning him down, grabbing his throat, ready to snap his neck, ready to—

"Gus, behind you!" Saoirse yelped, but it was a moment too late, something hard colliding with the back of his skull. The throbbing in his head intensified as pain ricocheted from the point of impact, Saoirse and the cannibals and the prison suddenly careening around him.

Involuntarily, he slumped forward, gritting his teeth as he fought to stay upright. The cannibal he'd been grappling with slipped out from under him with ease.

Someone took hold of him from behind and clamped what felt like shackles over his wrists. At first, the metal was cool, but then it grew hot as a stovetop, scorching his skin.

He called on his new strength again, strained to break apart the shackles, to keep on fighting, but the magic inside him was stunted, unable to move freely. *They're using iron on me*, he realized. *They're using it on me and it's suppressing my powers and they don't even realize it. Fucking hell, they don't even realize it.*

The cannibal who'd cuffed him yanked him up by

his shirt collar. "Door must've been flimsy," the cannibal said. "He got it open. That could've been bad. You have to check that stuff, all right?"

The man Gus had attacked retrieved his flashlight, shined it right in Gus's eyes. Red dribbled from his busted lip. "Yeah, all right."

"Let's just take 'em to the kitchen and finish this," one of the guys still holding Saoirse said, and then they all started down the hall.

# TWENTY-FOUR

Jagged nails dug into Gus's biceps as two of the cannibals hauled him through the building's dark hallways and adjacent chambers. Behind them, the other two dragged Saoirse along, one of them threatening to kill her right then and there if she even so much as thought about struggling against him, potential spoilage be damned.

"Don't you *dare*," Gus spat over his shoulder, though he was in no position to be making threats. The weight and pain of his new antlers was intense. The fact that the cannibals had hit him over the head and bound him with iron didn't help either.

Seriously, iron was something else. No wonder Saoirse seemed so bad off ever since she'd been bound with it. Not only did it burn his flesh, but it also felt as if it was conducting energy out of him, as if it was draining him of his life force.

How had Saoirse survived this long while trapped in the stuff, especially with the way her scars hurt her? *It's a testament to her strength. Be that mental, physical, or both.*

"What're you gonna do, freak?" the cannibal spat back. "Gut me with those little horns of yours?"

"Don't give me any ideas."

The cannibal chuckled. "You know what, Scars? Maybe you and me'll have some fun before we turn you into grub. What d'ya say?" Laughter from another cannibal. The last two didn't join in, but they didn't object either.

Gus pressed his lips into a thin line, his nostrils flaring as rage seethed through every inch of his body, the vehemence of it so fierce, so overwhelming, he hadn't known he was capable of it before now. *The second I get the chance, these bastards are dead.*

Soon they reached the prison's mess hall—an expansive area lined with long cafeteria tables. Gus couldn't make out much of the room because it was pitch dark outside and the cannibals only had a flashlight to illuminate their way, but as they forced him and Saoirse back toward what had to be the kitchen entrance, he caught sight of rusty cylindrical beams holding up the hall, of inoperative empire lamps hanging from the ceiling. Like the rest of the prison, it smelled moldy in here, and it had to be at least several degrees cooler than the rest of the building.

They stepped into the kitchen, which was a lot

smaller than the mess hall, narrow-ish and rectangular. The floor and walls and ceiling were made of concrete, the various aluminum appliances corroded with age and disrepair.

At the far end of the room stood what could only be the freezer the cannibals had stolen. The horizontal contraption reminded Gus of a trunk, and it stood at least four feet tall and had enough volume to hold the meat of a couple of large animals. It also emitted a low electrical hum, a tangle of wires coiling out from behind it. The cables looped all the way up to a counter littered with butcher knives, and beside the knives sat what seemed to be some kind of battery, the battery's transparent cells bubbling with glowing green liquid that cast a faint but nauseating veil of light across the kitchen.

The cannibals restraining Gus halted and looked up at the ceiling. "Aw, shit," the one with the flashlight said.

"Mikey, you moron!" the other snapped. "First the flimsy door, now this. You were supposed to set up those new rods and meat hooks!"

"I'll go get them right—"

"You won't do a goddamn thing." He snatched the flashlight from Mikey, then turned to the cannibals holding Saoirse. "Pat, you help Mikey restrain this guy while I'm gone, and Derek, you check the freezer. I told Jess to throw out the rest of that guy—he's too rotten now—but the stupid bitch never listens."

"You got it, Otis," one of them said.

Otis nodded at them, had just begun stomping away, when a bloodcurdling scream echoed in the distance, followed by the popping of gunshots.

Otis froze. "What the—"

More screams, more gunfire. What was going on?

Letting out a long breath through his nostrils, Otis turned back toward the others. "Pat, you come with me." He pointed at Mikey, then Derek. "You two, don't worry about the hooks. Just be sure to check the freezer before you slit their throats and cut 'em up." With that, he and Pat hastened out of the kitchen, while Derek threw Saoirse aside so carelessly it was as though she were no more than a bag of trash. She let out a feeble whimper, her head smacking against the floor.

Fresh fury simmered through Gus as he took in Saoirse's appearance. Even under the dim glow of the freezer battery, he could see that her complexion had grown pallid, the rings around her eyes giving her the look of a corpse undergoing livor mortis. Sweat seeped from her pores, soaked through her dress, the skin around her shackles teeming with angry red blisters. No wonder Derek wasn't wasting the energy to drag her across the room with him—she didn't look as if she had an ounce of fight left in her.

Derek sauntered across the kitchen toward the freezer, seemingly unfazed by the fact that his fellow cannibals could be under attack. Did this kind of thing happen often?

Never mind, it didn't matter. Any second now, Derek would have his back to Gus, would be checking the freezer. *This might be my only chance.* Gus took a deep breath, slow and steady, adrenaline pumping through his veins. *It's two against one. I can do this.*

The moment Derek opened the freezer, propping its lid back against the wall, Gus whirled around and, with all the might he could muster, kicked Mikey in the groin.

Mikey howled, letting go of Gus and falling to the floor. Thin, watery vomit spewed from his lips. Gus booted him in the head for good measure, then pivoted to face Derek.

As Derek lunged across the room, Gus vaulted to the side. Mikey yelled again, Derek slipping and crashing into him.

A clanking noise from Saoirse, and Gus chanced a glance that way. She was crawling toward the counter that held the knives and freezer battery, limbs trembling with effort.

Derek had seen her too, had already leapt back to his feet. He hurtled in her direction. With a snarl, Gus tackled him from behind.

They hit the ground, Gus on top of Derek. Before Derek could shove him off, Gus threw his hands over Derek's head, wrapped the chain of his shackles around the cannibal's neck, and squeezed.

Derek kicked and bucked, and although Gus did his best to hold fast, to stay upright, the cannibal knocked him on his side. He lost his grip for just a few moments, but it was long enough for Derek to twist around and clamber on top of him.

Hands on his throat, throttling him, his skull banging against the concrete. He rammed his hands into Derek's face, shoved a finger into the cannibal's eye. Derek roared, and Gus scrambled out from under him.

As Gus wriggled backward, away from Derek, his antlers hit something solid. There was pressure, and the pain of them intensified tenfold, making his vision fade in and out. Clenching his jaw, he forced himself into a standing position, willed his sight to normalize so he could go on fighting, so they could get out of here.

Weight slammed into him, sending him tumbling backward. Spine-first, his legs in the air, he collided with what felt like a pile of oddly shaped rocks, some icy with frost, others wet with condensation.

Then the smell hit him. It was putrid—sweet as meat left out to rot, sickly as feces sitting in the sun.

He gagged as realization set in.

*Jess didn't throw away their leftovers.*

Sight finally returning, he hurried to shift out of the awkward position he'd landed in, but it was difficult with bound hands, and while he tried not to look at the dismembered human being beneath him, he still caught glimpses of stiff fingers and contorted limbs, of milky eyes and blue lips.

A furious wail, a man's. *"You're dead, Scars! Dead!"*

Saoirse yelped, and Gus saw red. Using the full weight of his body, he propelled himself out of the freezer, onto the floor. The appliance tipped over with him, the acrid body parts it held spilling out around him. The battery came down too, the glass of its cells splintering as it hit the ground in front of him, glowing green liquid frothing from the cracks.

Less than ten feet away, Derek knelt before Saoirse. It appeared that she'd stabbed him, that he'd taken the blade from her or perhaps ripped it out of his own wound; gore leaked from a gash in his side, and he had the bloody butcher knife raised, ready to attack her.

Except he didn't.

He was temporarily distracted, staring at the battery.

In the second of confusion, Gus leapt to his feet and charged forward, Saoirse scrambling out of the way.

Pressure and pain where his antlers met skull.

Bones crunching, guts squelching.

He tore through Derek's stomach and chest, then pulled back and collapsed, his glasses clattering to the side.

Through blurry vision, he watched as the cannibal's soggy, steaming insides plunked out in a heap. The cannibal fell over, went perfectly still.

Before Gus had the chance to feel any sort of relief, the agony in his head grew so strong that the room spun. He wasn't sure how long he lay there like that, unable to move, unable to think.

But eventually, the pain dwindled, became more bearable, and his vision returned to normal.

He took in his surroundings. Saoirse sat beside him. At some point she must have put his glasses back on, because everything looked perfectly clear. Derek's body was in the same spot as before, and Mikey had joined the cannibal in death, lying in a pool of his own vomit, the butcher knife Saoirse had stabbed Derek with sticking out of his left eye. It appeared she'd shut and locked the door as well, probably to keep Otis and Pat out when they came back.

Where were they, anyway? How long had it been since they'd left?

"Gus!" Saoirse rasped. She rested her cheek against his chest, as close to a comfortable embrace as two faeries could probably get while bound with iron. The sour scent of sweat radiated from her, but he couldn't care less. If it weren't for his shackles, he would have hugged her, would have buried his hands in her hair. "I'm so glad you're awake," she went on. "How do you feel?"

He winced at the burning of his wrists, at the throbbing of his skull. Opening his mouth, he meant to say *I'm fine*, but when he realized that that would be a lie, he decided to say nothing instead.

She lifted her head to look at him, and he wished she hadn't. He wished she'd have lain on him for at least a short while longer. "What am I thinking? You feel awful, of course. We both do."

With a great deal of exertion, he managed to sit up, then stared hard at the corpses before them. Perhaps he should have felt guilty for the deaths, sick as he gazed at the remains. Perhaps he should have been ashamed because he so brutally, so *easily*, took a life.

But he felt none of those things.

He was glad these men were dead.

"Do either of them have keys for our shackles?" he asked, though he was afraid he already knew the answer, considering both he and Saoirse were still bound.

"No," Saoirse replied. "But before I killed Mikey, I made him tell me where the keys are. He said Otis has them."

"How long has it been since they left?"

"A few hours, maybe?"

"And they haven't come back yet?"

"No, no one's even knocked on the door."

"Do you think the other Children could've tracked us down? Do you think they're searching the prison for us, and that's why we heard those gunshots and screams?"

"If they were here, I feel like they'd have found us already."

"Then something else must've happened."

"That's what I'm afraid of." As she finished her sentence, their eyes locked. Hers were wide with apprehension, and Gus was sure his were too.

Neither of them had to say more. They seemed to know what the other was thinking, seemed to share the same fear.

Gus climbed to his feet and helped Saoirse stand. "C'mon. We've gotta get out of here."

# TWENTY-FIVE

The silence of this place was more unnerving than a tomb. The yells and gunfire had long since ceased, and now there were no voices, no distant echoes to indicate the presence of other animate beings . . . not ones that made noise, at least. All Saoirse could hear were her and Gus's footsteps and the chains of their shackles clanking.

Leaning on each other for support, keeping one another from toppling over in fatigue, they limped out of the kitchen, into the dining hall. The foul odors of perspiration, gore, and decay mingled in the air around them, clung to them like burial shrouds. Saoirse hoped that she'd be able to wash off sooner rather than later.

As they approached the dining hall's edge, Gus raised the balled-up sunlight-net toward it. Retrieving the net had been excruciating for Saoirse, but she'd had to do it. They'd needed a light source.

No sound came from the next corridor, and based on what little they could see, it appeared to be devoid of threats, so they hobbled into the darkness, squinting at the shadows around them in case someone—or some*thing*—leapt out at them.

Wait a moment. Did she hear . . . a noise like footsteps?

Yes, there it was.

Farther down the corridor.

It reminded her of claws click-clacking against a hard surface.

Gus widened his stance and positioned his hands between his legs, preparing to throw the net in a swinging, pendulum-like motion. At the same time, Saoirse held her breath, her body rigid as she kept her gaze trained on the inky mantle before them.

The sound grew louder.

Faster.

Closer.

It reached a crescendo, and . . .

A small creature with black fur hastened into the light, a key ring dangling from his mouth.

Saoirse allowed her muscles to relax and sighed in relief. "Rem, it's you!" Gus exclaimed. He handed the net to Saoirse, knelt in front of Remington, and held out his hands, presumably to take the keys. "I can't believe you found this!"

The squirrel squeaked as though to say, *It was easy!*

and dropped the key ring in Gus's right hand. Gus hissed through his teeth—the keys must have been made of iron—but managed to keep hold of them, turning to Saoirse. "Let's get you out of these."

"Why not free yourself first?" she asked, though a part of her already knew the answer. That same part of her knew it wasn't wise to be encouraging or even acknowledging the affection growing between them, but the more time she spent with him, the more she couldn't resist.

He glanced up at her, and their eyes met, his gaze softening in a way that made moths flutter in her belly. His antlers weren't done growing, and they were covered in blood, but they suited him, made him even better to look at. "I'm more worried about you than me," he said.

She should have protested. She should have told him that first and foremost, he needed to be concerned with his own health and safety. That *he* was important because he was the last living Child of the Lord of Corpses, that *she* didn't matter in the grand scheme of things because she was nobody.

But before she knew it, he'd already found the key they needed and unlocked both sets of her shackles.

She cast them aside, feeling as if a crushing weight had been lifted from her. While the burns the iron made would take time to heal even after she returned to the Otherworld, and while her powers wouldn't return to full strength for at least a few days, she was still immensely grateful to be free.

Gus stood up, handed her the key ring, but she barely registered the iron searing her palm and fingers. Her heart pounded, his face inches from hers. *He only needs you to unlock his shackles.* Cheeks heating, she did. He shook off the iron and stretched his arms.

On the floor, Remington began chattering frantically. "What is it?" Gus asked. "What's wrong?" In reply, the squirrel stopped screeching and bolted ahead, out of sight.

"I think he wants us to follow him," Saoirse said.

Gus nodded, offering her a hand. "He probably knows the way out."

She laced her fingers with his, and together, they plunged into the unknown.

By the time Remington led Gus and Saoirse outside, all the way to the fenced-in prison yard, dawn was breaking. Smog diluted the yellow light that outlined the horizon, but Gus could have shed tears of joy at the sight. It was crisp and cool and smelled fresh as rain out here, with dew on the grass and mist in the distance. *We made it*, he thought. *We're alive and—*

A woman lunged out from behind one of the makeshift shacks in front of them.

They ground to a halt. It was the woman from before, the one who'd refused to let them go, staring blankly at them as she blocked their path.

Except it wasn't *really* her.

Never would be again.

The monster had stolen her features, her frame, a labyrinth of purple veins etched beneath her bare, blue-stained skin.

Four more shard-raised corpses came into view. Gus recognized "Otis" among them, but he didn't feel even a speck of sympathy for the man. Otis had more than deserved his fate.

The shard-raised stalked toward Gus and Saoirse. Grunting in effort, in agony, Saoirse retrieved sunlight-nets from her hair. She gave two to Gus and kept the rest for herself, and they trapped the corpses with the objects.

"*Help,*" wheezed a man on their left.

They looked over.

It was Pat.

He lay nude inside one of the pens, his limbs broken the same way Tamara's had been when Gus and his teammates found her. Five skeletons—not shard-raised, these ones were lifeless, bones gleaming as if licked clean—lay around him, and it dawned on Gus that the corpses must immobilize any extra people around so that their skeleton friends didn't have to work so hard.

"*Please,*" Pat went on. "*Don't leave me here.*"

Gus didn't even bother responding. Hand in hand with Saoirse, he followed Remington through the rest of the yard to the fences. There were jagged breaks in the wiring, as if something had gnawed through the metal, and he wondered whether that was the work of Remington or the shard-raised.

Either way, it provided a path of escape, and they fled across the clearing, into the forest.

# TWENTY-SIX

Gus and Saoirse raced after Remington for what felt like hours, never letting go of each other. Gus struggled to keep his balance because the iron's effects hadn't completely worn off, and because if he wasn't careful, his antlers made him totter. They'd certainly take some getting used to; he felt as though he'd had a pair of small hammers fused to his skull.

But every time he stumbled, Saoirse was there to steady him.

He did the same for her.

At last, they reached a winding stream, blue spruces and quaking aspens lining the bank, and Remington stopped in front of the rocks at the water's edge, chirping as if telling them to do the same.

He truly was no ordinary squirrel.

It took a while for Gus and Saoirse to catch their breath. After they did, they drank from the stream until their stomachs ached. Gus probably should have boiled the water first, but Saoirse didn't seem concerned about it. Maybe bacteria didn't affect faeries the same way it did humans?

He tried to see his reflection in the water as well. How did he look now, with the antlers? But the currents moved too fast, distorting him to nothing more than a blur.

About twenty minutes passed before Remington let out another squeak and started hopping across the stream by way of rocks jutting out of it.

Heart in his throat, Gus glanced at the woods around them. Had any of the cannibals survived and tracked them down? Had the shard-raised corpses escaped the sunlight-nets and come after them? "Do you think we're being followed?"

"We could be." Saoirse still sounded exhausted and didn't look much better than before. She gestured at Remington. "Or he could be taking us exactly where we need to go."

"How would he know where that is? Unless . . ." Malachi *had* said that some faeries could see through the veil, could see what was on the other side of the gates. Had Gus been his biological parents, had he needed to choose a guide for his changeling son, he would have picked someone with that ability.

The thought made him wonder: Who were his real parents? Would he get to meet them? Were they even still alive?

Gus and Saoirse staggered against the stream's currents after Remington. Then they were on the move again, the squirrel traveling at a slow enough pace that they didn't have to run to keep up with him anymore.

"Saoirse?" Gus asked while they walked.

"Mm?"

"Do you know my biological parents?"

"I—I never had the chance to meet them."

"Are they . . . even around anymore?"

"No. They were murdered. They knew that it was going to happen, and that if they kept you, you'd be stolen afterward."

*They really were protecting me.* He didn't ask about it again, didn't need to know anymore. Not right now, at least.

Maybe he'd do more digging later, when things weren't so dire. But, at this very moment, his real family, the man who'd always been there for him, was in trouble. He needed to focus on saving Ronnie.

And to do that, he needed to reach the isle Saoirse had told him about—the Isle of Bone and Blood—and harness the power of the last two shards of the Cauldron of Rebirth.

Then he could stop the shard-raised.

"So, the Isle of Bone and Blood, huh?" He helped Saoirse climb over a particularly large fallen tree. "Sounds kinda creepy."

She snorted. "That's an understatement."

"Yeah?"

"Yeah. It's my least favorite place in the Otherworld, and considering I've seen the Unseelie Court, that's saying something."

They trudged on, Gus pushing up his glasses. "You've been there before? To the isle?"

The small bit of color that had been returning to her face drained away. "Once, in preparation for—well, for this. We searched every inch of it until we found the cauldron shards, and the only good part about it was the lake. Here."

She reached into her hair and grimaced as she produced a piece of paper, then handed it to him. It was a map, an elegant black-and-white rendering of the Isle of Bone and Blood. The isle was taller than it was wide, slanted to the west, and had four labeled locations: the Forest of Ghosts, Moth Lake, the marshes, and the Mound of Skulls. The forest took up the southern half of the isle, while the lake sat close to the middle and the marshes and mound were up north.

He studied the map. "Question for you."

"Go ahead."

"Since you've been to the isle, and you even have a map of it, you know where it is, right?"

"Right."

"Then why are we using gates to get there? Why not stay in the Otherworld and sail there? Or fly?"

"Because the Skeleton Faerie placed shard-raised around it to deter others from reaching the shards," she explained. "They guard it from the sea and sky."

Gus raised a brow. "Uhh, how does that work?

Shard-raised in the sea and sky, I mean."

"Simple. The Skeleton Faerie used the bones of sea monsters and sylphs with bat wings."

Gus could think of several sea monsters from Celtic mythology, all of which he did *not* want to encounter—especially as reanimated, indestructible skeletons. And as for the sylphs with bat wings . . . well, he couldn't wait to see them (from afar, of course). Centuries ago, when artists began depicting faeries with wings, most gave them insects'. However, he did remember reading that a couple of artists gave them bats'.

There had at least been the one instance, the statue of a faerie child holding a torch. He was pretty sure it had been sculpted by Harriet Hosmer, and it referenced will-o'-the-wisps and how they led travelers off safe paths. He could picture the photograph of the statue clearly—the white marble chiseled to perfection, the devilish bat wings protruding from the faerie child's shoulder blades.

"Why do they stick around and guard the isle?" he asked. "Why aren't they out hunting people or other faeries? They aren't *that* intelligent, are they?"

"No, they're not," she replied. "An illusionist created impressions of faeries for them to chase, which keeps them close to the isle. But if someone tried flying or sailing there, they'd almost certainly see them and attack."

He gave the map back to Saoirse. "One more question for you. Where on the isle are the shards located?"

"In the Mound of Skulls," she said, and grimaced, putting the map away. He hoped it wouldn't be long before she started feeling better. "And Gus . . . before we get there, you should know that harnessing the cauldron's power won't be a pleasant experience."

"How so?"

"From what I understand, the process is incredibly painful. Magic is in the body, and body in the magic, so the shards—the mound has to crush them, fuse them with your flesh."

He considered her words before saying, "That does sound painful, but if it means stopping those things, it'll be more than worth it."

Soon the two of them stumbled across Saoirse's lost flare-wand but decided not to send another signal, as they didn't dare risk exposing their location and being captured again. "I think we'll be fine without the others," she said. "We might even be better off." Gus couldn't help but agree, thinking about the strange way they'd treated Saoirse, but didn't say so out loud.

Later on, they found the sunlight-net she'd dropped and the gate they'd last traveled through. Gus stopped before the tree as its bark parted for him, tiny flickers of white dancing out of it like snowflakes in winter winds.

Gus pointed at the flurry of lights. "What're those? They weren't there before."

"Oh, they were," Saoirse replied. "You just couldn't see them because you were still so human. They're bits of the Otherworld's magic being sucked into this realm."

Remington let out an irritated sound. He'd paused his scampering, was looking back at them expectantly.

"What?" Saoirse cocked her head, feigning confusion. "You don't want us to go through this gate?"

The squirrel screeched and bolted back to them. He placed himself between their feet and the tree, chittering angrily.

With a shrug, she said, "I'll take that as a 'no.'"

"Safe bet, I'd say," Gus remarked.

They kept going, following Remington past more gates (which he did *not* want them to enter), the portals leaking magic like the one in the tree had been. The more Gus noticed the sparkles, the more he realized they weren't just at the gates either. They floated around Saoirse, Remington, even him, and they reminded him of the "stars" he had seen trailing behind the moths of Tír na nÓg.

"I can't believe you ever doubted that this creature was your guide," Saoirse said after Remington had finished scolding them for getting too close to yet another gate. "You mentioned that you visited him in the library sometimes?"

"Yeah, it seemed like he lived there."

"Perhaps he was always around, watching over you. Is he the one who led you to the books in the first place?"

"No, but . . ." He narrowed his eyes at Remington as the squirrel trotted up ahead. "But . . ."

"But what?"

". . . Umm, it's nothing." And it wasn't. The thought he'd just had—it was crazy. He shook his head, pushing it from his mind. "Let's keep moving. Rem's gonna leave us behind."

Around midday, they arrived at a clearing in the forest, a circle of rubbery white caps poking out of the grass in the center of it. Gus squinted at the mushroom ring, and sure enough, he saw that it glittered.

Remington chattered at Gus and Saoirse, almost seemed to be motioning at the mushrooms with his paw, then darted into the ring and disappeared, leaving flecks of magic in his wake.

"We can't risk losing him." Saoirse grabbed Gus by the forearm and dragged him into the ring.

The feeling of falling, the sound of liquid gushing over rock, and suddenly it was night and Gus and Saoirse were plunging through the air, down toward a dark pool, a reflection of the moon and stars rippling upon its surface.

Gus held tight to his glasses as he and Saoirse splashed into the pool. A shock of cold, and the force sent them sinking toward black depths. Icy water bit the bare parts of Gus's skin, soaking his clothes and flooding his nostrils.

Saoirse let go of him, and they swam toward the surface. As soon as they made it into open air, they started coughing, trying to expel any unwanted liquid from their bodies.

After recovering for the most part, Gus took in their

surroundings. Mossy, cliff-like boulders towered over them on both sides, forming a sort of gorge, and a tall curtain of cobalt cascaded between the stone walls, waterfall foaming where it hit pool. A short distance ahead, the boulders receded and the pool met land, giving way to forest that, even in the night, appeared as abundant as that of Tír na nÓg.

With one last coughing fit, Saoirse slapped the sopping hair out of her face and tucked it behind her ears. Then she looked around, her eyes going big.

Gus followed her gaze to the waterfall behind them. What was so shocking about it? Other than those sparkles funneling into it, he didn't notice anything strange.

"You okay?" he asked her. "You seeing something I can't yet?"

She jerked around to look at him. "N-no. It's nothing like that. I just recognize this place."

"Really? Where are we?"

"Annwn."

Realization washed over him, more frigid than the water they treaded. "Annwn" was the Welsh name for the Otherworld, so they must have been in the part of the realm that, before the Nuclear War, had mirrored Wales.

This was the land of his ancestors.

The land of Arawn.

An exasperated sound from the bank. Gus looked that way but couldn't make out Remington in the dark. Another squeak, and Saoirse started swimming, with

Gus following close behind.

The water grew shallow as they neared land, and before long they stepped onto grass. Remington waited for them by the trees, tapping a paw impatiently, but once they reached him, his attitude improved. He let out a satisfied noise, whirled around, and strode into the woods.

Saoirse produced a sunlight-net to help brighten their path, and its glow revealed their burns from the iron. Gus blinked in surprise at the still-present injuries. Shouldn't they be gone by now? "If we're injured by iron, the Otherworld can't heal us," Saoirse explained. "We have to heal on our own." He nodded in reply, and with that, they headed after Remington.

These woods probably should have unsettled Gus, yet he felt perfectly at ease. He gazed into the dark without his eyes playing tricks on him, without feeling as though something sinister were watching him. Of course, he was sure to stay alert for anything that might jump out of the shadows and attack them, but other than the occasional small animal scuttling by, they seemed to be alone, the only sounds those of the whistling wind and their padding footsteps.

It was so peaceful, in fact, that he had time to notice the way Saoirse's wet dress hugged her curves. But she wasn't the only thing on his mind. He was in Annwn, after all. This was where his parents had lived, where he had been born. If he met any of the faeries here, would they recognize him? Would they know who he was and why he was back?

"Gus, look," Saoirse whispered, pointing at something above them. He glanced that way, and there they were—some moths, or were they butterflies? He couldn't tell from here—fluttering about. Waving the sunlight-net, she greeted the creatures, and they lit up with a soft yellow glow, trails of magic sweeping behind them.

The extra light revealed that they were definitely butterflies (their bodies were slender, their antennae long and clubbed) and that there were nine of them. But why were they out at night? Weren't butterflies usually active during the day?

Come to think of it, he'd only seen butterflies in the Otherworld at night, and he'd only seen moths in the Otherworld during the day. But weren't moths primarily nocturnal?

He asked Saoirse about it, and she waggled her eyebrows mischievously, making him grin. The compound, the shard-raised, the cannibals—those seemed like distant memories now, nightmares he'd suffered long ago. Here, with Saoirse and Remington, in this enchanted place, he almost felt . . . safe. "I was once told that moths and butterflies are messengers between the realms," she said. "It's nighttime here, yes, but what if, where these beauties are from, it's daytime?"

The butterflies stayed close enough that Saoirse could put away her sunlight-net, and what felt like about an hour passed before she started to seriously tire. Her breaths grew heavy, her strides cumbersome.

Gus took her by the arm to keep her upright. "Is it your scars?" he asked.

"Always," she answered in a bitter tone.

The visions he'd had in the prison—the ones with the vines and skulls, the ones he suspected were Saoirse's memories of how she got her scars—flashed through his mind, and he wondered whether he should bring them up to her. The fact that he'd seen them felt like an invasion of her privacy, and he wanted to clear the air.

Except she'd sounded so defeated, so *hopeless*, after he'd mentioned them the first time. Should he wait for her to bring it up? Or should this be something the two of them never discussed?

"Hey, Rem?" he called, and the squirrel glanced back at him. "We need to stop and rest."

Remington had them walk for a few more minutes, leading them to an especially dense area of forest where Gus suspected they would be well hidden.

While the butterflies nestled into a nearby bush, Gus helped Saoirse sit against the base of a tall leafy tree, and Remington scurried into a large cluster of plants beside the tree, presumably to rest. But then the plants rustled, and wild strawberries—red and fat— began tumbling to the ground. Remington snatched a few with his teeth and darted up into the tree.

"Eat up." Saoirse picked out a strawberry and took a bite.

Gus's mouth watered. These were the biggest, shiniest, most delicious-looking strawberries he'd ever seen. He sat down next to Saoirse and grabbed one, was about to start eating, when he recalled yet another detail from old folklore: people weren't supposed to eat anything from the Otherworld unless they wanted to be bound to it.

"Something wrong?" Saoirse asked.

"It's just . . . eating this won't trap me here, right?"

She stared at him for a second, startled, then threw her head back and laughed. "How could it trap you here? This is where you were born. You're part of this place."

That was a good enough explanation for him. In no time, he devoured over two dozen strawberries (they tasted as good as they looked). Then he wiped his mouth on his shirt, grateful that he'd essentially gotten to rinse off in that pool with the waterfall. He shuddered to think about all the nasty shit that had been stuck to him before. Was it really only yesterday that they'd been trapped in the prison?

"You missed some." Saoirse gestured at the space between her bottom lip and her chin.

He rubbed his mouth on his shirt again. "Did I get it?"

"No," she said, giggling. "Here."

She reached up and wiped it for him, a pleasant sensation prickling across his skin. Cast in the glow of the butterflies, she was golden, ethereal.

Her thumb lingered on his bottom lip a moment longer than necessary. With a sharp inhale, she pulled her hand back to her side. "There. It's gone."

He swallowed hard. "Appreciate it. You, uhh—you gonna rest now?"

"Someone needs to stay awake and keep watch. If you'd like to sleep for a few hours, I can take first—"

"No way. I'll be lookout for a while. You need to relax, after everything."

"But what about your antlers? They're still growing. You should—"

"Saoirse, I'm fine. Just rest."

She gave him a gloomy little smile that made his breath catch, then got comfortable under the tree, closed her eyes, and fell asleep.

Strangely enough, keeping watch was wholly uneventful. Remington snored up above, and though Saoirse frowned and muttered as she slept, she didn't stir. The woods were calm, quiet, so soothing that Gus almost drifted off a couple of times.

That is, until he realized he needed to urinate.

Not wanting to do so in front of Saoirse (yes, she was asleep, but what if she suddenly woke up?), he climbed to his feet, crept a short distance away from their camping spot, and hid behind a tree.

Just as he was finishing up, he thought he saw a glint in the shadows to his left. He knit his brow, took a closer look.

A pair of luminescent red orbs shone out from a cluster of bushes. The orbs were small and circular, like a pair of eyes glowing in the dark.

The sight of them should have startled him, should have made him want to run away. But instead, he found himself drawn to them. He buttoned and zipped his pants and tiptoed over to investigate.

The bark of a dog cut through the air. He hadn't heard many of those—whenever there were dogs in the compound they were relegated to farming—but the sound was unmistakable.

And then the ghost jumped out at him.

# TWENTY-SEVEN

Growing up in the compound, Gus had always been told that there was no such thing as ghosts. They were supernatural beings, and the elders actively discouraged people against belief in the supernatural.

But that didn't mean he was terribly unfamiliar with the concept of them.

Ghosts were a common motif in Celtic folklore. From everything he'd read, the ancient Celts believed in reincarnation—when someone in the Mortalworld died, their soul was reborn in the Otherworld, and vice versa—but spirits could also linger between lives.

All that to say, this was why he knew the creature jumping out of the bushes was a ghost. It appeared as they were often described: a foggy mass. He should have been startled by it, especially because it was leaping toward him, but just as he felt perfectly at peace here in Annwn, he felt perfectly at peace in its presence.

Abruptly, it stopped, right in front of him. It wasn't too small, but it wasn't big by any means either. Standing at fourteen, maybe fifteen inches tall, it gazed up at him with glowing red eyes as round and expressive as Saoirse's.

The ghost let out a delighted bark, and that was when Gus really started to see it—it was a dog, with floppy ears and wisps of long curly fur, and it didn't have paws, not in the traditional sense. Its "legs" faded into twines of haze that hovered just above the ground. It was also translucent, the grass beneath it obscured by the white haze of its shape.

"Hey there." He knelt before the ghost-dog. It almost seemed to be smiling at him, lips spread wide in a big toothy grin. It cocked its head, its ears dangling to the side. They matched its eyes, as if the tips of them had been dipped in red dye. "I'm guessing I can't pet you?"

He reached for the ghost-dog, and in an instant, it seemed to solidify. Suddenly it was no longer translucent, the fog that formed its "limbs" snapping together to make four regular legs with four regular paws. He petted its neck, and his fingers disappeared into soft, thick fur.

"What are you?" he asked, mostly to himself since the ghost-dog probably didn't talk. It couldn't be a Cŵn Annwn—one of those spectral hounds of Welsh myth—right? It had the right coloring, but he'd always imagined those to be ferocious and bigger than a horse, and this creature was neither of those things.

After a minute or so, he stopped petting the ghost-dog and stood up. "Well, it was nice to meet you, but I've gotta head back, okay?"

He took a few steps toward camp.

The ghost-dog took a few steps after him.

He took another few steps toward camp.

The ghost-dog took another few steps after him.

He paused and stared down at the ghost-dog.

The ghost-dog paused and stared up at him.

"Are you hungry or something? Do ghost-dogs even need to eat?" The creature transformed into a phantom once more, barking as it glided in a circle around him, and he put a finger to his lips. "Shh! If you wanna hang out, you've gotta be quiet, all right?" It seemed to understand him, because it didn't make another peep as it followed him the rest of the way back.

At camp, Saoirse still slept under the tree. But the ghost-dog must not have liked that, because it solidified, leapt on top of her, and started licking her face.

Gus hastened over to stop the creature, but it was too late. Saoirse was already coming to. "Why, would you look at that?" she said, and sat up. The ghost-dog settled into her lap. She smiled, began petting it behind its floppy ears. "I think you've made yourself a new friend."

"H—sh—*it* found me, actually." He plopped down

next to them. "I think it's a ghost."

Saoirse examined the ghost-dog. "*She* is a Hound of Annwn. I thought you'd have known that, since she's white and has red eyes and ears?"

"Well, yeah, I noticed her coloring. But she looks . . ." The creature was grinning at him again, pink tongue lolling out of her mouth. "She's just not how I imagined the Hounds of Annwn. Weren't they, like, part of the Wild Hunt? Shouldn't she be scary?"

"Not if she doesn't want to be." Saoirse scratched the ghost-dog's chin. "What are you going to name her?"

"I'm supposed to name her?"

"You named the squirrel, didn't you?"

"Sure, after he'd been around for more than five minutes."

"She's not going anywhere," Saoirse asserted. "You're a Child of Arawn, and the Cŵn Annwn were known to be his servants for years. I wouldn't be surprised if she sensed your arrival and sought you out."

"You really think so?"

"Mm-hmm. She's chosen you. She's yours now, and you're hers. That's how it goes with dogs—even the ghost ones."

"If anything, she chose *you*." As though in agreement with Gus, the ghost-dog returned to licking Saoirse's cheek. "She just followed me back."

Saoirse's smile fell. She pushed the ghost-dog's face away from hers. "She's yours, Gus." She said it with such finality that he couldn't argue, and the creature hopped out of her lap and into Gus's.

He stroked the ghost-dog's back. "Okay, fine. I guess she's mine, then. If you had a pet, you'd probably pick a moth or a butterfly anyway, huh?"

"What gave you that idea?"

"It's obvious you like them."

"I *love* them. Moths, mostly. But butterflies are lovely too." She narrowed her eyes in suspicion. "How did you know?"

"It's pretty obvious to anyone paying attention."

"Are you saying you've been paying attention to me?"

"Who wouldn't?"

She flushed, and they were quiet for a while.

Finally, he broke the silence. "So, why moths over butterflies? Aren't they just about the same thing?"

"They are *not* the same thing." If it weren't for the impish gleam in her gaze, she might have looked offended. "Moths are much, much cuddlier."

He chuckled. "Cuddlier?"

"Yes, cuddlier," she said with a mock huff.

More chuckling, and he asked, "How long have you loved them for? Have you been interested in them your whole life, or is it a recent thing?"

She sighed, almost wistfully. "I've loved them for as long as I can remember. One of my earliest memories was watching an emperor moth fly straight into the flame of a candle. I got so upset! I couldn't understand why it would do such a thing, but now . . . I mean, it would be nice to be done and to never have to . . ." She trailed off, seemed to reconsider her words. It unsettled him; what had she meant to say? "Hey, you like 'folklore,'" she went on. "I bet you'll appreciate this. Have you ever read about what the Irish used to believe white butterflies held?"

"No, actually," he replied, deciding not to worry about whatever had just happened. It was probably nothing. Merely a slip of the tongue. "What did they believe they held?"

"The souls of dead children."

"Huh, interesting. What does that have to do with your love of moths, though?"

"I was getting to that. Other cultures from around the world had similar beliefs—about both butterflies *and* moths—and I don't think it's coincidence. I think that they might really hold the spirits of the dead. Perhaps they even transport souls from one realm to the next, allowing them to visit loved ones left behind."

It was a beautiful notion. "I like that idea." Another, shorter lull, and then he said, "Okay, here's something I want to know. Of all the moth species out there, which one is your favorite?"

"What kind of a question is that? How am I ever supposed to pick?"

"Just say one off the top of your head."

"Hmm. Probably the . . . um . . . the luna moth. Yes, yes, the luna moth! They're big and green, and they come from North America. After reaching their final form, they only live for about a week, but they're so pretty. I just wish I could see one with my own eyes. I've only seen pictures of them."

"Pictures? Like, illustrations?"

"Yes?"

"Where'd you get those from?"

"Oh, Gus Brandon." Playfully, she tsk-tsked. "You aren't the only one with access to books, you know."

He smiled. "You like to read?"

"Love to. But I must admit, I'm partial to books that document species of insects over anything else."

At that, something warmed deep in his chest. "I completely understand."

"Here, let me show you." She reached into her hair and pulled out a book, brown and leather bound. "I keep this with me always. I must have read it cover to cover at least a dozen times."

And so she flipped through the book, hovering a bit longer on her favorite pages—some were about the luna moth, which he had to admit *was* quite pretty. She showed him pictures, read him passages, and for a little while at least, he forgot about their troubles, absorbed in what she was telling him, captivated by the way joy had replaced melancholy in her droopy green eyes.

# TWENTY-EIGHT

Gus ended up falling asleep. He'd fought it for as long as he could, wanting to listen to Saoirse talk, wanting to ask her questions until he couldn't think of any more. She'd noticed him drifting off, insisted that he rest, that she be lookout for a bit. Then she'd taken off his glasses and set them aside, and he'd succumbed to sleep.

When he woke up, the sun was rising in the watercolor sky. Rays beamed through branches, warming his face, the smell of grass and soil thick in the air.

He rolled over to check on Saoirse but found she was gone, an impression in the greenery where she'd been sitting. The ghost-dog, solid for now, slept on the impression, curled up black button nose to long fluffy tail.

"Good, you're awake," Saoirse said from behind him, and he sat up and turned around. Her cheeks were pinker than they had been yesterday, but she still had the burns and the rings under her eyes. She gathered strawberries that littered the forest floor, stuffed them into a sack he'd never seen. *Must've pulled that out of her hair too.*

He located his glasses and put them on. "Why use a bag to carry those when you have magic?"

"You mean the packing spell?"

"Yeah, that. You'll have to show me how to do it, and how to use glamour and everything."

"We'll start with glamour today, and I'll teach you how to cast spells when I'm feeling stronger." Her voice held an anxious tremor. "As for why I'm not using the packing spell on the strawberries—well, you can only cast spells on nonliving objects."

"But strawberries aren't ali—"

"Their seeds are."

"Huh. All right. Hey, is everything okay?"

She paused, strawberries in one hand and the bag in the other. "We need to leave. A horde of shard-raised passed by earlier."

Realistically, he'd known that it wasn't truly safe anywhere they went. He'd been stupid to let himself feel as though they might be out of harm's way here. Even still . . .

He cussed under his breath.

She put the strawberries she'd been holding into the

bag and inhaled deeply. "I know. You feel at home here, and you should. This *is* your home. It's not fair that the shard-raised roam free, but everything will be better once you've harnessed the power of the cauldron. And, with any luck, that will be soon. Now eat something so we can get out of here."

Despite everything, her words put him at ease, and he scarfed down another dozen strawberries (there were so many!). Then he woke up the ghost-dog and she had some, and Saoirse stashed more away. She must have eaten while they slept. "Remington?" she called. Gus couldn't see Remington from here, but he'd heard the squirrel snoring before breakfast. "You ready to go?"

Remington came scuttering down the tree. The ghost-dog barked, running toward the squirrel, and a rush of panic went through Gus. How hadn't he thought of it before? The ghost-dog was a hunting hound, and Remington was the perfect small game.

Gus darted forward, but thankfully, he didn't need to separate the animals. Remington nuzzled the ghost-dog's legs as if she was an old friend, and the ghost-dog let out a contented whimper and licked his nose.

The whole exchange astounded Gus, and his expression must have reflected that, because Saoirse giggled at him. "What's so funny?" he asked, grinning.

"The way you look . . . your face . . ."

"This is exactly what I was afraid of." He shook his head in mock disappointment. "I'm not near as pretty as the merrows say, am I?"

More laughter—this time from both of them—and with that, Remington led the group away from their camping spot, farther into the forest.

"So," Gus began after several minutes of walking, "you said something about showing me how to use glamour?"

The ghost-dog pranced next to Saoirse, hopping up every few steps to lick her fingers. It made her smile every time. "There isn't really a way to 'show' you how to use glamour. It happens in the mind and requires a great deal of focus."

"What do you mean by that? Like, I just think about making a tree look like a bush, or turning someone invisible, and it works?"

"Um, not quite. You can't use glamour on anything other than yourself."

"Really?" She nodded, reaching down to scratch the ghost-dog behind the ears. "That's weird," he continued, "because in the stories, faeries use glamour on everything."

"The stories you're thinking of are probably referencing glamour *powder*, which is a tool of the gods. Very hard to come by these days."

"I remember you mentioning 'tools of the gods' before. Isn't that what your sunlight-nets are?"

"Yes, they were made by Lugh, long ago. And my flare-wand was made by Brigid. The gods used to craft all sorts of tools for the faeries."

Gus thought for a second, trying to recall everything that Lugh and Brigid were known for. He knew that they were part of the Tuatha Dé Danann, that Lugh had a lot of useful skills and had defeated the mighty Fomorian named Balor, that Brigid was associated with fire and spring and healing, that—

*Not important right now*, he told himself. *We were talking about glamour.* "Okay, so I can't change the appearance of anything except for myself?"

"You can *conceal* things about your appearance, so long as it's a part of your body, but it's only an illusion. You can't actually change your form. You'd have to inherit the power of transformation from a divine ancestor to do that."

"What about objects, like clothes?" he asked. "When you used glamour to make yourself invisible in the library, your dress disappeared with you, but technically, your clothes aren't part of your body."

"That's right. I had to cast an invisibility spell on my dress to make it look as if I'd completely disappeared. But let's just focus on glamour for now. Like I said, we'll worry about spells later."

As it turned out, Gus had at least understood one aspect of glamour usage. Saoirse explained that he did, in fact, only have to think about the "change" he wanted to make to his appearance for it to work. "When you're just starting out, it's best to practice in front of your reflection," she said. "Why don't you try it the next time we stop for water?"

"Sounds good to me," he replied.

Over the next several hours, they kept their eyes peeled for shard-raised and passed all sorts of gates and wild animals. Surprisingly, the ghost-dog was friendly with every creature they came across: deer, rabbits, squirrels, toads, foxes, crows. They also saw a wide variety of insects, including a group of butterflies that Gus joked about with Saoirse.

"Tell me," he said, motioning at the butterflies as they flittered from bush to bush, "what moth species are these?"

She returned his teasing smirk. "Weren't you paying attention to anything I showed you last night? Those aren't moths, they're butterflies. Meadow browns."

Two of the insects swooped down in front of the ghost-dog then flew back up again, and she immaterialized and floated after them, pretending to bite them. In return, they glowed orange and taupe and stars trailed behind them.

Soon the trees began to thin. They reached a meadow bursting with wildflowers, the blossoms' sweet scents wafting in the breeze. Here, the landscape rolled like waves, long green grass swaying rhythmically, and in the distance, a pair of stags grazed.

At the sight of the meadow, the ghost-dog solidified, and she and Remington began frolicking about, popping flowers off stems and into their mouths. Although Gus thought Remington would be fine to consume the blossoms, he wasn't sure whether it was safe for dogs to eat them—but then again, she wasn't a normal dog, was she?

"Have you decided on a name for her yet?" Saoirse asked as they caught up with the animals.

He shook his head. "No. I've been thinking about it, though." And he had. He'd decided that as a Hound of Annwn, the ghost-dog needed a Welsh name. He'd named Remington in a similar manner: since he'd thought the squirrel lived in the destroyed city, he'd given Remington the name of one of its still-standing street signs.

The only issue was that he didn't know any feminine Welsh names outside of the ones he could remember from mythology. "Branwen" and "Rhiannon" were the first to come to mind, but neither of those seemed like suitable titles for this creature. He guessed there was also "Arianrhod," but again, it just wasn't a good fit for her.

Then, as he watched her snap her jaws around a white blossom, it hit him. *Olwen*. From the tale "Culhwch and Olwen." Gus couldn't recall all the details of the story, just that it was about a prince named Culhwch who was cursed to never marry—that is, unless he could win the heart of Olwen, the daughter of an evil giant named Ysbaddaden. Olwen was so kind and gentle that white flowers sprouted wherever she walked, and with the help of the famous King Arthur, Culhwch managed to thwart Ysbaddaden and marry Olwen.

"Olwen," Gus said aloud, testing it on his tongue.

Saoirse glanced over at him. "Hm?"

"Olwen," he repeated. "That might be a good name. For the ghost-dog. Do you think it fits her?"

"I do. But what do you think, girl?" Saoirse smiled

down at her. "Do you like the name 'Olwen'? Would you like us to call you that?"

The ghost-dog barked and offered them a goofy grin. "Guess that settles it," Gus said. "We'll call her Olwen."

They made it across the meadow and into another mountainous, woody area, and the rest of the day was fairly calm. There were some close calls with wayward skeletons, but Saoirse took care of the monsters with her winds. Then they'd keep walking, passing gate after gate after gate. They ran into a group of does and fawns and heard the bays of wild dogs (which Olwen promptly responded to with melodramatic howling). When they grew hungry, Saoirse retrieved strawberries from the bag, and the only instances in which they stopped were when they saw water, not only to get a drink but also so Gus could practice glamour usage in front of his reflection. However, to his disappointment, all the water sources they passed moved so quickly that he couldn't see himself in them, so he didn't have the chance to try.

For the most part, all seemed to be going well . . . until they ran into the shard-raised corpses.

It was right when Saoirse's scars began badly hurting her. The sun was setting anyway, so they started searching for a place to rest and stumbled upon a river. Figuring they'd better stop and drink before settling down for the night, they approached the water, and a pair of hands broke the surface.

At the sight, Gus staggered backward. He narrowed

his eyes at the hands, and sure enough, purple veins snarled across their blue flesh.

Another pair of hands appeared, then another, and then the three shard-raised corpses the hands belonged to emerged.

The faeries they'd devoured had probably been beautiful before, with their long brown hair and shapely figures. But now these forms were terrifying, their unblinking eyes wide, their open mouths slack. They lumbered through the water toward the riverbank.

Olwen barked, actually sounding ferocious for once, and Remington screeched and gestured with his paws as if to say, *"Run, you idiots!"* Gus was about to grab Saoirse and do just that, but stopped when he realized she was holding three sunlight-nets.

The shard-raised reached the riverbank. Saoirse threw the nets at them, trapping them. Gus seized her by the hand. "Let's go!"

But as they sprinted back into the forest, the skeletons surrounded them.

# TWENTY-NINE

There were too many skeletons to count, the stench of them overwhelming Gus's senses. They came from every direction, emerged from the shadows between trees as if they'd been watching, waiting. *How're we gonna get out of this?*

Had Saoirse recovered enough to fly them both away? To take down a throng of these things by herself? Because as much as Gus hated to admit it, he was useless against the shard-raised. Would be until he had the power of the cauldron and knew how to use it.

Olwen growled and stepped in front of him, and Remington scrambled up onto his shoulder. Beside him, Saoirse waved her arms, already looking ready to pass out as she sent wind through bone. But despite her efforts, the skeletons kept coming. It seemed that for every monster defeated, two more appeared.

As they closed in, Olwen barked furiously, and she seemed to be . . . growing? With each utterance, she got taller, wider. Her fur straightened, shortened, her floppy ears shrinking and morphing into upright triangles, and before Gus knew it, she was taller than him, appearing lean and muscular and dangerous.

Exactly how he'd have imagined the Hounds of Annwn.

Olwen snarled and solidified, then lunged at two of the skeletons. She brought them down with a thrust of her front paws, their ribs snapping beneath her weight. They clacked their teeth at her, tried lifting their heads to bite her, but she immaterialized at the last second, their jaws going straight through her wispy form. They began to stand, and she resolidified and smacked their skulls off their spines. That seemed to occupy them for the moment; rather than trying to attack, they crawled around, groping for their skulls until, seconds later, the enchanted mist that animated them pieced them back together.

Saoirse and Olwen immobilized more of the skeletons—Saoirse with her winds, Olwen with her paws, and while Olwen's method wasn't permanent, it bought time. Together, the two of them cleared a path of escape, and Gus dragged Saoirse through it, Remington clinging to him for dear life.

Was Olwen behind them? He looked over his shoulder, and his gut clenched.

The ghost-dog wasn't fleeing the skeletons.

She was fighting them.

Based on the way she'd handled herself, he knew that she wasn't in danger, that she could get away at any time, that she was only protecting them. But what if they lost her? What if she couldn't find them again?

He didn't vocalize these questions, partly because he feared he already knew the answers, but mostly because right after he thought them, ten shard-raised broke off from the horde to shamble after him and Saoirse.

They sped up as best they could, and Saoirse waved her free arm. A gale ripped through two of the closest skeletons. Another wave, and more bones scattered. But before she could summon a third gust, she stumbled, a frail yelp escaping her lips.

"Saoirse!" He caught her by the biceps.

Her head slumped to the side. "I'll be—okay. Just no—more wind."

With a nod, he grasped her waist. She threw an arm around his neck, careful not to hit Remington. They pressed on.

It wasn't long before dusk turned to dark and they reached an especially rocky area, the cliffs obscuring much of the twinkling sky. Saoirse retrieved a sunlight-net to help them see while Gus glanced over his shoulder—the skeletons still shuffled along behind them.

Remington jumped off Gus's shoulder and darted to the left. "Rem!" Gus cried as he and Saoirse ground to a halt. "What are you doing?" Saoirse shined her sunlight-net at the squirrel, and he chattered irritably at them, making upward motions with his paws.

Gus looked that way, and then he saw it. Forty feet above them, a cave had been carved out of a jagged cliffside, sparkles funneling into the arched entrance.

Remington hopped across the stones at the base of the precipice and started scrabbling up it.

Panting, trembling, Saoirse untangled her body from Gus's and tucked away her sunlight-net. Gus took her hand and squeezed. "I'll carry you. It'll be hard with the antlers, but—"

She yanked him into the air and fluttered toward the cave. *Never mind.*

They reached the cave opening, and she dropped him next to Remington and collapsed. He lunged for her, caught her before she hit rock. Her breaths were growing faster, her skin slick with sweat. Could they rest here a while and wait for Olwen to reach them? Or would the shard-raised climb up after them?

He looked back and caught glimpses of ivory struggling to mount the cliff. It might not happen fast, but sooner or later, the shard-raised would reach them.

They had to go through the gate, had to leave Olwen behind.

It wasn't at all what Gus wanted to do, but he and Remington couldn't incapacitate the shard-raised even temporarily, and Saoirse couldn't keep stripping away their magic. *Please be okay, Olwen. Please find your way back to us.*

Remington screeched at him, plunged farther into

the sparkling cave. He scooped Saoirse into his arms and rushed after the squirrel.

Light so bright it made his eyes water, and then he was slipping, sliding, skidding down a mound of unstable matter. He tried to gain his footing, tried to stop himself, but hard objects gave way beneath his boots, and he kept tumbling, holding Saoirse tight as she buried her face in his chest.

As quickly as their descent began, it ended, Gus crashing to the ground tailbone-first. The collision knocked the wind out of him, and pain caromed through his body from the point of impact.

Saoirse scrambled out of his arms, gave him space to recover. It only took a minute to catch his breath but felt so much longer.

He blinked at their surroundings, finding heaps of debris everywhere—brick and wood and concrete and rusted Golden Era automobiles piled like garbage as far as the eye could see, reminding him of the destroyed city near his compound but worse. From what he could tell, it was morning, the atmosphere polluted with smog once more, and a few feet away, Remington stood on his hind legs, sniffing the air as though he sensed danger.

Saoirse gasped. At first, Gus thought she was still struggling to breathe, but then she yanked him to the side.

She ducked behind another pile of rubble, dragging him down with her. That was when he saw it.

One of the shard-raised skeletons had made it up to

the cave and through the gate. It hobbled out of a glittering mushroom ring atop the mound of wreckage Gus and Saoirse had just been sitting at the bottom of, then tripped, toppled over debris, and hit the ground as they had.

It got up, carried on.

Gus held his breath until it disappeared.

He and Saoirse stayed there for a while, hiding behind rubble, their stares trained on the mushrooms, but no other skeletons came out of them.

Neither did Olwen.

Saoirse sagged against the debris. Sinking to the ground, she put her face in her hands.

"Hey, it's okay." Gus sat down next to her, wanting to put his arm around her, to hug her, but hesitated, afraid to make things worse. "I don't think more of them are coming after us."

"I know," she said, her voice quivering.

"Then what's wrong? Is it—is it Olwen?"

She let her hands fall, looked up at him. Tears glistened in her eyes but she did not cry. "It's that, but it's everything else too, Gus. It's how weak I feel, how much I hurt. It's the shard-raised and the Skeleton Faerie and the state of the realms. I'm just . . . so tired. I can't keep doing this. I'm ready for it to be over. If I could just go to sleep and never . . ."

She didn't finish the thought, so he asked, "And never what?"

No reply.

He recalled something she'd said last night. Or

rather, something she'd *almost* said. *"I couldn't understand why it would do such a thing, but now . . . I mean, it would be so nice to be done and to never have to . . ."*

Oh no, she couldn't have meant—

*Stop*, he thought. *Stop thinking into it so much. Stop jumping to conclusions.* As she'd said, she was tired and in pain. A monster made of vines (or that controlled vines? He wasn't sure which) had torn her apart, had traumatized her, and she'd been dealing with everything regarding the shard-raised and the Skeleton Faerie for much longer than him. If he were her, he'd be tired too. He'd be ready for the Skeleton Faerie's demise so that he could really, truly rest.

*You know what? Fuck it. She's hurting.* And maybe she didn't want comfort, maybe she didn't need it, but he wanted her to know that he cared, that he was here.

He wrapped his arms around her, held her close.

She melted into him.

Could she feel his heart pounding? If so, he hoped she'd attribute it to the fact that they'd just escaped a mob of shard-raised. Not that he wanted to brush her hair behind her ears and cup her cheeks in his hands. Not that he wanted to know how her lips would feel against his, how her body would—

*Dammit.*

*I'm in trouble, aren't I?*

A chirp beside them. It was Remington, urging them along. They pulled away from each other and stood up, and Remington led them through the ruins, in the opposite direction of the skeleton.

They didn't get far, maybe a mile or two, before they reached an area that wasn't so demolished. Rather than appearing to have been bombed, this place looked abandoned, and it reminded Gus of the apartments section of his compound, buildings clustered together and pathways winding between them. The only differences were that this place had streets with old parked cars and its structures were quite a lot smaller than the compound's apartment complexes. *Houses*, he realized. *These are houses from the Golden Era.*

He'd studied photos of Golden Era houses while training for his job in construction, and he decided now that they looked much shinier, much more perfect, in pictures. Polished and bright and colorful, as if freshly built, freshly painted.

Though he supposed that a century ago, these structures had also been spectacular, because despite their smashed windows, flaking paint, and drooping ceilings, they were far more congruent than the compound's buildings. They'd been methodically constructed with complementing colors and materials, not smashed together with whatever old scraps were available.

As they trudged farther into the neighborhood, the smell of decay assaulted Gus's nostrils, and for a moment he panicked. Had they come upon more shard-raised?

Then he saw them—the lifeless human corpses—strewn across the paths and streets. It seemed there had been a gunfight of sorts, bullet holes riddling the bodies, the cars, the houses.

"I have—to rest," Saoirse said between labored breaths.

"How about in a house?" Gus motioned at the closest building, the one to their right, which might have been pastel blue before fading to pewter. Two men still clutching their handguns lay dead on the cracked concrete driveway. "You can stay out here. I'll make sure there's no one inside and yell for you if there are any shard-raised."

She nodded, leaning on the hood of an automobile, and he headed up the driveway, pausing only to rip the guns out of the corpses' stinking, bloated hands. He should have gagged as their flesh tore, as their bones crunched, but he didn't. He barely flinched. Handling them felt like nothing compared to everything else he'd experienced over the past few days.

His lack of disgust was probably a good thing anyway, right? After all, he was supposed to be able to raise an army of the dead.

Pattering from behind him, and Remington hopped onto his shoulder. "You're coming in with me?" he asked, and the squirrel chittered as if to say, *"You bet!"* "Okay, then. If you're sure."

He kept hold of one gun, stuffed the other into the holster at his belt. Each firearm only had a couple of rounds left. Hopefully, that would be enough in the event of a non-supernatural threat.

The front door's locks were rotted through, so he and Remington walked straight in. Despite the fractures on the walls and ceilings from the house settling over the years, its interior was nice, nicer than both apartments he'd lived in and roomy to boot. The building was long and rectangular and only had one floor, but there were two living rooms, three bathrooms, and five bedrooms, all of which were more than twice the size of Ronnie's kitchen. Some of them had plain beige walls, while others were decorated with intricately designed papering, but all of them were populated with mold-and-dust-covered furniture and graying photographs of a four-person family that was surely long deceased.

After Gus finished searching the house and determined it was safe, he helped Saoirse inside. The doors couldn't be locked and the windows had been shattered, so they opted to camp out in the only room that didn't have windows: the smaller living room. It was on the left side of the building, sandwiched between the kitchen and the garage.

Saoirse retrieved the last of the strawberries, and the three of them finished off the fruit in minutes. Then she crumpled onto the couch and drifted off almost immediately, and Remington disappeared into the house, presumably to leave and hunt for more food.

And as for Gus? Well, he had no interest in rest, had far too much work to do. Gun in hand, he set his jaw, went into the closest bathroom, and faced his reflection in the mirror.

# THIRTY

The crack in the glass split Gus's face down the middle, the rest of the circular mirror smeared with filth. Thankfully, he could see himself just fine, but his reflection was jarring, to say the least.

On the one hand, he looked as normal as always. Messy hair, brown eyes, aviator glasses. But on the other hand, he didn't look quite . . . real. Probably because of the antlers. Six inches long, they jutted from the puffy red skin above his temples and forked into three sharp tines, the branch-like appendages stained with lingering gore.

*What about my ears? Have those changed too?* It was hard to tell with his hair hanging over them. He set the gun on the counter and pushed his hair back, and sure enough, the tips of his ears were no longer rounded.

They were pointed.

He wasn't sure how long he stood there, stupefied as he examined the changes to his appearance, thinking, *Faeries are real, and I'm one of them*, over and over. But after he came out of his daze, he began practicing his glamour usage.

For hours, he stared at his reflection, picturing how he'd looked without antlers in his mind's eye. By and large, nothing happened. However, in four separate instances, he felt chills beneath his skin. Then the air around his antlers shimmered and the bones vanished.

Saoirse hadn't been kidding when she'd said that this trick required a great deal of focus, though. Each time he successfully concealed his antlers, they reappeared as quickly as they'd disappeared, and he had to start the whole process over again. He figured it would be a while before he could hold the illusion for more than a moment.

Eventually, he decided he wanted to try something else. He slipped the gun into the side pocket opposite his holster and headed outside.

If it weren't for his newfound strength, it would have been far more difficult to drag the corpses into the house. The men from the driveway weren't particularly large, but deadweight was a thing. Still, he had no trouble once he concentrated on his strength. As magic coursed through him, he hauled them inside without issue.

He hadn't wanted to bring them in initially, hadn't wanted to risk disturbing Saoirse. But at the same time, he needed to be able to defend her in the event of an intruder. So he decided to bring the bodies into the kitchen. It was . . . unsanitary at best, but the place was already run down, and he'd be close to her this way, as she was just around the corner.

He placed the bodies in the middle of the tile floor and, for a solid twenty minutes, studied them. He imagined them twitching to life and following his commands, but ultimately, he couldn't make them move an inch, couldn't even feel magic beneath his skin.

Did he have to be touching them? He knelt before them, placed his hands on their heads, and tried again.

No such luck.

"What are you doing?" Saoirse asked from behind him.

He flinched at the sudden noise but recovered quickly, then climbed to his feet and turned to face her. The couch pattern was etched on her cheek, her hair a nest of tangles. "Uhh, I'm trying something," he said.

"Trying what?" She walked up beside him, examining the bodies. "To make yourself an army of corpses?"

"The start of one, yeah. I thought it would be good to practice and prepare myself, but it's not really working."

"Hmm. You said before that you didn't realize Arawn was a death god, right?"

"Yeah?"

"Then part of your problem could be that you need

to connect with the past. Your death-magic is present, but to use it, you might need to learn more about Arawn, about his other descendants. You also need to practice more—powers are like muscles. They have to be used, challenged, to grow stronger. It's rare for someone to master them immediately."

"Why could I channel my strength so quickly, then? That's a power too."

"Yes, but it's the easiest to use. Glamour and spells are harder, and unique abilities . . . those take the most practice."

"I managed to use glamour earlier, for a few seconds. If you're feeling up to it, maybe you could teach me a spell?"

"I'm much better than earlier, and you need to learn anyway. Let's do the packing spell first." Trying to smooth her hair with her fingers, she led him into the living room, and they sat down on the couch. "Where's Remington?" she asked.

"Out hunting for more food, I think."

"Ah."

"So, are there a lot of limits to what we can do with spells, like there are with glamour? I know you said they don't work on nonliving objects. Anything else?"

"They don't work on dead bodies either, on things that once had a soul. You need to be touching whatever it is you're casting the spell on, and objects made mostly of iron are immune. But outside of that, the possibilities are practically endless—for instance, we can preserve objects from the elements. That's how

I've kept my book and the map of the isle from deteriorating. We can also make things invisible, or transform them, or change their size."

"Or pack them away," he added.

"Mm-hmm." She produced a sunlight-net. "First things first, choose a spot on your body to store the object. I recommend the hair."

"Why the hair? Why not an eye, an ear?"

She giggled. "This would hurt terribly going in and out of an eye or an ear!"

"Fair enough," he said with a chuckle. "Hair it is. What's next?"

"You envision what it is you want the spell to do while touching the object you're casting it on. But when you're first getting started, it's best to say the spell out loud as well, like this." To his surprise, she didn't raise the sunlight-net to her own head; she raised it to his. It felt like warm silk against the nape of his neck. "Tool of Lugh, you're so small you can't be seen by the naked eye, and you're packed away safely and securely in the hair of the faerie called Gus Brandon."

Suddenly the object wasn't touching him anymore, but her fingers were. They lingered there, and her gaze fell to his lips, and—

She dropped her hand. "Does that make sense?"

"Yes." He swallowed hard, adjusted his glasses. "Should I try after you take it out, or . . . ?"

"You could disable it yourself."

"Disable it?"

"The spell. To disable it is to reverse it."

"Okay." He placed his hand where hers had just been and pictured what he wanted as he said it. "Tool of Lugh, you're back to your regular size, and you sit in my hand." Cold energy glided through him, and the object rolled out of his hair and into his palm.

"Good, now try packing it away," Saoirse instructed.

"Your hair or mine?"

Her stare stayed on him as she considered the question. "Mine."

He took a deep breath and brought the sunlight-net to the nape of her neck, her still-messy blonde strands tickling his fingers. Heart skipping, he imagined the sunlight-net shrinking down and vanishing safely into her tangles, and as he described what he pictured aloud, the object obeyed.

Saoirse reached up and took his hand in hers, then pulled it into her lap and ran her thumb across the knuckles. As she looked up at him again, he realized they were closer than before. There was a flush in her cheeks, and she leaned forward, and so did he, and for a moment he thought she might kiss him, thought—

A clatter from somewhere in the house.

They jumped to their feet.

"Rem?" Gus called, but all he got in response was a second clatter. He could hear now that it came from the other side of the building.

He grabbed the gun from his pocket. "Stay close to me," he whispered to Saoirse, and they crept in the direction of the sounds.

Was it wise to actively search for danger rather than flee the house and hope nothing followed them out? Gus thought no, probably not. Especially because he wasn't even close to mastering his abilities, and he and Saoirse hadn't finished healing from the iron.

Yet they couldn't just *leave*, not without Remington. He was Gus's friend, but more importantly, he was their guide to the Isle of Bone and Blood. They needed to be here when he came back from wherever he'd run off to.

And so they tiptoed down the house's narrow main hall toward the commotion.

Soon Gus heard hisses between the clangs. Was it a snake? A bobcat, a mountain lion?

He got his answer as a huge four-legged animal stalked into the hall from a room twenty feet ahead. Muscles rippled beneath its short sand-colored fur as it turned its head toward them.

No, wait—not its head.

Its *heads*.

It had two of them, round and unmistakably feline. They protruded from separate necks, with erect ears that curved at the tips, matching sets of yellow eyes, and triangular pink noses.

The second the mountain lion saw him and Saoirse, its ears went flat against its skulls. Growls rumbled from its throats, and its lips peeled back, mouths bared to reveal long, sharp fangs.

On instinct, Gus raised his gun and fired.

The bullet missed the animal and hit the wall behind

it, which should have been enough to deter it. The roar of the weapon—especially in this enclosed space—was deafening.

But the gunfire only seemed to anger the mountain lion. Mouths foaming, tail twitching, it drew closer, pumped its legs as though preparing to pounce.

He muttered a slew of curse words as he and Saoirse staggered back. *Does it have rabies, or is it just hungry?* He discharged again. This time, the shot hit its target.

The animal's left head slumped over, red liquid dribbling from a perfect hole between the eyes, and the remaining head unleashed a scream so loud and shrill he could hear it over the ringing in his ears. *That should do it. It'll go away now.*

Too bad he was wrong.

Very wrong.

With one head hanging limp, the mountain lion bounded toward them.

Gus pulled the trigger a third time but nothing came out. Before he could drop the gun and scramble for the one in his holster, Saoirse leapt in front of him, wind whooshing toward the mountain lion.

The gust sent the animal streaking backward. It crashed through the bathroom door at the end of the hall, splintered wood careening through the air. Surely, now it would retreat?

To his dismay, it did not. It unleashed another spine-chilling shriek, forced itself to its feet, and stomped toward them. *What the hell is this thing made of?*

He hurled the empty gun aside and seized the other

while Saoirse conjured a second gale. The wind tossed the mountain lion sideways, ramming it heads-first into the wall. Saoirse grabbed his free hand and they darted away, toward the entrance of the house.

Snarling behind them. He chanced a glance over his shoulder. The mountain lion couldn't move as quickly as it had before their attacks, but it still stumbled after them.

They reached the entrance and burst out the door. He slammed it shut behind them, and they sprinted down the driveway.

Again, the mountain lion screamed. Pulse pounding, he looked back, caught sight of it hurtling through one of the smashed-in windows. He whirled around and shot twice at the animal, but if the bullets hit it, he couldn't tell, because it didn't react, it just kept coming.

Saoirse blasted it with more wind. It skidded backward across the fractured pavement, struck the front of the house. Saoirse grabbed a sunlight-net and readied herself to throw the object.

"Wait!" Gus said, and she paused. "Didn't you say you have a limited amount of those? Don't waste it. Let me shoot this thing."

She nodded and put it away. At the same time, the mountain lion struggled to its feet, and Gus raised the gun and aimed for the animal's right head.

But in the end, he didn't get to kill it.

Because a giant white dog with glowing red eyes barreled into sight and tackled it to the ground.

# PART FOUR

# THE ISLE

# THIRTY-ONE

Gus watched, astounded, as the ghost-dog made quick work of the two-headed mountain lion. With her teeth, she shredded open its belly and throats, and it fell lifeless.

Then she turned to Gus and Saoirse and grinned at them like a loon, blood dripping from her jaws and staining the fur around her mouth.

"Olwen!" they shouted in unison. How had she found them? Not that he was complaining. He felt lighter suddenly, and before he knew it, laughter began bubbling out of him.

Olwen went on smiling and shrank down to her smaller size, and that was when Gus saw Remington. The squirrel sat on her as one would sit on a horse, clinging to the back of her neck with his front paws.

The sight was absurd, and it only made Gus laugh more. "We were wondering where you'd gone," he said. In reply, Remington chirped, hopped off Olwen's back, and scampered over to Gus, and Gus returned the gun to his holster, picked up Remington, and cuddled the squirrel to his chest.

Olwen immaterialized, the mountain lion's blood spilling to the ground. She floated straight to Saoirse and resolidified, not a trace of gore left on her, and Saoirse knelt down and hugged her. Warm with relief and contentment, Gus walked over to them and scratched Olwen behind the ears.

They stayed that way for a while, hugging Olwen and Remington and expressing how happy they were that the animals had made it back safely. Olwen ate it up, her grin growing wider as they petted and praised her.

After their encounter with the mountain lion and their reunion with Olwen, the rest of the day proved to be uneventful. Saoirse suggested that Gus rest for a while, and he agreed. With Olwen at his spine and Remington by his head, he slept for several hours.

When he woke, he returned to practicing his magic. He'd pretty much mastered the packing spell (both casting and disabling it), but his ability to hold glamour hadn't improved, and when he tried to raise the corpses in the kitchen again, nothing happened. "You'll just have to keep at it," Saoirse assured him. "Maybe read more about Arawn when you can. It might take time, but you'll do it."

While Gus continued his work, Saoirse rested some more, and by nightfall, they decided it was time to leave the dilapidated house—partly because they were all hungry and thirsty, but mostly because Remington was agitated. Admittedly, Saoirse could have used more sleep in her condition, but they still hadn't reached the isle. "Remington isn't wrong for being frustrated," she said with a sigh of exhaustion. "We can't stay in one place for too long."

"Do you think we'll get there soon?" Gus asked.

She bit her lip. "I have no idea."

He thought of Ronnie, of how the old man was surely trapped somewhere in the compound, hiding from shard-raised. It made his chest tight. *Hold on, okay? I haven't forgotten about you. It's just taking a little longer to get back than I expected.*

They followed Remington for miles through deserted neighborhoods, which were as fraught with broken-down automobiles and bullet-filled corpses as the rest of the ruins here. As they passed dead bodies, Gus focused on resurrecting the lifeless husks, but just as before, he couldn't even make them twitch.

Saoirse must have noticed his disappointment; she put a hand on his shoulder. "Don't give up." Olwen solidified and jumped up to lick his fingers, though he couldn't be sure whether she did it to encourage him or because she wanted to taste whatever minuscule bits of decay might linger on him from when he'd been handling the dead.

Within a couple of hours they made it out of the

abandoned neighborhoods, into a moribund meadow, and then into more woodland. They washed up and drank generously from a stream, ate and packed away acorns, crabapples, and black trumpet mushrooms, and by daybreak, Gus knew they must be getting close to a gate—presumably an old one—because the vegetation was getting thicker, healthier, the colored leaves that fell from the trees some of the most vibrant he'd ever seen.

Before long, Remington led them to a massive glittering oak adorned with burnt orange and yellow. As they approached it, its trunk opened like a deformed mouth, revealing a gate swirling with more sparkles.

Remington and Olwen hopped right into the gate and disappeared. Lacing their hands together, Gus and Saoirse walked in next.

A shock of something wet, cold, the ground crumbling beneath them. Everything went dark, even darker than before, in the tree. There was no sunlight behind them, no forest, and they were . . . floating?

Yes, "floating" was the right word for it. They had to be underwater, because freezing liquid that tasted of salt—and rot?—flooded his mouth.

Gold glimmered in his peripheral. He looked that way to find Saoirse holding a sunlight-net in her free hand. Every pink stitch scar on her face and neck lay bare, exposed as blonde wisps drifted around her head.

They appeared to be in a smallish underwater cave. The entrance was to his left, and Remington and Olwen already swam toward it. Holding tight to each other, he and Saoirse followed them.

Something that looked like bone flashed at the entrance. They all snapped backward through the water, the last of Gus's oxygen escaping his lips. Was that . . . ?

*Oh shit.*

It was.

In the dim light, he saw the side of the skull. White mist circulated around it, and it wasn't human, wasn't even any animal he'd come across before. It was so big that he doubted it could fit through the entrance, and the shape of it reminded him of an illustrated dragon he'd seen in one of his books.

The shard-raised caught sight of them. It turned and jolted toward the entrance of the cave.

The four of them lurched backward again, but just as Gus had suspected, the shard-raised couldn't fit its skull inside. It only managed to cram in the front of its long nasal and jaw bones, though its outermost teeth came dangerously close to impaling Remington.

Rumbling all around them as the shard-raised tried jerking its skull from side to side, and Gus thought he might pass out, thought his lungs might burst.

He started turning around so they could swim back through the gate—there was no way they'd be able to get past this thing, and if they waited around much longer, they'd be either drowned or crushed—but then Saoirse yanked her hand out of his and motioned at the shard-raised.

A frothy current ripped through its skull. Its white

mist dispersed, and the cave stopped shaking.

Right away, Remington and Olwen darted through the skull's jaws and out of the cave. Saoirse snatched Gus by the wrist and they did the same.

As they all swam upward, toward the surface, Gus couldn't help but wonder how Saoirse had used her wind-powers just now. She was a sylph, and they were underwater. He supposed there was *some* air in water, but still, he hadn't expected that.

They reached the surface within seconds, and Gus coughed up what he'd swallowed and gasped for breath, Saoirse and Remington doing the same. Apparently, ghost-dogs didn't need much oxygen, because Olwen seemed completely fine as she hovered above the water beside them.

It was brighter up here thanks to the twinkling night sky, but Gus soon realized that it was still difficult to see more than a few feet in all directions due to the dense haze that blanketed the gently tiding water. He thought that, in the distance, there might be the outline of land, but again, the mist made everything so murky he couldn't be sure.

Strangely enough, this fog smelled too, faintly of death, almost reminding him of the shard-raised, of their—

That's when it hit him.

"Is this the isle?" he cried.

"It—is," Saoirse said, then finished catching her breath. "We need to get to shore before another sea monster shows up."

*That's right. She said the isle is guarded, to keep others from trying to fly or sail to it.* He should have known where they were right when the dragon-like skull appeared.

They paddled frantically (except for Olwen, who *floated* frantically) toward the dark shapes that formed the Isle of Bone and Blood, and more questions crossed Gus's mind. For instance, why had Remington led them here through an underwater gate? If he could see through the veil, and if he knew there were sea monsters around, he must have known it wasn't entirely safe. Didn't the isle have other entry points? Or was Remington in that much of a hurry to reach the shards? *At least this means I'll get back to the compound faster.*

They arrived at a shelf of rock and sand, the water shallow enough that Gus and Saoirse didn't have to swim anymore. With his free hand, Gus scooped Remington out of the water to carry him the rest of the way.

Finally, land overcame liquid, and as Gus stepped onto shore, the ground *cruuunch*ed beneath his boots. *That's weird.* He looked down.

The ground here was a twisted cacophony of bone and beach. For as far as he could see, haze curled over human skeletons half-buried in the sand, their ivory frames decorated with barnacles and seashells and slimy brown kelp.

He held Remington close, and a whine sounded by his feet—it was Olwen. He could hardly discern her body from the mist, her ears barely more than red specks, but the glow of her eyes cut through the fog like flashlights.

"Let's get to the trees," Saoirse said, grabbing Gus's hand again. "Before the flying shard-raised see us."

With the brightness of the sunlight-net, the ghost-dog's eyes, and the moon and stars, the beach's edge came into view, sand fading into forest. The trees here were a stark contrast to the rest of the vegetation Gus had seen in the Otherworld; they stood crookedly, hunched over as old men ready for death do, their gnarled branches appearing so starved of nutrients not one leaf could have grown from them.

After Gus and Saoirse reached the cover of woodland, they were able to slow down. Remington climbed out of Gus's hand and onto his shoulder, and Olwen opted to glide next to Saoirse.

Fog inched along the forest floor. There were skeletons here too, semisubmerged in dirt. Dying grass, sagging mushrooms, and twisting vines grew around and inside of them, poking from their cracks and crevices. Even the trees were plagued by them, bones protruding from bark as though they'd always been there, as though they somehow *belonged* there.

Worst of all, however, was the moaning. It drifted through the woods, and to Gus, it sounded like a group of mourners, conjuring memories of funerals in the compound, of military police officers lowering bodies into farmland.

Then he noticed them, in the distance. Humanoid figures creeping between trees. They were feathery and see-through, almost as if they were an extension of the haze.

"Don't worry," Saoirse said. "They're just ghosts. I think we're in the southern half of the isle."

"The Forest of Ghosts," he said, recalling the map of the isle she'd shown him.

"Uh-huh. So we'll be seeing a lot more of them. We've got a bit of a walk ahead of us, too."

He realized something, tearing his gaze from them to face her. "The ghosts—they're the spirits of the skeletons I'm seeing everywhere, aren't they?"

"Unfortunately. They're trapped here, bound to the land."

"Why's that?"

"The cauldron's magic is the beating heart of this isle, and as Matholwch's resurrected soldiers from long ago, they're tethered to it, body and soul. Being placed in it tainted them, chained them to it. Now they're unable to move on and reincarnate. Their bones can't even turn to dust."

". . . That's awful."

She nodded solemnly. "Yes, it is."

As they continued through the forest, Gus could make out more of the ghosts' clouded appearances. They looked to be men and women of all shapes and sizes, and their forms were monochromatic—their hair, faces, bodies, *everything* about them cast in ghoulish shades of white and gray. They wore the simple fabric garb of ancient Irish soldiers, and they all had weapons too: spears, swords, axes, bows. They whispered to each other in a language he didn't understand—Irish

Gaelic, perhaps?—and they whimpered and wailed as he and Saoirse passed, clawing the air as though to grab the two of them.

"Should we just . . . *not* stop and make camp tonight?" he said.

"That might be for the best," she replied.

And so they didn't.

# THIRTY-TWO

The Forest of Ghosts wasn't any more pleasant in the day than it was in the night. For one, it was now apparent that this place was void of color. It was as if the sun had been swallowed by clouds, drowning the landscape with gloom, the contorted trees so brittle and black they could have been charred. Not only that, but Gus kept seeing glimpses of skeletons and shadows in the sky, of shard-raised sylphs with bat wings chasing . . . something. The illusions Saoirse had mentioned, probably.

The lamenting ghosts and the skeletons lodged in the terrain were also more visible in daylight. Being surrounded so thoroughly by them (and by fog—far too much fog) made him feel as though he were on the wrong side of an ancient burial site, groping through soil to get from grave to grave. The eerie feeling only intensified as crows swooped down from what seemed to be out of nowhere. The birds landed in the trees, lining the branches with ebony, cawing at him and the others as they trekked by.

Despite all this, they eventually had to stop and rest, and they made camp next to a creek that appeared to run with blood, not water.

"Uhh." Gus pointed at the creek. "Is that . . . ?"

"It's regular water," Saoirse said. "Safe to drink and everything. It just looks like blood because of the way it reacts to the minerals in the land—or was it the magic in the land? I can't remember exactly how it works."

He chuckled. "Must be why they tacked 'blood' on the end of the name, huh?"

"Probably, yes," she replied, laughing a little.

With that, they all drank from the creek, and it was, in fact, regular water, or at least it tasted like it. Then they ate some of the food that they'd gathered from before. Afterward, Gus insisted that Saoirse sleep first because of her breathing and fatigue, but also because he wanted to work on his magic. So she curled up with Olwen, the two of them making themselves as comfortable as possible, and Remington climbed up into a tree that housed fewer skeletons than the others.

As they slept, Gus practiced. He started with glamour, tried to make his fingers disappear. There wasn't much improvement there, so he moved on to raising the dead. He didn't bother removing any of the skeletons around him from their dirt and bark, as he figured that, in the event of success, they'd be able to get up and move around by themselves via his magic.

When nothing worked, he gave up and sat next to Saoirse, who looked troubled. He brushed some hair from her face, the tips of his fingers stroking her cheek, and the lines between her brows softened.

His gaze went to her lips. Again, he found himself wondering what it would be like to kiss her.

It was stupid, wasn't it? For at least half the time he'd known her, either she'd been teaching him the truth about himself or they'd been fighting for their lives. The compound was under attack, and the realms were quite literally falling apart. Yet somehow, he'd mustered the emotional capacity to topple head over heels for her, this sylph covered in scars.

Saoirse woke hours later and Gus took his turn to rest. Then, after he woke in what had to be sometime in the late afternoon, they proceeded through woodland. They saw a great many more ghosts, heard a great many more moans, but at some point, he started to tune out the torment. It wasn't that the dead soldiers were no longer unsettling, but after encountering so many, he'd gotten rather used to them.

They spent one more night and day like this. Walking through the forest, drinking from bloodred waters, eating their stored food, watching for shard-raised in the sky. Gus continued to practice but had no luck, and here and there, he saw more gates in the mist and water.

By sunset of the second day, the trees and ghosts

grew sparse before finally clearing altogether, and the four of them came upon a great mouth of liquid red. Ashen hills and cliffs blooming with equally ashen vegetation surrounded the water, more haze and skeletons peppering the cragged landscape.

Saoirse twirled in excitement, not a trace of sorrow in her eyes. "We made it! It's Moth Lake!"

"Definitely your kind of place," Gus said. "Despite, well, you know."

"Yes, the location isn't ideal. It's the only enjoyable spot on the isle, really."

"Then I'm glad we get to pass through."

"Me, too. Come on!" She took his hand and started jogging toward a cliff on the right edge of the lake, Remington and Olwen close behind them.

As they ran, Gus looked around, trying to catch a glimpse of the moths populating the area, but saw none. "Why's it called 'Moth Lake'? There aren't any moths around."

"You'll see after nightfall," Saoirse replied.

They reached the base of the cliff, and he realized why she'd come this way. A cave opened on the side of the precipice. They slowed to a walk and stepped through its rounded entrance.

The sun had almost finished setting now, its glow unable to reach very far inside the cave, so Saoirse produced a sunlight-net to help them see. From what Gus could tell, it was about thirty feet wide and fifty feet deep, with only a few bones wedged in the floor and walls, and on the far wall, there were more openings where the cave branched off into other chambers.

Olwen floated over to a corner. She made herself solid, curled up nose to tail, and fell asleep almost instantly. At the same time, Remington scurried out of the cave, back toward the lake. "Where's he going?" Saoirse asked.

"Who knows with him," Gus said. "But he'll be back. Do you think it's safe enough in here to have a fire tonight?"

"I don't see why not."

Together, they built their fire. Olwen joined them for dinner (and some attention) before returning to her corner. Then they watched mist drift across the lake as they lounged by the flames, soaking in the warmth and the smell of smoke.

Gus raised a brow at Saoirse as she sat beside him. "You know," he said, "the sun's been down a while now, and nothing's happening out there."

"Patience, Gus Brandon." She nudged his shoulder with her own, but rather than pulling away afterward, she leaned on him.

They stayed that way for a bit longer, until the vegetation at the edges of the lake rustled with movement. "There they are." Saoirse climbed to her feet. "Let's go say hello."

"You're not worried about the bat-wing shard-raised?"

"So long as we don't stay out *too* long or draw attention to ourselves, no. Now let's go, before we miss them!"

He stood up and followed her out of the cave, down the bank to the water. Even in the dark, he was beginning to see them, the moths this lake was named for. They fluttered from their hiding spots, hundreds of them, out from shrubs and grass and bones, and soared toward the moon above.

Saoirse waved at them. "Hello! It's nice to meet you! Safe travels!"

At the sound of her voice, dozens of the insects started to glow. They varied in size, in color, their wings embellished with a diverse array of markings. Some of them swooped down to whirl through the air around her, and she giggled, spinning in sync with them. As Gus watched her, warmth spread through him.

A flash of green in his peripheral. He glanced that way, nearly gasped. He recognized it from the pictures in Saoirse's book. "Oh my— Saoirse, look!"

It flittered down, in front of her, and she stopped to stare at it, awe in her expression.

She'd seen her luna moth.

# THIRTY-THREE

The paintings didn't do this creature justice. They'd failed to portray the delicate way it carried itself, the way moonlight filtered through its gossamer wings, highlighting every pattern, every vein.

Gus hadn't even heard of luna moths until a few days ago, yet he couldn't keep his eyes off it. Saoirse must have been overjoyed.

"It's . . . it's . . ." She lifted her finger, and the large insect perched itself there. But to Gus's surprise, her smile faded. "I can't believe this is happening."

"It's gorgeous," he whispered, not wanting to spook it. "Look at its wings, its colors. Aren't you happy?"

Her eyes grew wet, glassy, and a tear rolled down her cheek. "I think so? At the very least, I'll know I'll have gotten to see one before I die."

If the spell hadn't been broken before, it was now. "Are you . . . expecting that to happen soon? Some of the things you've said . . . Are you okay? Are you sick?"

She shrugged. "I wish that's all it was. For so long now, I've been forced to deal with this—this *hurt*. It never really goes away." She paused, nuzzled the moth with her nose. It seemed to nuzzle her back. "I just . . . think about it. A lot."

"You think about death a lot? About dying?"

"I do."

"Because you think it'll be a relief," he said, feeling as though he finally understood.

She lifted her hand, and the moth flew off, into the sky. "I don't *think* it will be a relief. I *know* it will be a relief."

Something deep in his chest tightened. "But then you'd be gone."

"The concept of reincarnation was mentioned in your books, wasn't it?"

"Yeah, it was."

"Well, that's all it would be. If I died, I'd be reborn. I'd live on, and I wouldn't hurt like this anymore."

"Saoirse . . ." He took her hand. "You can't really mean that. You *don't* really mean that. Right?"

She wouldn't look at him. "Does it matter?"

"Of course it does."

She seemed to consider his words before speaking again. At long last, she said, "I do mean it. There are things you don't know about me, Gus. Horrible things."

Without thinking, he let the words tumble from his mouth. "Like how you got your scars?" She met his eyes then, stared hard at him. "That's what those visions were of, right? When you were channeling your magic into me, the visions—they were memories. Memories of how you got your scars."

"Why exactly did you come to that conclusion?"

"Because of the way you reacted after I mentioned them."

"You weren't supposed to see them." She looked away.

"I thought not. I'm sorry."

"For what?"

"That any of it happened. That I saw what was done to you. That you went through it in the first place."

She tugged her hand out of his and stepped closer to the lake. "Can't say it's all right. That'd be a lie. I'm in pain, all the time, and it reminds me of that day, of everything that was taken from me."

He realized he was gritting his teeth, clenching his fists. He marched after her. "Where is it now, the vine-monster thing? Has it been killed? *Can* it be killed?"

"I think maybe it can. But trust me, you wouldn't want to do that."

"Yes, I would," he insisted. "That way I'd know it'd never hurt you again."

"But it *would* hurt me. Every day it would hurt me. Because even if you managed to destroy it, I'd still be in pain. So long as I'm alive, I'll be in pain."

"Then we'll find something for your pain." He

grabbed both her hands now, brushed his thumbs over the scars around her wrists, her knuckles, and she shivered. "There's got to be something, somewhere, that can ease it. A type of medicine, maybe. We'll find it."

She looked up at him. They were close enough that if he dipped his head, their lips might meet. "Why," she started, "would you say something like that?"

"Because I want you here, with me." He jerked his head at the moths above. "Around what makes you most happy."

She laughed then, but it wasn't a joyous, girlish giggle, as it usually was when she found something he said amusing. No, this laugh was strained, tight around the edges. It gave way to tears, and before Gus could stop himself, he was wrapping her in his arms and crushing her to his chest, and she was tilting her head toward him and pressing her lips against his, and he was kissing her back, fiercely, desperately, and she tasted of apples, smelled of smoke, felt like home, like hope for a better future, like everything good left in the world, everything worth fighting for.

*Stop this*, Saoirse thought. *Before it's too late. Before it hurts both of us more than it already has to.*

But she couldn't stop. She couldn't stop kissing

Gus. She couldn't stop biting his neck or tugging his hair or leading him back toward the cave where they'd made camp.

It was too late for her, wasn't it? And it had been for a while, since the moment he'd offered her that first lopsided smile. There was no way to drag herself out now, no way back up. She could only keep falling.

Breathless, they stumbled into the cave, dropped next to the fire in a tangle of limbs, him on top of her. Their eyes locked, and he brushed some hair behind her ear and whispered, "Is this okay?" He was so earnest about asking that it made her heart clench.

"It is," she replied. "I actually didn't think you'd stop. I hoped you wouldn't, anyway."

At this admission, he kissed her again, and then their clothes were off and their bodies were one, and for a while at least, Saoirse didn't dwell on how much she hurt or what she was, what she'd been forced to become.

A monster, a murderer.

The Skeleton Faerie.

# THIRTY-FOUR

Not so long ago, there was a faerie king and a faerie queen, and they ruled over Annwn. They also ruled over its inhabitants: the Tylwth Teg Family.

When the faerie queen gave birth to the pair's first and only child, they were overjoyed. So was the rest of the Family, for the baby had been marked with a most important destiny.

But there was no time to celebrate. Word of a newborn spread quickly, and Annwn's enemies planned to take it for themselves.

To protect the infant prince, the faerie king and faerie queen had him switched out with a baby in the Mortalworld. From that day on, the human girl was known as their first and only child, the faerie princess of Annwn.

Until she was stolen away.

SIX YEARS AGO

Fiadh was teaching, and Saoirse should have been paying attention.

But she couldn't.

History had never interested her, especially when it had to do with the politics of the Families.

"...and that concluded the thousand-year war between our Family and the Seelie Court," Fiadh droned on. While the older Child paced in front of the worktable in the castle library, Saoirse sat at it, doodling a cecropia moth in her notebook. She thought she'd spotted one in the woods beside the training grounds the other day. It had flown through a mushroom-ring gate, greeted her, and promptly returned to where it came from.

Had insects been the subject of all her studies, she would have never been bored.

"Saoirse," Fiadh snapped, "did you hear anything I just said?"

Slamming her notebook shut, Saoirse whipped back into focus. "Yes, sorry. You were talking about the end of a thousand-year war."

"Between?"

"Uhh . . ."

Fiadh sighed, shaking her head. She'd donned a dress that matched her midnight-blue irises, styled her brown hair in a braid down her back. "Darling, please. There's a reason for everything I teach you. You're meant to—"

"—'lead the Family to a glorious destiny,'" Saoirse interjected. "I know, I know."

"Why aren't you taking this more seriously, then?"

She glared down at the table. "How am I supposed to take it seriously when I'm not even sure what it is I'm going to be doing?"

It was a fair question. For as long as she could remember, she'd lived with the Children of the Death Gods—a subset of the Aes Sídhe Family that consisted of faeries who possessed their death-god ancestors' unique abilities—but they'd never told her which deity she was related to, or what kinds of powers she'd have. She didn't even know who her parents were, had always been cared for by Fiadh and Niall.

It was especially frustrating because the other Children her age (who had only been here for a few months!) knew the goddess they were descended from and what their abilities were. The three of them were related to the Phantom Queen: Margaret could transform anything, could turn rocks into crows if she so pleased. Moira sent warriors into frenzies, helping them win even the most challenging of battles. And as for Malachi? He was capable of stopping a heart with a single touch.

Then there was Saoirse. She had decent enough strength, and she utilized glamour and cast spells as well as anyone else. But she had no idea why she was *here*. She didn't belong. Never had, never would.

"Perhaps it's time Niall and I had our talk with you," Fiadh said. "Tell you about where you came from."

That night, Saoirse's caretakers finally told her the truth. She'd thought for years that she'd been born into the Aes Sídhe Family, but as it turned out, she'd actually been born into the Tylwth Teg Family. The death god she was descended from was the Lord of Corpses, her parents had been the late king and queen of Annwn, and she'd been stolen by the Children of the Death Gods because the Aes Sídhe needed what she supposedly had—the power to raise the dead. That, apparently, gave her the ability to properly control the old, fragmented magic of the Cauldron of Rebirth.

"You must understand, Saoirse," Niall said, adjusting his small round spectacles as the three of them sat in Saoirse's bedchamber, "the Tylwth Teg were planning to use your power to kill us. In a way, they forced our hand. We had no choice. We *had* to take you."

Saoirse felt numb. This was too much to process at once. "But then . . . I mean, what am I meant to do for the Family? To lead them to glory? You don't expect me to—to kill the Tylwth Teg, or any of the other Families, do you?" The Families were always fighting each other, squabbling about one thing or another. She'd often hoped for it to stop, but certainly not by genocide.

"Oh no, of course not," Fiadh insisted. "That would be unimaginably cruel. You'll only be ensuring that the Aes Sídhe has authority over the other Families." Whatever relief Saoirse had felt a moment ago dissipated. Was that really much better? "But before then," Fiadh continued, "you'll have to fulfill the prophecy."

"Prophecy? What prophecy?"

Niall smiled more mischievously than a leprechaun, his thick black mustache curling up with his lips. "Why, the one foretold upon your birth, my dear. The one that says you'll eradicate humanity before they destroy what's left of the realms. Because what's the good in governing the Otherworld if we're all dead?"

### THREE YEARS AGO

Saoirse hadn't wanted to go to the Isle of Bone and Blood. She'd wanted to be done with all this "raising the dead" and "eradicating the humans" nonsense.

But her caretakers had dragged her here anyway, along with the other Children her age, to try and bring her unique ability to fruition. Niall said the cauldron shards were located somewhere on the isle, and the idea was that if she absorbed them now—even though it was early, even though her antlers hadn't come in yet—it would stimulate and, ultimately, manifest her power.

Since they had no way of flying, they'd sailed; only the faeries with sky-god lineage had wings, and none were a part of the Children of the Death Gods. They'd landed on the southern tip of the isle and traveled through what the map called the "Forest of Ghosts" and "Moth Lake," but they hadn't found the shards in either place.

Now they were farther north, searching the marshland. Like the rest of the isle, a fetid stench plagued this place, reminding Saoirse of departed warriors left unburied on a battlefield.

"I'm sure we'll be on our way back any day now," Malachi said, trying to reassure her as they trudged through gray mud. Mist and bone riddled the landscape, and scarlet pooled in its valleys, the red shade in dramatic opposition to its colorless peaks. "If Niall thinks the shards will help your power manifest," he went on, "don't you want to find them?"

"Not really, no." She hugged her sides. Though the clouds blocked the sun, it wasn't cold. Still, she kept shivering. "I . . . I have a bad feeling."

"Aw, little moth. Is it because of the skeletons staring at us?" He chuckled and put an arm around her shoulders, giving her a modicum of solace. "You have to stop letting these things affect you so much. Perhaps, when your abilities manifest, you'll feel better about it all?"

"Perhaps," she said.

But later on, when they reached the "Mound of Skulls," when they found the cauldron shards inside, she discovered that it would not make her feel better.

It would make her feel much, much worse.

ONE YEAR AGO

The Children of the Death Gods had made a grave error.

Saoirse wasn't related to the Tylwth Teg—she wasn't even related to the faeries.

She was a human-born changeling, switched out with the Lord of Corpses' real descendant to protect them from enemy Families.

Her true lineage should have been obvious to Niall and Fiadh when her antlers never appeared, when the Mound of Skulls spit her out in pieces, when she only fused with two of the four cauldron shards. But it wasn't until she began channeling the cauldron's magic, until she realized she couldn't resurrect or control corpses, that they pieced it together.

They didn't know what to do at first, so they held a meeting with the rest of the Children of the Death Gods, hoping for guidance. Many faeries suggested returning her to the Isle of Bone and Blood, then searching for the Child the Family really wanted. But others pointed out that she had a bit of the cauldron's magic, that she could control the skeletons. Sure, doing so hurt the new scars covering her body, fatigued her beyond comprehension, but she could still be of use— that is, until her changeling counterpart was tracked down. Once they were found, they'd be forced to kill her and absorb her power.

Just as it seemed Saoirse's fate was sealed, her caretakers had an idea. They concocted a plan that, if successful, would keep her alive *and* give the Family what it needed.

That plan had led her here, to the dense forests of Annwn.

Hunting creatures she didn't want to kill.

"I don't think I can do this," she whispered to Malachi, who crouched next to her in a cluster of wildflower bushes. The scent of the blossoms turned her stomach, the glare of the sun making her head pound. Or was it her apprehension doing all that?

"You don't have a choice," he replied, his stare locked on the pool ahead. "It's you or them. If we can't prove that this will work on you, you're dead." She wondered, briefly, if death would be better. "Besides," he continued, "all four of us need their powers if we're going to survive the search in the Mortalworld."

Hours went by before the sylphs arrived. They undressed, giggling about swimming in the pool and splashing in the waterfall. There were four of them, just as Malachi said there would be. He'd been watching them for a while now.

As per the plan, Saoirse and the others leapt out of hiding; Margaret and Moira had been standing behind the trees across from Saoirse and Malachi. Then the four of them threw their sunlight-nets, trapping the sylphs at the water's edge.

The sylphs cried out as they realized that the golden netting sliced through their winds and kept them bound to the forest floor. They tore at their confines, but it was no use. They were helpless.

Malachi stalked toward them, iron dagger in hand, and one of them screamed. It was a frightful sound, making the hair on Saoirse's neck stand straight. She looked into the sylph's eyes, big and blue and full of terror, and that's when she realized for certain—she couldn't do this. She *wouldn't* do this. It wasn't her, never had been her.

She'd rather die than carry out such a monstrous act.

"Stop!" she yelled, stumbling after Malachi. "This isn't right! They're innocent in all this!"

But he didn't listen to her. "Hold her back," he said, and suddenly the others were grabbing her, dragging her away from him.

"No!" She kicked and thrashed, but they held tight. "NO!"

Malachi killed the sylph who had screamed, the sylph with the big blue eyes full of terror, far too easily. He hacked off her wings without flinching, drank a cup of her blood without gagging. All the while, Saoirse begged him to stop, tears blurring her vision, snot dribbling from her nostrils.

She knew then that she'd never known him, not really. He was callous. She could never love someone so callous.

He restrained her while Margaret and Moira killed their own sylphs. At least *they* seemed to have a guilty conscience. They trembled as the sylphs begged for mercy, but still, they followed through.

Last came Saoirse. "It has to be done by your hand, Saoirse," Moira said, giving her the dagger. Despite the leather wrapped around its hilt, the iron burned her skin. "Otherwise, it won't work."

She stood as tall as she could manage and hurled the weapon aside. "I was b-born human, so there's *still* a ch-chance it w-won't w-work. Just let her g-go. It's not w-worth it. I'm n-not d-doing it!"

"Yes, you are," Malachi hissed, and then he forced her to.

And when it was done, when all four sylphs were murdered and their wings were severed and their blood was drunk, when Saoirse and Malachi and Moira and Margaret grew wings of their own and had wind-powers and could fly, Saoirse found that, for the first time in her life, she wished that she weren't breathing, that her heart weren't beating.

For the first time in her life, she wished she were dead.

It would not be the last.

# THIRTY-FIVE

Remington's chatter yanked Gus into consciousness. Groggily, he blinked, processing where he was, how he'd gotten here.

He lay on his back, naked in the cave by Moth Lake, muted light leaking in through the entrance. Saoirse slept in his arms, her head on his chest. Her bare skin felt warm and a bit sticky pressed against his. Remington stood on their left, mushrooms piled around him (he must have gone foraging), and Olwen stretched and yawned on their right.

Saoirse came to, and as she looked around the cave—at Olwen, at Remington—she seemed to remember she was nude. Flushing, she shot out of Gus's arms, grabbed her dress, and pulled it over her head.

A twinge of disappointment as the green fabric concealed her. Last night, he'd discovered that those pink stitch scars wrapped around her entire body, but honestly, they didn't detract from her beauty. Their jagged edges cut through her softness, producing the kind of antithesis found only in great works of art.

"Don't cover up on my account," he teased, reaching for his own clothes. "I was enjoying the view."

She smiled a bit but wouldn't make eye contact. "It'll only take about two more days to reach the Mound of Skulls. We should probably leave soon."

*Shit.* Had he messed up? Had he misread her, misread the situation? He wasn't sure how he could have, considering *everything*, but . . .

Wait, was she concerned about pregnancy? If it weren't for his regular birth control shots, he would have been too. Should he try to put her mind at ease?

"You know, you don't need to worry about getting pregnant," he said, and she turned toward him sharply. "In the compound, they give us shots that prevent it until we're married. They estimate the ones for men are over ninety-nine percent effective, and they work even better if you pull out, which . . . I did."

She furrowed her brow. "I wasn't concerned about that."

"Oh. Uhh, did I—did I do something wrong, then?"

"Not at all." She softened her gaze, as if to reassure him, and it worked. Relief surged through him. "I just wish it didn't have to end so soon. Being here, with you."

He nodded, began dressing. "I wish that too. Maybe, when this is all over, we can spend more time together? Preferably in fewer life-or-death situations."

"Yes." Her tone was flat, distant. "Maybe."

He finished putting on his clothes and knelt next to her. "Are you sure everything's okay?"

"It will be," she said, then kissed him so deeply and for so long that he forgot to ask more questions, forgot to wonder what "it will be" meant.

Saoirse wanted to share her plans with Gus. She wanted to tell him that she was the Skeleton Faerie, that she was his changeling counterpart, that she wasn't a true sylph.

She wanted to tell him *everything*.

And what was stopping her, really? Malachi, Margaret, and Moira weren't around to overhear her, or to keep her from betraying them. Remington was Gus's guide, so he certainly wouldn't object to what Saoirse wanted. And Olwen . . .

Well, Olwen wouldn't like it, but when the time came, Saoirse could conjure shard-raised for the Hound of Annwn to fight. Perhaps that would distract her long enough for Gus to finish this without interference.

So why, then? Why keep the rest of the story from him any longer? *Cowardice*, she thought. *You're a coward, Saoirse. Afraid that for the last days you have him, he won't look at you the same.*

*But you're only prolonging the inevitable.*

It didn't take long for them to travel around the remainder of Moth Lake, walk through a patch of woodland, and head into the marshes. "Without trees, we'll have to watch more closely for shard-raised," she said. She ended up doing most of the watching, but she didn't mind. Gus needed to practice his magic.

When the sun went down, they stopped for the night. It was cold and wet and uncomfortable, but they didn't dare make a fire. Instead, they cuddled for warmth, Saoirse's head nestled beneath Gus's chin. Olwen lay beside Saoirse, and Remington beside Gus, but every so often, the squirrel gave Saoirse a knowing glance, as if passing judgment. *Don't look at me like that. Do you think I meant for this to happen?*

The next day came far too quickly, and Gus rose in high spirits, ready to reach the Mound of Skulls. Saoirse should have been ready too—after all, wasn't this what she wanted? She'd been planning for this, plotting against the Family, against her fellow—

Splashing behind them, and Saoirse's heart sank. *We just passed another gate . . .* She swung around, and a wave of distress threatened to knock her off her feet. *No, they can't be here!*

Except they were, all three of them.

Malachi.

Margaret.

Moira.

They emerged from a sparkling pool a short distance away, clawing through the mud toward Saoirse and Gus.

Gus knew that Malachi and the others must have been searching for him and Saoirse this whole time. He *knew* that. But after a few days away from the three of them—after a few days alone with Saoirse—he'd started to forget about them.

Well, maybe "forget" wasn't the right word for it. It wasn't that he'd forgotten about their existence, per se. He'd just been so absorbed with Saoirse's company that he hadn't been thinking about them.

But now they stood before him, drenched with scarlet water and marsh sludge, and an uneasy feeling settled in the pit of his stomach. And, looking over at Saoirse, he knew his feelings were justified. Her eyes were wide with fear, her lips parted in shock. Remington must not have wanted the other sylphs around either, because the squirrel clacked his teeth at them as he sat on Gus's shoulder.

"Don't look so happy to see us," Moira said with dry sarcasm, wiping the muck from her face.

Margaret threw back her braids and stuck her

tongue out at them. "We've been looking everywhere for you!"

"I was so worried." Malachi hastened toward Saoirse. Muscles tensing, Gus stepped forward and rested a hand on her shoulder, but he wasn't the only one feeling protective. Olwen snarled and solidified, planting herself between Saoirse and Malachi.

Malachi paused, glared at Olwen. "You have a mutt now."

"We call her Olwen," Gus began, "and she's no mutt. She helped us escape a horde of shard-raised and saved us from a two-headed mountain lion."

Malachi turned his scowl on Gus, but Gus held his stare. "Saoirse, aren't you glad we're here?" His voice was dangerously low, almost threatening. He placed a hand on the sheathed dagger at his belt.

"She's just shocked," Gus said. "So am I."

Saoirse moved closer to Gus. "A-apologies. We just—we weren't expecting you to find us so soon." Right after she finished her sentence, she clamped her mouth shut. Had that been the wrong thing to say?

Apparently, it had been. "Were you even trying to find us?" Margaret cried. "How long have you been on the isle already?" She tramped forward through the mud, then halted. It appeared she'd noticed Remington. She pointed at the squirrel. "What is *that* doing here?"

Remington hissed, which Gus had never heard him do. "This is my guide, Remington," Gus said, petting him to try and calm him down. "After we got separated from you guys, we were taken by cannibals living in an old prison. Rem brought us food and the keys so we could escape more easily. That's why we weren't looking for you. We were busy trying to, you know, not get eaten."

Moira crossed her arms. "Well, you obviously escaped and found your way here. It's been almost a week, Saoirse. At no point did we see a signal anywhere."

This was infuriating. They were being ridiculous. Before Saoirse could respond, Gus snapped, "What was she supposed to do? Put a target on our backs? We'd already been captured once, and they threatened her, they . . ." He paused, took a deep breath. "We could've died. We almost did."

"Is this true?" Malachi asked. "Or is he lying to us?"

"It's true," Saoirse managed to get out. "I don't—I don't think he could lie anymore, even if he wanted to."

Moira cocked her head. "Probably not, now that his antlers are coming in. They suit you, 'Gus Brandon.' Help balance your appearance, what with those long limbs of yours."

"They really do make him extra pretty, don't they?" Margaret's anger had dissipated, replaced by her usual bubbliness. She laughed—an airy, tinkling sound. "And look, his ears are pointy now, too!"

Nostrils flaring, Malachi rolled his eyes. "Saoirse, you've been on the isle for a while now. Do you have any idea how much longer it will take to reach the Mound of Skulls from here?"

"I'd guess by—by the end of today," she said.

"Then let's go." He shoved past Gus, stomped in the direction Gus and Saoirse had been traveling in before. Moira and Margaret followed him, and Saoirse started to as well, much to Gus's surprise.

He grabbed her hand to stop her, leaned down to whisper in her ear. "They're clearly up to something. We've gotten this far without them. Why don't we just leave?"

A guilty expression crept across her face. She shrank in on herself. "No. They'll think we're working against them."

"Maybe we should be."

"We can't do that, Gus."

"Why not? I don't trust them."

"I can't tell you why." She squeezed his hand. "Not yet. It would put your life at risk. You just . . . Don't trust them all you want. I don't blame you. But you have to trust *me*, okay? For a little while longer."

Up ahead, Malachi, Moira, and Margaret had stopped, watching them disapprovingly. *She really is their prisoner,* Gus thought. *She thinks she's not, but she is. We both are.*

*What're they planning to do to us? What's* she *planning to do to them, to fight back? Something, obviously.*

*Something that could get me killed if I knew about it.*

"All right." He had to force out the words, his instincts screaming at him to flee from the others. "For a little while longer."

# THIRTY-SIX

The last thing Gus wanted to do was enter the Mound of Skulls.

One of his books that documented bits of Irish history talked about the country's ancient burial mounds. More specifically, it talked about Newgrange. According to the text, Newgrange was old, older than Stonehenge, older than the Pyramids of Giza. Human remains had been found inside, both cremated and non-cremated, and the mound was said to have once been home of the Dagda—the Good God—but was stolen by his son Aengus.

The book had pictures of Newgrange too, with notes about how it had been built. But to Gus, it didn't look as if humans had constructed the massive building; it looked as if it had risen from the soil, summoned from the land by a divine force. Circular in structure, it was made of earth and rock, with grass sprouting from the top.

This place reminded him of those pictures . . . had they been macabre.

Like Newgrange, the Mound of Skulls appeared to have been crafted with soil and stone, but instead of grass on the top, dead vines wrapped around the whole building, skulls threaded through them like beads on a necklace. More forest laced with skeletons surrounded it, and more ghosts floated across the mist between trees, murmuring in that language Gus couldn't understand.

The sun had set while they'd been walking across the marshes, the moon visible between clouds. To better see where they were going, Malachi, Margaret, and Moira had conjured sunlight-nets for themselves, but Saoirse had produced one for both herself and Gus. The two of them trailed behind the others, had barely said a word in hours. Neither Remington nor Olwen left them for even a second.

As they drew closer to the mound, Gus heard scratching noises. Pushing up his glasses, he peered at the structure, and that's when he saw it.

The vines covering the mound seemed to squirm of their own accord, scraping against its exterior.

"You're sure this is where we'll find the shards?" he asked, forcing a chuckle. His breaths came out in little clouds, making his glasses misty.

Malachi sneered. "What is it, changeling? Don't like

it here?"

"No, I don't. Do you?"

"Not particularly. I just thought you might be able to . . . *appreciate* it for what it is, considering your lineage. Saoirse told you all about that, didn't she?"

"She did."

They neared the pitch-black arched entrance, so small only one of them could pass through it at a time. Fog leaked out of it in droves, the smell of the isle growing stronger than ever. Did the stinking haze originate from this place?

Saoirse grabbed Gus's hand and, shoving past everybody else, yanked him to the entrance. "You go first," she said. "Lead the way."

He glanced back at the others. As Olwen floated through their legs to reach his side, they smiled at him in a way that made his skin crawl.

Margaret gestured at the entrance. "What are you waiting for?"

He gulped, his instincts once again urging him to run. But how would he do that, realistically? These three would easily overpower him.

*Saoirse told you to trust her.*

*Just follow along.*

With Remington on his shoulder, Olwen at his heels, and a light source in his grasp, Gus crept into the dark.

It was even colder in here than outside, and almost immediately, he felt as if he'd been dropped in a labyrinth. Rather than a relatively open, easy-tonavigate layout, the inside consisted of a narrow dirt-and-rock tunnel—a cramped path that twisted and turned incoherently, except it was built at a gradual upward slant, giving the effect that, slowly but surely, it led to the crest of the mound. *That must be where the shards are.* Wedged between the stones and jutting from the packed earth were more skulls, all of which looked human. Vines slithered out of their hollow eye sockets, their open jaws, hissing across the walls and ceilings.

A prickling on his neck, as if he was being watched, and he looked back. Saoirse was behind him, but Malachi was behind her, and sure enough, Malachi glowered at him.

He narrowed his eyes at the sylph before returning his attention to the path. If only those three had never made it to the isle.

The farther he went, the more it seemed the walkway was shrinking, closing in on him. He crouched slightly, the tips of his antlers tearing the vines and scratching the walls. Was it just him, or had the fog worsened as well? He could barely see the glow of Olwen's eyes now, and the stench had reached a peak. It coiled around him, dank and suffocating. Everyone gagged.

They went on that way for what felt like hours, until finally, the tunnel led them into an open cavern. It was disk shaped and infested with vines. It was also fashioned with stone and earth and bone, but it had to have a circumference of at least a couple hundred feet, so it was large enough that the five of them could stand comfortably and move around in it.

White light pulsed from the center of the ceiling. It flared through the gaps between skulls and vegetation, lanced through the haze twining across the ground, there and gone in the blink of an eye. The cavern quivered, humming beneath their feet.

Olwen whined and hid behind Saoirse, and Remington leapt off Gus's shoulder and disappeared into the mist.

At that moment, he knew for certain.

*The shards . . .*

*Let's get this over with.*

He looked back at Saoirse, handed her his sunlight-net. She gave him a nod of encouragement.

Another pulse of light that vanished as quickly as it came.

He walked toward it.

The white glow kept pulsing, on and off like a giant light bulb, and as he stepped beneath it, as he peered up at it, he realized that it came from two jagged pieces of silvery hammered metal. The shards were embedded in the ceiling and had to be at least four feet tall and wide, the earth around them throbbing in sync with their flashes. It was as if they were the heart of the mound, as if they were pumping blood to the rest of the structure.

Except how could they be moving the ceiling like that? Wasn't the building rock solid? It sure as hell felt like it. Maybe the phenomenon was just another aspect of the cauldron's magic?

Again came the flare, but this time it didn't go away, so bright he had to cover his eyes. The tremors in the ground became stronger, the humming louder. It nearly knocked him off-balance.

A sound like a whip cracking, and a dry bristly vine snapped over one of his wrists, then the other. Then more were wrapping around his arms and legs, enveloping the rest of his body, yanking him toward the shards, the stones and bones parting and the soil opening as if inviting him to join them.

And so up he went.

Soon the light dimmed enough that he could look around without his eyes watering. That was when it dawned on him—he recognized his surroundings.

He'd been here before.

Everywhere he turned there were vines. Writhing like a den of snakes, they laced through skulls, made the bones sway around him as if in morbid celebration.

It was Saoirse's memory, how she'd gotten her scars.

*But that means she's . . .*

Cold realization set in, spearing through his chest, his gut, his mind racing with memories of Saoirse. Saoirse dancing, Saoirse talking, Saoirse giggling.

Saoirse, Saoirse, Saoirse.

The thoughts came to a jarring halt as vines lurched down his throat. They dug deep, into his organs, his insides, and tore him apart.

# THIRTY-SEVEN

White light
Flesh squelching
Sharp pain
Nothing.


White light
Leaves rustling
Sharp pain
Nothing.


White light
Vines scraping
Sharp pain

Nothing.


White light
Bones crunching
Sharp pain
Sharp pain
*Sharp pain*
*Oh fuck*
*THE PAIN*
*WON'T STOP—*


The next time Gus was conscious and aware enough to process his surroundings, he was falling from the ceiling of the disk-shaped cavern in the Mound of Skulls. It was no longer glowing, no longer had the silvery metal shards embedded in it. *Because they're inside of me*, he realized, and hit the ground sideways, left antler banging against rock and making his head spin, glasses flying off his face and vanishing into the fog.

He tried to crawl over and retrieve his glasses, but he didn't have the strength. His bones ached, his muscles ached, his skin ached. He felt as if he'd been ripped apart and put back together.

Then he remembered that's exactly what had happened.

A pretty face covered in stitch scars appeared in front of him, and his heart clenched. After quickly examining him, Saoirse located his glasses and returned them to their rightful place. Her lips moved—she was saying something—but he couldn't hear her. He wondered why and realized his ears were ringing.

How had she managed to fake what had happened between them? How had she so convincingly pretended to care about him? Faeries couldn't lie. *But that doesn't mean they aren't deceitful.*

*I should've never trusted her.*

The ringing in his ears reached a crescendo, then stopped altogether. He caught the tail end of her words. "—really worked! There's not a scratch on you!"

He raised a trembling hand, gestured at her. "When were you planning to tell me that you're not just a sylph?" It was hard to speak, felt as though nails had been driven into his esophagus. "That you're the Skeleton Faerie?"

She looked stricken. He knew it wasn't real, but it made his heartache worse. How long had it taken her to perfect the act? "It's not what you think, I swear. I can explain every—"

She yelped and dropped her sunlight-net as Margaret and Moira landed beside her, seized her by the arms, and dragged her away from Gus. A flash of gold above him, mesh opening and trapping him where he lay. Despite his weak, shaking hands, he tried to pull the netting apart, even focused on his strength to do it, but it was no use.

"Don't touch him!" Saoirse cried, struggling against her captors, and for a moment he had hope.

Hope that maybe she hadn't only been pretending to care.

He suppressed the feeling as quickly as it came. She was the Skeleton Faerie. They were supposed to be enemies.

Right?

"I'm sorry, little moth," Malachi said, stepping into Gus's line of sight. "Hopefully, this is the last time we have to do this, but it's for your own good." He pulled the dagger from the sheath at his belt. It looked to be made of iron. "Bring her here. We need to work qui—"

Black fur vaulting up Malachi's body.

The dagger falling.

Remington hissing.

The squirrel swiped furiously at Malachi's face with his claws, and then, before Malachi could retaliate, jumped all the way from Malachi to Gus and began gnawing on the sunlight-net Gus was trapped in.

Howling in shock and fury, Malachi stumbled backward. His right eye hung from the socket, the stringy muscle it dangled by swinging in tandem with his movements. He fumbled with the organ, tried to put it back. It slipped through his fingers again and again.

At the same time, Olwen snarled, appearing behind Moira and Margaret in her much larger, much more fearsome form. They didn't even have the chance to turn around before the Hound of Annwn mangled their wings with her teeth.

As they wailed, Saoirse escaped their grasp. She was back at Gus's side in an instant, Malachi's knife in hand. *What's going on? What the hell is she planning?* Olwen lunged toward Gus too, stopping only to rake her claws through Malachi's wings, and once she reached Gus, she joined Remington in trying to free him.

With Olwen's help, the mesh was shredded in seconds. "Appreciate it, you two," he rasped, and tried to stand. But the effort made his head spin, and his legs gave way beneath him. Olwen hunched in front of him protectively, Remington standing at attention beside her.

Whistling beneath them, and Gus looked down. The fog was moving, crawling outward, toward the edges of the cavern, and Saoirse was waving her hands—she must be the one directing it.

The mist curled up the walls, the ceiling, and as it reached the skulls lodged there, they seemed to awaken, twitching, opening their jaws, sucking in haze through their nasal bones as if it were a delectable fragrance.

Then the tremors started.

Bony hands erupted from the packed earth around the skulls. They shoved aside rocks, ripped apart vines. The force of it all intensified the quakes. Dirt showered everyone like rain, and moonlight poured into the cavern through fissures in the ceiling, fissures that hadn't been there a moment ago.

Quivering with hurt, her wings in tatters, Margaret shrieked, "Saoirse, what are you doing? This wasn't part of the plan!"

"Maybe it wasn't part of *your* plan, but it was always part of mine." Saoirse held her head high, her shoulders back. "Now stand down and unbind the pooka from his animal form, or you die here and now."

The pooka? What pooka?

In Irish, Cornish, Welsh, and even some other mythologies, pookas were shape-shifting trickster faeries. When they weren't in their humanoid form, they were said to appear as horses with either white or black fur, but some stories described them as other animals, such as goats or rabbits.

Wait a second . . .

He glanced at Remington.

He'd never heard of a pooka appearing as a squirrel, but . . .

"Come on, little moth," Malachi said with a strained laugh. He'd gotten his eye back in the socket—or had it healed on its own?—but his wings weren't healing so quickly. Gus didn't feel the least bit sorry for him, for any of them. "Drop the act. We all know you don't have it in you. You can't even bring yourself to murder strangers, let alone the ones you love."

What did he mean, she couldn't bring herself to murder strangers? She was the Skeleton Faerie! From the beginning, they'd made her out to be a monster.

Then again, the Saoirse he'd come to know was far from a monster. She'd also said that she could explain, that it wasn't what he thought . . .

Could there be more to this than meets the eye?

"I don't love you," Saoirse spat. "And I never did. Not the real you."

Just as she finished the sentiment, the shard-raised skeletons in the walls and ceiling finished exhuming themselves and toppled to the floor, more chunks of earth falling with them. Half a dozen climbed to their "feet" and stalked toward Malachi, Margaret, and Moira, all of whom were still too injured to fly.

Desperately, the three sylphs conjured gales, blasted the shard-raised with them. But the attacks only slowed the skeletons' gaits.

It had never been Saoirse's winds that had defeated them; she'd only made it look that way. It had been the cauldron's magic all along.

The other ten shard-raised began marching toward Gus, Saoirse, Remington, and Olwen, but Saoirse took them down before they could get close. "Unbind the pooka, or I promise I'll let them kill you!"

"Don't do it, Margaret!" Malachi sent more gusts toward the shard-raised closing in on them. "She's bluffing! She'd never—"

A skeleton snatched him from the side and sank its teeth into his throat. Red spurting from him, he screamed, the sound fading into gurgles as the monster dragged him to the ground.

"Margaret, *now*!" Saoirse demanded.

Malachi stopped struggling, went still as the skeleton feasted. Margaret and Moira glanced between him and Saoirse with wide eyes, then turned to each other. Moira nodded, her expression pleading with

Margaret to oblige.

Margaret raised a hand.

Silent, stunned, Gus watched as the black squirrel he called Remington grew taller and wider, stretching and straightening, body contorting and fur fading away, until he resembled the man Gus called family.

Until he resembled Ronnie.

# THIRTY-EIGHT

"Hey, kiddo," Ronnie said, kneeling next to Gus. He looked exactly as he had the last time Gus saw him, wore the same clothes and everything. "I guess I have some explaining to do, don't I?" The way he spoke sounded different now. He had an accent that reminded Gus a bit of Saoirse's, but they definitely weren't the same.

"That . . . is a fucking understatement," Gus replied. His voice sounded better, and his body didn't hurt so much anymore. He managed to sit up but had to lean on Olwen's legs.

He should have been relieved, should have been weeping with joy, should have been grateful he hadn't lost his family. But he felt numb, anesthetized, the world as he knew it crumbling around him yet again.

He stared dumbfounded at the old man—no, the old *pooka*—barely registering the fact that Saoirse had tossed Malachi's iron dagger aside, had trapped Margaret and Moira and the skeleton eating Malachi in sunlight-nets, had taken care of the remaining shard-raised.

How could this be? Ronnie was a faerie. Ronnie was Remington. Ronnie was Gus's guide.

Sure, Gus had had his suspicions. Mostly when "Remington" had first been leading him and Saoirse from gate to gate, when Saoirse had asked him if the squirrel was the one who'd led him to the library and the books. At that moment, it had dawned on him that no, Remington hadn't done either of those things, but Ronnie had. Then he'd wondered: *What are the odds that Ronnie's a faerie? That Ronnie's Remington in disguise?*

For a second, it had made sense. Ronnie had been an outsider of the compound, hadn't joined until after Gus was born, and faeries could use glamour, could even shape-shift sometimes.

Except then he'd realized that that was crazy, that it actually *didn't* make sense, the more he thought about it. Because if Ronnie was Remington in disguise, wouldn't he, at that point, have revealed himself? Wouldn't he have done more to break Gus and Saoirse out of the prison?

But even more than all that, Gus had thought that if Ronnie was a faerie, if Ronnie had been sent by Gus's biological parents as a guide, he would have taken Gus away from the compound long ago, away from the caregivers who didn't love him.

Yet here Ronnie stood, a faerie.

And he'd done none of those things.

Well, that wasn't entirely true. Margaret had bound him in his squirrel form (which, how had she done that? As far as Gus knew, that wasn't a sylph power), so he'd at least helped Gus and Saoirse as much as possible during that time. While bound, Ronnie presumably hadn't been able to reveal himself either, so it wasn't as if he'd abandoned or purposely deceived Gus then.

But what about the years before that? What about the years Gus spent miserable and neglected? Ronnie had been around, sure, but things had never had to be that way. He could have told Gus the truth, and they could have left the compound together.

So *why*? Why here, why now?

Gus wanted to ask all these questions and more, but when he opened his mouth, the only thing to come out was, "So you're a faerie too?"

Ronnie chuckled, the air shimmering around him. Suddenly Gus could see his nonhuman features. Instead of regular ears, or even pointed ones, he had the furry ears of a black squirrel, and a long bushy tail curled out behind him. "Sure am," he said. "Is that all you wanted to ask me?"

"Huh? Oh, no." Gus shook his head. "Why didn't—why didn't you *tell* me?"

"If I had, would you have believed me? Would you have been able to keep it a secret from everyone in the compound, including Beverly?"

"Everyone in the . . . But why would we have had to stay in the compound? We weren't happy there. I mean, *I* wasn't."

"Didn't matter if you were happy. Staying there was part of the job."

"Part of the job," Gus repeated in a flat tone.

"That's right. Your parents—your *real* parents— entrusted me with bringing you to the compound. It was the safest place they could find. I was supposed to protect you and prepare you for the truth."

"You're the one who brought me to the compound?"

"I am."

Anger broke through the numbness, twisting his insides. "And you made me live with *them*? With Mom and Dad? You couldn't have just taken me there as your child, or your grandchild? I couldn't have lived with you from the beginning?"

"There was more work for me to do before I could stay with you permanently. Besides, I had to bring your parents Joel and Sofia's blood daughter so the Family could pretend she was you. Unlike you, she was disposable. She could be stolen away, and it wouldn't have mattered."

Disposable? Was that really how Ronnie had felt about that baby girl, whoever she was? The prospect of having children terrified Gus, but that didn't mean they were *disposable*. That didn't mean he'd be okay with any of them being *stolen away*.

"Granted," Ronnie went on, "I had to use the last of your parents' glamour powder to make the switch believable, right as she was born. But it worked out in the end. It kept you safe."

"That's—right," Saoirse cut in. "It kept—him safe. But not—me."

But not her? What did she mean by that? Gus looked at her as she stumbled toward them. She was sweaty and out of breath, but her expression was one of resolve. Behind her, the shard-raised gorging itself on Malachi had started to transform, while Moira and Margaret clawed at the golden mesh around them.

Saoirse continued, "It was—*me*, Gus. He gave *me* to—your real parents."

"Wait, what?" Gus's head spun with confusion, then comprehension. "Are you saying that I—that we—" He turned to Ronnie.

"She is," Ronnie said. He was only a few feet away from Gus, but suddenly, the distance between them felt like miles. "She's Joel and Sofia's blood daughter. Your changeling counterpart."

The words were a gut punch. They stole the air from Gus's lungs. Had he not been leaning on Olwen, he might have collapsed again.

"That's why she's bonded to half of the cauldron shards," Ronnie continued. "The faeries that stole her from your parents—the Children of the Death Gods— they thought that she was your parents' child, that she had your lineage, and they brought her here, to the Mound of Skulls. By the time they discovered the truth, it was too late. The shard-raised were out of control.”

Gus reminded himself to breathe. “But—but humans living among faeries—I mean, from what I understand, they'd only be able to develop basic magical abilities. Not unique ones. And Saoirse—you have wings, wind-powers. You'd have to be descended from a god to have those, right? A sky god or something? So you couldn't have been born human.”

“She *was* though, Gus,” Ronnie insisted. “She stole those wings from a real sylph.” He pointed at the others. “And so did they. None of them inherited their wind-powers.”

A guttural sob escaped Saoirse. Despite everything that was happening, Gus found himself wanting to go to her, to comfort her. “It wasn't my choice!” she shrieked, no longer gasping. “I didn't want to! Malachi overpowered me. He held me down and he *forced* me to kill her, to cut off her wings, to drink her blood. I begged him to stop, begged them all to stop, to leave those sylphs alone, but they wouldn't listen!” She dropped to her knees and put her face in her hands.

“I'm so sorry, Saoirse.” Gus didn't know what else to say. There was far too much information being thrown at him in far too short a time. But what she'd just described . . . it was horrific. No wonder she'd let Malachi die the way she had.

Had she also been forced to use the shard-raised for murder? Was that why Malachi had thought she was bluffing when she'd threatened him with them earlier?

A new thought struck Gus then. Instinctively, he

reached up to touch his antlers. "You said these are the seat of my power. Did they want you to—"

"I was never going to do it." She lowered her hands to look at him. "I was never going to hurt you."

"Then what was your plan?" He feared he already knew, but he needed to hear her say it.

Fresh tears trickled down her cheeks. "For *you* to kill *me*. For *you* to take *my* power."

He'd known what she was going to say. He really, truly, honestly had. But still, when the words actually left her mouth, he couldn't believe it. Or maybe he *could* believe it, and he simply hated it.

Yes, he decided. He hated it. He hated it so damn much.

Before he could stop himself, he let out a cold bark of laughter. "That's your plan? You want me to murder you? To cut the cauldron's power out of you and drink your blood? You honestly think I'm capable of that? After *everything*?"

"You have to be capable of it," Ronnie said. "You don't have a choice."

"Oh yeah?" Gus faced Ronnie again. The pooka was standing now. "And how's that?"

"The cauldron's magic has been split between the two of you, and so long as that's the case, neither of you can harness it to its full potential. One of you *has* to kill the other and absorb their half of the power."

Gus swallowed hard, forcing down the lump that had formed in his throat. He couldn't sit here anymore, needed to move around. Arms and legs trembling, he forced himself to his feet. "I don't see why we'd have to kill each other to do that. Can't we just combine our halves another way? A way that keeps both of us alive?"

"No," Ronnie answered tersely. "That's not how it works."

Saoirse dried her tears with her sleeves. "Gus, please. My pain . . . it's not only physical. All the deaths I've caused, even though I didn't *want* to cause them . . . I carry that guilt with me every day. I'm ready for it to be over. Besides, look at me." She gestured at her scars. "I wasn't made for this, like you were. I doubt my body would survive much more."

"I can't," Gus said, his voice cracking. "I . . ."

She stood, took his hands, and stared hard at him. "Think about it. Your compound was attacked because of me. The humans who died at the hands of shard-raised that day—they suffered because of me. The skeletons I raised are out of control, searching for hosts. Not only that, but Malachi—he led them right to your compound. He opened that door and let them in, claimed it was a distraction so we could get you out more easily, and I couldn't stop him. I only had enough strength to save you. I don't deserve to live."

"But like you said, this was forced on you," Gus countered, squeezing her hands. "It isn't your fault."

Ronnie sighed in exasperation. "This conversation is pointless. Saoirse, it doesn't *matter* if the people of the compound are dead because of you. You know they're all meant to die anyway, and it will be by Gus's hand. It's his destiny to annihilate the human race."

"What?" Gus cried. "You're in on that too? You think all of humanity has to die? Even the innocent ones?"

"I *know* they have to die. They've caused too much trouble for us already, and they've had enough second chances. Trying to save them is idiotic."

Gus couldn't believe what he was hearing from Ronnie. He'd called Saoirse disposable, and now this? "But they're—they're living beings."

"Doesn't matter. They're a plague on the realms, and they need to be eradicated." Ronnie glanced over at Margaret and Moira, who were still trying to get out of their nets. The skeleton that had eaten Malachi resembled the "sylph" now, scratching at the mesh that kept the monster trapped. "Gus, please, we're running out of time." He picked up Malachi's iron dagger and offered it to Gus. "You know what you have to do, kiddo. This is the last hard thing. You care about her, right? This is what she wants. What she *needs*. Help her end her pain, and I'll be with you every step of the way. I promise, I'm not going anywhere. Now let's get this over with."

"I'm not killing Saoirse! There's gotta be another way."

"Even if there were, you'd never be able to find it with the shard-raised running around the way they are," Ronnie said. "You have to be able to control them."

Gus shook his head and returned his attention to Saoirse. "Is this really what you want? Or are you doing it because you feel like you have to?"

She let go of him and hugged her sides, considering the question. "It would end my guilt, my pain. I would no longer exist, in this way. I'd have the chance to reincarnate. I'd have a new life and no memory of the things that have happened to me . . . that I've been made to do."

"But is that what you *want?*" Eyes burning with tears, he tried not to yell at her. "I've seen your smile, your passion. I've seen the way you laugh, the"—he choked back a cry—"the way you dance when you think no one's watching. And forgive me if I'm wrong, but because of what I've seen, I don't think that, deep down, you want any of that. Not really."

She began to weep. It almost broke him. "Th-this is for the b-best, Gus. F-for you, f-for the Otherworld—"

"I don't care about any of that right now!" he shouted, no longer able to control his temper. "I care about *you*. We can find another way!"

"W-what if there isn't another w-way? You w-wanted to try and save b-both our realms, r-remember? What if you c-can only do that b-by killing m-me?"

"I'm not sacrificing you to do that! I'm not, okay?" The two of them locked eyes, and he hoped that what he said next would get through to her. "I think you wanna live, Saoirse. I think you always have, and that's why you let me in. Will you stay with me? Please?"

At his words, her tears stopped, and a ghost of a smile turned up her lips. They parted slightly, as if she was about to reply.

But she never got the chance.

A flash of movement, the sickening sound of a blade tearing through flesh, and Ronnie backed away from her with a bloody dagger in hand.

Saoirse clutched her ribs. Scarlet seeped through her dress, stained her fingers. *"Gus?"*

# THIRTY-NINE

Ronnie swung around and thrust the knife into Gus's hands. Even through the leather-covered hilt, Gus could feel the blade's burning energy, the heat threatening to leak out and sear his skin. "There, I started it for you," Ronnie said. "Now finish it."

Realizing just what Ronnie had done, Gus dropped the iron weapon. "No, no . . ."

"Now, Gus," Ronnie barked. "End her pain. Take her power. She already told you this is what she wants. She planned this from the beginning."

Saoirse whimpered, staggered, collapsed. He caught her before she hit the ground and set her down as gently as possible. With one hand, he put pressure on her wound, and with the other, he cupped her cheek. Her eyes were growing distant, the soul in them withering away.

"Don't go." His words were little more than a croak. He realized he was crying. Behind him, Olwen whimpered as though confused. "Stay. We'll fix this. We'll fix everything."

"I'd like—that," she managed to get out. "I'd like—to stay—with you."

Someone grabbed the collar of his shirt and jerked him away from her. Suddenly he was looking at Ronnie, a bewildered expression on the pooka's face. "I said *now*, Gus." He shoved the dagger at Gus once more. "I don't want to have to make you, but I will if need be. Do you understand? This is important."

It was then that something snapped inside of Gus.

He accepted Ronnie's knife, but he didn't use it on Saoirse.

In two quick motions, he wrenched the blade across Ronnie's chest and stomach, shredding through fabric and flesh.

"*Get out of here!*" he screamed in a voice he barely recognized as his own. "*Get away from us!*"

Red bloomed from Ronnie's wounds, the confusion in his expression intensifying. "What are you—"

"*I SAID GET AWAY FROM US!*"

A gale roared. The force of it pitched Gus and Ronnie and Olwen into the air. As he barreled backward, Gus caught sight of Moira's and Margaret's nets in shreds, of the two of them flying out of an opening in the ceiling. Were they carrying something?

He didn't get the chance to look closer, because he

slammed headfirst into the cavern's curved wall. Sharp shooting agony arced through his antlers, his skull. Then there was black.

When he gained consciousness again, he registered the throbbing in his head first, Olwen hovering over him second. In her smaller form, she whined mournfully, solidified, and licked his face.

*Saoirse. Is she okay?*

He shot up, looked around.

His heart almost shattered when he saw she was gone.

Margaret and Moira must have taken her. The only one of the group who remained was "Malachi," still captive to his mesh.

*This can't be happening. Not when she finally realized that she wants to live, that she's wanted to live this whole time.*

She'd said it herself. She'd like to stay with him. But she was bleeding out, quite possibly dying, and he wasn't there, with her. He couldn't hold her, couldn't protect her, couldn't do *anything* for her.

To the right, Ronnie muttered something under his breath and climbed to his feet. Palms pressed to his wounds, he took in the scene before them. "Now look what you've done!" He pointed at the empty space where Saoirse had lain before. A puddle of scarlet was all that remained of her. "They've made off with her. And we were so close!"

"They're going to kill her, aren't they? Take the

cauldron's power for themselves." The thought of it paralyzed Gus, made him numb again.

"And waste months—maybe even years—learning how to control the shard-raised skeletons as well as she does? No, they wouldn't do that. They wouldn't put their lives at even more of a risk."

At this, Gus felt his shoulders relaxing. *Maybe there's hope.*

"Besides, she's proven herself to be weak-willed," Ronnie went on, "which they can use to their advantage. They'll do everything they can to keep her alive, break her down, get her under their control again. Then they'll come after you."

Weak-willed? Had Ronnie been paying attention to the kind of person Saoirse was at all? She'd been forced to endure heinous torture and had, for the most part, still come out the other side a gentle soul. That wasn't weakness; it was strength.

With a grunt, Gus managed to stand up. "I have to save her. If it weren't for me, she wouldn't be in this mess. I have to fix this."

Ronnie turned to Gus, his features warping with fury. "Save her? You're still on about that? What is *wrong* with you? The fate of the realm is at stake, and here you are, losing your mind to lust!"

"What's wrong with *me*?" His nostrils flared, rage breaking through the numbness once more. "No, what's wrong with *you*? You stabbed her, you prick!"

"I stabbed her to help you," Ronnie spat. "For years, that's all I've done. Help you. I lived in the

Mortalworld for you, restored the library for you, gathered books for you. I pretended to be friends with the idiots that raised you and shielded you from their abuse whenever I could. I cast tracking spells on you and defended you and—"

"Wait, you cast tracking spells on me? But that—that doesn't—"

"Of course I did. How else would I have found you when I needed to?"

"But *how*? Spells only work on nonliving—"

Then it dawned on him.

*The watch.*

It hadn't been a gift. Not a sincere one, anyway.

What else hadn't been genuine? Nausea clawed through Gus as he flipped through his memories with Ronnie—every interaction shared, every word uttered. Had he even meant it when, all those years ago, he said he didn't want to live in a world without Gus? Surely, he had, but now the sentiment was tainted, all because of Gus's "destiny." What if Ronnie had only meant that he didn't want to live in a world where the shard-raised were out of control? Where humanity wasn't forced to extinction?

What if Ronnie had never cared about Gus for who he was, but for what he would someday do?

Chest aching, he whispered, "You're not who I thought. Are you?"

Ronnie threw his hands in the air. "Obviously not! Neither was Saoirse, neither were your—"

"That's not what I meant." He stared sadly at the

broken device on his wrist. "Everything you did for me—you didn't do it because you cared about me."

"Now wait, hold on. Just because it was my job to protect you doesn't mean that I didn't come to care about you. You're incredibly important, the closest thing I've ever had to a—"

"Do you honestly believe that humanity deserves to die?" Gus interrupted. "All of them, even the ones who haven't done anything wrong?"

"Don't you? I mean, think about it. *Really* think about it. Consider everything that you know now. Can't you see that their existence is a plague on the realms? That they have to be stopped?"

"Sure, we have to stop them from doing more damage to the veil, but that doesn't mean we have to *kill* them. Don't they deserve to know what's going on? Don't they deserve a chance to change?"

Ronnie opened and closed his mouth as though struggling to form a response. Finally, he said, "No, they don't."

He'd heard enough. He tore the watch off his wrist and chucked it at Ronnie. "Don't look for me."

Ronnie glanced at the watch on the floor, then at Gus, then at the watch again. "You can't do this. I won't let you."

"Goodbye, Ronnie." He focused on his magic. No—he focused on the magic of the cauldron.

This energy was so much easier to tap into, and conjuring it took barely any effort. Could it be that it had a mind of its own, that it had been waiting for the moment he summoned it?

Like his regular magic, it sent chills through him, but it didn't conjure images of ghosts in his blood. It was sharp, prickly, as if the remaining cauldron shards had been smashed into tiny fragments and stirred into his veins.

The mist beneath them whistled, answering his call. Satisfaction coursed through him.

"Don't you dare!" Ronnie snarled, but it was too late.

The fog crawled into the scattered bones around Ronnie, and four new shard-raised—*Gus's* shard-raised—twitched to life.

At first, they were clumsy, staggering about as they tried to gain their footing. But it wasn't long before they balanced themselves, and when they did, they lumbered toward Ronnie.

"What do you think you're doing?" Ronnie yelled as the skeletons came after him. "Stop this!"

Gus shook his head. "Not until you leave."

Ronnie gave him one last incredulous look before shrinking down into a squirrel, scurrying up the wall, and disappearing through one of the fissures in the ceiling.

The skeletons turned on Gus then. He remembered the way Saoirse had stripped them of their magic and waved his arms, trying to do the same.

It didn't work.

He called on the magic again and tried a second time, then a third.

Still nothing.

But before he could panic, Olwen (back in her larger form) pounced on the skeletons and knocked their skulls off their spines, one by one, then barked as if to say, *"Let's go!"*

Despite his aching flesh, he didn't waste another moment. He vaulted into the twisting, turning hallway of the Mound of Skulls, Olwen bounding close behind him.

# FORTY

Saoirse couldn't remember much after the pooka stabbed her. She'd been fighting to stay awake, fighting to breathe, and then darkness swept over her.

The next time she opened her eyes, she was in bed, in her room in the castle of the Children of the Death Gods. The sun shone through her window—she thought it must be very warm outside—but she was shivering, frigid and clammy, thick wool blankets wrapped around her.

Footsteps padded against the stone floor, and then Margaret and Moira were standing over her, watching her.

Searing agony in her ribs as she tried to sit up, the burning sensation a stark contrast to the chills in the rest of her body. She groaned and clamped her eyes shut. "Gus? What have you done with Gus?"

Moira was the one to answer her question. "We haven't done anything with him. We didn't have time. You were dying, so we had to leave him behind."

*Then he had the chance to escape.* That at least brought her some comfort.

A tap on her shoulder, and she opened her eyes to find Margaret offering her a cup of water. She wriggled her arms out from under the blankets and accepted it, her throat parched. "The Family isn't happy with you," Margaret said. "You didn't follow their instructions."

She smiled wryly. "No, I suppose I didn't."

"They're going to make sure it doesn't happen again."

"Oh? And how do they plan on doing that? By killing me? Good luck."

Margaret's expression turned solemn. "There have been . . . *breakthroughs* in Moira's abilities. While influencing weaker minds, she's been able to do more than just send warriors into frenzies."

That made Saoirse's blood run cold. She gazed up at Moira. "So they want you to—to what? Alter my thoughts? My emotions?"

"They want me to try," Moira said, and sat down on the bed next to Saoirse. "Now that you're awake, let's get started, shall we?"

This walk was long, and it would have been far more perilous had Gus been in different company. Olwen never left his side, gliding so closely to him that sometimes he stepped right through her. When that happened, she'd let out a yip—not in pain, but as if she was saying, *"Hey, watch it! I'm right here!"*

Yet even with Olwen's company, he was lonely, more so now than ever. He'd thought the neglect of his "parents" had hurt, but it was nothing compared to Ronnie's betrayal. When he'd stabbed Saoirse, he might as well have driven an iron dagger between Gus's ribs too.

*Saoirse.* Gus saw her smiling when he closed his eyes, heard her giggling when he sat in silence. Did he love her? He thought so. He hadn't known her long, but she felt like understanding and belonging, comfort and home, and he'd been drawn to her since the moment they'd met. Had a small part of him, even then, known that their fates were entwined? That they had been since birth?

Yes, she'd hidden things from him. But she'd only wanted to escape her pain. Like him, she was imprisoned, a changeling trapped by destiny.

He hoped he could find a way to liberate them both.

He spent weeks going on like this, trekking from gate to gate with his ghost-dog, searching for familiar landmarks that would help lead him to his destination. He foraged for food and practiced his magic when possible, but he still couldn't raise the dead without tapping into the power of the cauldron. He still couldn't entirely control the shard-raised either.

It was hopeless, wasn't it? The compound and everyone in it. At this point, there was no way anyone could have survived. Still, he'd make his way back when he got ahold of his abilities. If by some chance there was anyone left, he'd save them.

The days in the Mortalworld became shorter and the temperatures lower, and in the Otherworld, the opposite occurred. His antlers seemed to finish growing; from skull to tip, they were about two feet long, and whenever he caught sight of his reflection, he didn't recognize the person staring back at him.

He was not a man but a monster, a beast in a faerie tale book.

Surely, his story would be one to inspire nightmares.

At last, a gate took him to a place he recognized— the river at the edge of the ravine. He and Olwen swam to the surface, then to land. He half expected to find Adam's, Lewis's, and Tamara's mutilated bodies there, but all traces of carnage had been washed away.

By daybreak, he reached the library in the destroyed city. Trudging through its shattered doors, across its cracked flooring, past its sagging bookshelves, he felt more optimistic than he had since . . . well, he couldn't even remember when. *A long time*, he thought. *Too long.*

Because if this worked—if this helped him master his abilities—then perhaps he could rescue Saoirse. Perhaps he could save humanity. Perhaps he could fix everything.

He strode to the back of the library, to his favorite

section, and located the book he'd left behind the last time he'd been here: the illustrated encyclopedia of Celtic deities. Then he looked through the index, located Arawn's page, and flipped to it, ready to connect with the past, ready to change the future.

To be continued in the second installment of the
Children of the Death Gods series . . .

# THE CORPSE CHANGELING

A. P. Mobley is the Halloween-loving, rock-music-obsessed author of dark fantasy inspired by mythology. She doesn't only write about her favorite myths, folktales, and fairy tales in her books, though; she discusses them on her podcast, *Myths (& Folktales & Fairy tales)*, as well as on her blog and newsletter. She grew up in Wyoming and Nebraska and currently lives in South Dakota, and when she's not up to her elbows in research for her next project, she can be found consuming dangerous amounts of coffee, reading speculative fiction, or rewatching *The Good Place*.

# ALSO BY A. P. MOBLEY

You can find A. P. Mobley's other books at
www.apmobley.com/books


# JOIN A. P.'S NEWSLETTER

Never miss an update from A. P. by joining her
newsletter at subscribepage.io/aTKktx

# ACKNOWLEDGMENTS

I'd like to start by thanking someone who wasn't involved in the feedback/production process of this book but who was an integral part of its creation nonetheless. Siân Esther Powell, the amazing host of the *Celtic Myths and Legends* podcast, thank you so much for sharing your passion and expertise regarding Celtic stories with the world. Five or six years ago (I can't remember exactly how long it's been), when I first had the idea for *The Skeleton Faerie*, I didn't know where to begin in my research. I was more familiar with other world mythologies and only knew the basics of the Celtic stories—not nearly enough to write a book—but then I discovered your podcast, and it was the best place I could have started. Your storytelling abilities captivated me and made the characters of Celtic myth feel like living, breathing beings. Your "rambling" never failed to bring a smile to my face, and it made the research process that much more enjoyable, because I felt as if I were listening to a good friend tell a story by a campfire, not slogging through a textbook. Without you and your podcast, I'm not sure the book would exist in the same way it does now, as you ignited my imagination with your episodes—especially the ones about the pobel vean and the *Mabinogi*. So thank you, thank you, thank you for being you!

Now, on to the folks who were involved in the feedback/production of the book:

This book was hard for me. I mean, every book has its own challenges, but in many ways I felt as if I were a debut author again with *The Skeleton Faerie*. Granted, some of that was to be expected. I'm transitioning from YA to adult, after all, and the amount of research I did before even writing the first draft was ungodly. But I also had a lot of health issues while writing this book (still working through them), on top of mountains of self-doubt and wondering if this is even what I'm supposed to be doing.

There are a lot of people who helped me work through those negative emotions, who believed in me and didn't let me give up, and they must be mentioned here.

Mom, thank you for the long phone calls and venting sessions. Every time I fell down during this process, you helped me get back up. I don't know what I would have done without your support through this process.

Kelsey, my gorgeous friend (one of my best friends!), thank you for reading chapters of the book before anyone else and for supporting me every time I posted about the book online. The chapters you read needed work, but you saw the potential there, and you hyped me up every chance you could get. Your excitement for the story definitely helped me get through some of those harder days!

Tory, my husband, my love, thank you for giving me the honest, brutal feedback I needed while first writing this book, and for being so understanding and supportive when I had to stay home from gatherings to work. Being an author is isolating, but with you, I never feel like I'm alone.

Thank you to Dillan, my writing buddy and one of my best friends, for reading the earliest drafts of this manuscript, pointing out its strengths and weaknesses, and always talking me off a ledge when I started spiraling.

Nikki, my editor (how many books has this been now? Nine? OMG!), thank you so much for helping me take the story and characters in the direction they needed to go. You were incredibly patient with me, even when I sent you novel-length emails of notes and questions and was *way* too late on deadlines, and your feedback was crucial in getting this book to a place where I finally felt happy with it. I really don't know what I would do without you and your thoughtful critiques!

Last but certainly not least, thank you to Gabrielle,

the incredible artist who's brought all my books to life with gorgeous illustrations. We've been working together for almost a decade now, and your skills have (somehow) become even more remarkable with each passing year. You completely outdid yourself with the cover illustration and map and interior art for this book, your passion for the story evident in every line and brush stroke—and, of course, in the feedback you gave me as a reader! I can still hardly believe the fact that you read earlier drafts of the book. But I'm immensely grateful for it; your comments helped me strengthen some important characterization. I just hope you know how much I appreciate you!